THE
DESERT MOON
MYSTERY

THE
DESERT MOON
MYSTERY

Kay Cleaver Strahan

COACHWHIP PUBLICATIONS
GREENVILLE, OHIO

The Desert Moon Mystery, by Kay Cleaver Strahan
© 2024 Coachwhip Publications edition

First published 1928
Kay Cleaver Strahan, 1888-1941
CoachwhipBooks.com

ISBN 1-61646-586-7
ISBN-13 978-1-61646-586-5

1
The Cannezianos

I knew, that evening in April, when Sam got home from Rattail and came stamping snow into my kitchen, his good old red, white, and blue face stretched long instead of wide in its usual grin, that he had brought some bad news with him: a slump in the cattle market; moonshine liquor discovered again, down in the outfit's quarters; a delayed shipment of groceries from Salt Lake. I, who in the months that were coming, was to live through more shock, and fright, and distress and disaster than should fall to the lot of a thousand women in all of their combined lifetimes, was worrying, then, for fear we should have to be doing without olive oil and canned mushrooms for a few weeks in the ranch-house!

"I had a letter to-day," he said, "from the Canneziano twins."

I am like a lot of folks who say that they are not superstitious, who just happen to think that it is bad luck to walk under a ladder. More than likely the shivery, creepy sensation I felt, when Sam said that, was due to the cold he had brought in with him, and was not due to the fact that those words of his were the forerunners for all of the grim mysteries and the tragedies that made the Desert Moon Ranch, before the end of July, a place of horror.

"How much do they want?" I questioned.

"No, Mary; they want to come here to live."

"Lands alive! For how long?"

"Danielle wrote the letter. She says they want to come here and rest, indefinitely. There was quite a bit in it about the peace of the deserts and the high mountains here in Nevada. She says she longs for it with all her soul, or something like that."

"Danielle," I said, "always was the best of the two. You going to let them come, Sam?"

"Anything else for me to do?"

"Not a thing—for you. There'd be plenty for others. Those girls are no kin of yours. Let me see—they must be able-bodied young women by now. Eight years old when they were here in 1909, makes them twenty-four years old now, according to my figures. Why a couple of women twins, aggregating forty-eight years, should decide to come here and rest their souls, at your expense, is beyond me."

"I have plenty."

"So has Henry Ford. Why don't they go rest their souls with him? They've got as much claim on him as they have on you. None."

"I reckon."

"Where are they now, anyway?"

"Switzerland."

"Lands alive! I don't pretend to know much about foreign geography, but I've understood that there were a few mountains in Switzerland. Leave those girls rest their souls right there where they are, Sam."

"No—I don't know, Mary. I guess I'll write them a letter and tell them to come along. Lots of room."

I didn't argue any more about it. For twenty-five years I had been housekeeper of the Desert Moon ranch-house, and I had learned, during that time, that there was only one subject, concerning Sam, or the place, on which I could never hope to have any say-so. Trying to argue with

Sam about anything that had to do, in any way, with Margarita Ditsie, when she was Margarita Ditsie Stanley, or when she was Margarita Ditsie Canneziano, was about as sensible as hoisting a chiffon parasol for protection in the midst of one of our Nevada mountain cloudbursts.

Margarita Ditsie was of French-Canadian parentage; a dark-haired, big-eyed beauty. Her father kept a gambling hole in Esmeralda County in the early days. Her mother had run away from a convent, after she had become a nun, to marry him. The girl had some of the nun, some of the runaway, and some of the gambling house proprietor in her. It made a queer combination.

When she was eighteen years old she came from Carson to visit Lily Trooper, over on the Three Bars Ranch, in northeastern Nevada, about sixty miles from here. Sam met her there, at one of Ben Trooper's big barbecues. She and Sam were married two weeks later. She was a lot younger than Sam; but, even then, he was the richest man in the valley, with every unwedded woman for a hundred miles around setting her cap for him.

Whether Margarita married him for his wealth, or whether it was to spite the other girls who would have liked to marry him, I don't know. All I know is that Margarita never had a mite of love for him. She stayed with him, though, and acted decently enough for two years, until Dan Canneziano came to the ranch and got a job on it as cowpuncher.

It was during those two years that Sam built this ranch-house for her. He had an architect in New York draw the plans for it; and though now on the outside, with its towers and trimmings, it looks kind of old fashioned, I think it is still the finest house in Nevada. Sam's lead and silver mine had just come in, and there was not anything, from Italian marble fireplaces to teakwood floors, that was too grand for what Margarita called the Stanley Mansion. She left it, all the elegance and the luxury, and she broke her marriage vows, for love of this wop cowpuncher. That, I guess, is fair and full enough description of Margarita Canneziano.

I don't blame her. I quit blaming folks for things a good many years ago when, after firing three Chinese cooks in six weeks, I decided that, if we were to live healthy and wholesome, I'd have to take over the job of cooking as well as housekeeping for the Desert Moon Ranch, and set about it, and learned to cook. In other words, when I became a creator myself, I got to know creations and so quit blaming all of them. If I forget to put the soda in the sour milk pancakes, it isn't their fault if they don't rise. They are as I made them. Margarita was as the Lord made her. He, I suppose, either had His own good reasons for turning out such a mess, or else He was tired, or flustered, or, maybe, was just experimenting on the road to something better when He did it.

I should explain, I suppose, wishing to be as honest as possible in spite of the fact that I am writing a mystery story, that Canneziano was different from the ordinary breed of cowpunchers. His father, he claimed, had some hifaluting title in Italy, before he got into a peck of honorable, patriotic trouble and had to skip to the United States to save his neck. That may be true, and it may not. Canneziano had a good education; he talked poetry, and played the violin. Margarita heard him playing, down in the outfit's quarters one day, and had Sam invite him up to the house to play. She accompanied him on the grand piano that Sam had bought for her.

Before long, Dan Canneziano was spending a good part of his time at the ranch-house. Sam, being nobody's fool, soon saw how the land lay; but he, according to his custom then and now, kept his mouth shut and his eyes open. Sure enough, one evening they tried to elope together.

Sam went after them and brought them back. I remember, yet, how the three of them looked, coming into the house that night.

Margarita, her head high, defiant, but pretty as a fire's flame. Canneziano, slinking in at her heels, like a whipped cur, expecting worse; and Sam, following behind them, calm as cold turkey. The three of them had about half an hour's talk together. Then Sam herded Canneziano down to the outfit's quarters and, I suppose, told the men to keep him there, for there he stayed until Sam was ready for him again.

The next morning Sam started to the county seat. He reached there that evening. The following morning he got his divorce. He came back to the Desert Moon on the third morning, with his divorce and with a preacher. He sent for Canneziano, and stood by, while the preacher married Margarita Stanley to Daniel Canneziano, decent and regular, according to the laws of Nevada.

There it should have ended. It didn't, because Sam never got over loving Margarita. I don't hold that to his credit. I see no more virtue in keeping on loving a person who has proved unworthy of being loved, than I see in hating a person who has turned out to be blameless, or in continuing to do any other unreasonable thing.

At any rate, Sam did it. So when, nine years later, she came back to the Desert Moon, with twin girls, Danielle and Gabrielle, and said that Canneziano had deserted her and the children Sam took them all right in. I don't know, yet, whether or not they took him in.

Certainly he did not show much surprise when, in about ten days, Canneziano put in an appearance. Sam allowed him to get a good start with his threats, and then he took him across his knees and gave him a sound spanking, and passed him over to Margarita to dry his tears, and washed his own hands and went fishing.

That evening he had one of the men hitch up and take the whole kit and caboodle of Cannezianos to Rattail in time to catch the east-bound train. I am ashamed to say that Sam gave them money. I don't know how much. I shouldn't be surprised if it was more than they had expected to get from their blackmailing scheme. A tidy sum, I'll be bound, for shortly after we heard that Canneziano had opened the finest gambling house south of the Mason and Dixon line, in New Orleans.

Sam wanted to keep the children. He offered to adopt them. Margarita would not consider it. But, several times after that, pale yellow, perfumed letters came to the Desert Moon, and Sam answered those letters with a check. Me he answered, each time, with, "It is for the little girls, Mary. I can't let little girls go needing."

When Margarita died, in France, seven years after she had paid us her blackmailing visit, Sam, the ninny, wrote to Canneziano and again offered to adopt the girls and give them a good home on the Desert Moon. He got a few insulting, insinuating lines for an answer. Canneziano had his own plans for his daughters, who had developed into rare beauties. He would thank Sam to keep his hands off, mind his own business, and so forth.

It would have made a milder man than Sam Stanley fighting mad. Sam went around all that day, swearing to me that he was through; that he had made his last offer of help to the Canneziano family, had sent his last contribution. I know for certain, though, that he sent five hundred dollars to Gabrielle, after that, in answer to a letter she wrote to him. But, if Sam was soft with the women, he was not soft with Canneziano. He had showed up here, beaming and broke, about three years ago. He had left, suddenly, after having seen Sam and no one else, less beaming but quite as broke as he had been when he had come. I thought, maybe, Sam was forgetting that side of the family, and that this might be a good time to remind him.

"Is Canneziano planning to come on later, too, and rest?" I asked.

"Just at present he is in San Quentin, serving a three years' term. Danielle didn't say for what deviltry. His term's up this summer. That is another reason the girls want to come here. Somewhere safe from his persecutions, I think the letter said. Poor little girls," Sam went on, "I reckon we haven't any idea of what they've been through, all these years."

"I reckon not," I agreed. "But they aren't little girls any more. Seems queer to me, with all the beauty their father was bragging about, that neither of them has married. Twenty-four is getting along."

"I'll bet," Sam answered, "it is because they have never had any decent opportunities. You know how pretty they were as little girls, and how good—"

"Danielle was good enough," I said. "Gabrielle was a holy terror."

Sam let that pass. "Considering," he continued, "the life that they've had to lead, and all, I think it speaks pretty well for them that they have come through straight and clean."

Instead of asking him how he knew that, I said, "You'd be willing, then, to have John marry one of them?"

John, Sam's adopted son, was the apple of Sam's eye. He would have the ranch, and Sam's fortune, other dependents provided for, when Sam died. Whether or not the girl he married would be contented to live on the ranch, and help John carry it on and keep up its traditions, making it one of the proudest spots in Nevada, was a mighty important thing to Sam.

He waited so long before answering my question that I was sure I had hit the nail on the head.

"John," he finally said, "is old enough to take care of himself."

"With that he turned and went out of my kitchen, not giving me a chance to say that, though I had lived through fifty-six years, I had never yet seen a man at the age he had just mentioned. I did not care. I felt too vimless for even a spat with Sam. I knew that if these Canneziano girls came to the Desert Moon, they would bring trouble with them. I was right. A merciful Providence be thanked that, for a time at least, the knowledge of how terribly right I was, was spared me.

2
John and Martha

I am not an admirer of men. Looking at most any man, I find myself thinking what a pity it was he had to grow up, since as a little, helpless child he would have made a complete success.

Sam Stanley is different. There is some of the child left in Sam, just as there is, I think, in any good man or woman—a little seasoning of simplicity, really, is all it amounts to—but there is a quality about Sam that makes a person feel that he set out, early in life, to follow the recipe for being a man, and that he has made a thorough job of it. Physically, alone, Sam would make about three of most men, with plenty left over for gravy. But it is not that. It is the something that makes him stroll up, unarmed, to a cowpuncher who is bragging wild with moonshine and clinking with firearms, and say, in that drawling, gentle voice of his, "What's the trouble here, son?" And the something that makes that cowpuncher get polite first, and evaporate immediately after. And Sam whiteheaded, now, at that.

Why he, as a young man, with a pretty fair education and a tidy sum of money left him by his father, who had been a well thought of lawyer in Massachusetts, should come out here to Nevada, take up his homestead land, and settle content for the rest of his life, has always been more or less of a mystery to me. I will warn you, though, that it is a mystery that doesn't get solved in this story, unless you care to take Sam's explanation of it.

He says that, when his father died, it left him without a relative, whom he knew of, in the world. He was twenty years old, and he owned a set of roving toes and an imagination. So he went to California, seeking romance and gold. Finding neither, he took a small boat named *The Indiana,* and went up to Oregon, where he joined a friend of his, named Tom Cone, who had a place on the Columbia River near Rooster Rock.

One day Sam was out in the woods—he said there was nothing to be out in except woods or rain in Oregon in those days—and he heard a noise behind a thicket. He thought Tom, who lived for practical jokes, was getting ready to pull one. So Sam crept up to the thicket, stooping low and making no noise, and shouted "Boo!" at the biggest bear he had ever seen in his life. Sam says he has forgotten what the bear said. He decided, then and there, that the Oregon forests were no place for a man with no more sense than he had; he left them, and came down here to Nevada.

"No forests, no fences, no folks, and a free view for ten thousand miles," is the way Sam puts it, "so, I stayed. It was the first place I'd ever found where I didn't feel hampered for room."

He staked out his hundred and sixty acres with Boulder Creek tumbling and roaring through them. He built his cabin, out of railroad ties, in a grove of quaking aspen trees. He hired help, and built fences, and dug ditches, and planted crops, and bought stock. He bought more land. He hired more help, dug more ditches, planted bigger crops, bought more stock. He has been doing that, regularly, ever since. And, of course, he located the lead and silver mine, on his property, that made him millions,

if it made him a cent, before it played out. But, in spite
of the money that "Old Lady Luck," as he called his mine,
made for him, Sam never gave his heart to it. It was the
Desert Moon Ranch that he loved, and the money he made
from it that he was proud of. That was why, when the
honor of the ranch went under, during those terrible weeks
last summer, Sam all but went under with it.

After Margarita left the place from her visit of 1909,
taking the twins with her, Sam went around for a week or
two, with his head cocked to one side as if he was listening for something. I knew what he was missing, and I was
not surprised when, one day, he told me he had decided
to send to San Francisco and get a couple of children and
adopt them.

He wrote to a big hospital in San Francisco and got in
touch with a trained nurse who would be willing to come
up and live on the ranch and take care of the two children. He had her go to an orphan's home and select the
children and bring them with her when she came. Sam's
specifications concerning them were that they were to be a
boy and a girl, under ten and over five years old, healthy,
American, and brown-eyed. (Sam's own eyes are the color
of ball-bluing, giving his face, with his red cheeks, and his
white beard, the patriotic effect I have mentioned.)

The nurse came early in September with the two brown-
eyed children, named Vera and Alvin. Sam at once re-
named them. John, he said, was the only name for a boy,
and Mary the only name for a girl. But, since my name
was Mary, he would let the little girl have Martha, which
meant, according to Sam, "Boss of the Ranch."

The nurse's name was Mrs. Ollie Ricker. If you can
imagine a blue-eyed, pink-cheeked, yellow-haired bisque
doll, turned old, you will have a good idea of her appearance at that time. I don't know how old she was then. I
don't know how old she is now. Younger by many years

than I am, I am sure; and yet she has always seemed old
to me; old with the sudden but inevitable oldness of a
wrecked ship, or a burned-down house, or a felled tree,
that makes a body forget that a year ago, or perhaps only
yesterday, it was a fresh, new thing. She never talked. I
do not mean that she never chatted, or gossiped. I mean
that she never said one word, not, "Good-morning," nor,
"Good-night," nor, "If you please," nor, "Thank you," if
she could possibly avoid it. At the end of sixteen years of
daily association with Mrs. Ricker, that is, up to the time
of the second murder on the Desert Moon, I knew exactly
as much about her past life as you know at this minute.

John, at that time, was nine years old. He was as bright,
and as upstanding, and as handsome, as any little fellow to
be found anywhere; bashful at first, but ready and glad to
be friendly, with an uplifting smile that wrinkled his short
nose and that would wheedle a cooky out of a pickle jar. I
may as well say, now, that this description of John, at nine
years old, is as good a description as I can give of John at
twenty-five, if you will draw his height up to six feet, and
put on weight accordingly.

Martha, when she came to us, was a frail, white-faced
mite, with enormous brown eyes that looked as if they had
been removed from a Jersey heifer and set in her white
face. The papers from the orphanage gave her age as five
years; but even I, who knew less about children than it was
decent for any woman to know, soon saw that something
was wrong. She walked well enough, but she could scarcely
talk at all. Her ways and her habits were those of a two-
year-old infant, yet she was far too large for that age. Before she had been with us a week I knew that Martha was
not quite right in her mind.

Mrs. Ricker knew it, too. Her excuse was, that she had
chosen Martha because she was so pretty; that she had
had no opportunity to judge her other characteristics. She

insisted that she thought, with proper care, Martha would develop normally.

I knew better. Sam knew it, too. But, when I begged and besought him not to adopt her, he brought out an argument good and conclusive for him.

"If I don't adopt her, and take care of her," said Sam, "who the heck would?"

So adopt her he did. And he spent a small fortune on doctors, specialists, for her. None of them could do anything. It was, they said, a hopeless case of retarded development. So, at twenty-one years of age, Martha, though the care and doctoring had given her a fine healthy body, had the mind of a child of five or six years—not too bright a child, either. That was at best. At worst— Well, no matter. Entirely harmless, the doctors said; but I always had my doubts.

Sam tried all sorts of teachers for her, too; bringing them from back east and paying them sums to stagger. But, in the end, we found that Mrs. Ricker was better with her than anyone else. She never pretended any particular love for Martha, but she took care of her, and kept her sweet and clean, and put up with her tempers, when many a better woman than Ollie Ricker would have gone away in disgust. I am not saying that, if there is a Judgment Day, as many say and some believe, I'd care to be standing in Ollie Ricker's shoes, if she is wearing them at that time; but I do say that her gentleness, and her patience, through all those years with Martha, should be counted to her credit, whether or no.

3
Hubert Hand

It was three years after Mrs. Ricker came to the ranch, bringing John and Martha, that Hubert Hand put in his appearance. He had got Mr. Indian Chat Chin, as everybody called him, to bring him up from Rattail in his old surrey. Hubert Hand was something of a dude in those days, though he has well outgrown it since, and I remember yet how comical he looked, sitting up there so stiff and fine in his light gray overcoat and gray Fedora hat, with that big Roman nose of his protruding out and up, disdainfully, above his little moustache, and apparently above all consciousness of dirty old Mr. Indian Chat Chin and the rattle-trap rig.

Mr. Indian Chat Chin stopped his old nag at the entrance to the driveway, and Hubert Hand climbed carefully down and came up the road, swinging a walking cane like he was leading a parade.

Sam and I, as was our custom, went walking down to meet him.

He took off his hat to me, and said to Sam, "I wish to see the owner of this ranch."

"Nobody ever mistook me for a fairy before," Sam said. "But go ahead. Your first wish is granted. What are the other two?"

Hubert Hand got out his card then. Besides his name it had "Clover-blossom Creamery," and the San Francisco address printed on it.

"Now, Mr. Stanley," Hubert Hand went on, after the embarrassing minute of general introductions, "I am going to be honest with you—"

"Hold on, stranger," Sam interrupted, "you're not. You are going to be as dishonest as heck. Otherwise, you wouldn't bother to tell me you were going to be honest. Go ahead."

Hubert Hand laughed, but he didn't like it. He went ahead, though, and explained that he had an up-and-coming creamery business in San Francisco, but that his physician had told him that he had to live in a high, dry climate with plenty of sunshine and no fog. He had, after inquiries and investigations, decided that the Desert Moon Ranch, altitude seven thousand feet, sunshine three hundred and sixty-five days in the year, to say nothing of the marvelous view of the Garnet Mountains, the hunting, the fishing, and the pure snow water, would fill all his requirements.

"Thanks," Sam said. "When I get ready to start a Gold Cure Sanatorium, I'll drop you a line."

"You won't do business, then?" Hubert Hand questioned.

"I hadn't heard anything about doing business," Sam said.

Hubert Hand's proposition was that he start a creamery, on the Desert Moon Ranch, and supply the valley with ice-cream, butter, and other dairy products. Sam had the ranch, the cows, and the big ice plant. Mr. Hubert Hand had the knowledge and the equipment. They could divide the profits.

Next to sheep men, I guess there is nothing that cow men hold in lower contempt than they hold dairy farms. Sam was too much disgusted to swear very long.

"But, do you realize, Mr. Stanley," Hubert Hand insisted, "that this entire valley has to depend on Salt Lake City, or on Reno, for its dairy products?"

"Listen, stranger," Sam said. "I wouldn't turn the Desert Moon into a place to slop milk around in if the entire valley had to depend on Hong Kong, China, for its ice-cream cones. Forget it, and come in now and have some supper."

To my knowledge, Hubert Hand, from that day to this, has never again mentioned, on the Desert Moon, anything that had to do with creameries. Neither, from that day to this, has he been off the ranch for more than a couple of weeks at a time.

"By the way," he began, trying to make it sound unimportant, when we had finished supper, "I heard, in Telko, that you were something of a chess player."

"I am, when I can get a game," Sam said. "But chess players, in these parts, are as scarce as hen's teeth. My neighbor, thirty miles east of here, and I used to play regular, two nights a week. But the son of a gun struck it rich, and like most loyal Native Sons of this state, he moved to California to spend his money. I'm teaching my boy, John—but he is just a kid. Here, lately, about all I've done is work out the puzzles by myself."

"I play a little," Hubert Hand produced, right modestly.

Sam jumped up and got out his chess table, inlaid ebony and ivory, made special, and his ebony and ivory chess-men.

Hubert Hand beat him the first game in about half an hour. They set up their men again. It took Hubert Hand over an hour that time to beat Sam, but he did it.

"Heck!" Sam said, at the end of that game. "You're hired."

"Hired for what?"

"For whatever you want to call it, except the slopping of milk around. Send for your trunk and name your pay.

Why didn't you say, in the first place, that you were a blankety-blank crack chess player?"

I realize, right here, that I am not going to be able to get through with this entire story, with Sam in it, and continue to modify his vocabulary into hecks and blankety blanks. Wrong, I think it is; but it is true, that men out here do not talk like that. Sam cusses, swears and damns, just as naturally and as innocently as he breathes. The only real trouble about Sam's profanity is that he uses up all his strong words day by day in ordinary conversation; so, when occasions arise that call for something really emphatic, Sam hasn't any words to do them justice. If the demands are not too serious, he reverts and finds a little "Pshaw!" or, "Shoot!" unusual enough to meet the need. If it goes beyond that, he opens his mouth in silence and keeps it open, hoping for a word, until his pipe drops out and scatters ashes and burned and burning tobacco all over everything. I pay no attention to his profanity and small attention to his "Pshaws," and "Shoots." But when his pipe drops, I get right down interested.

To return to Hubert Hand: he accepted Sam's offer, then and there. The next day he titled himself assistant ranch manager, and named his salary at two hundred and fifty dollars a month. Sam paid it without blinking; and kept right on managing the ranch, and everything on it, except, perhaps, myself, without any assistance, the same as he had always done.

4
Chadwick Caufield

Chadwick Caufield, the other member of our household, who was present on the Desert Moon Ranch at the time of the first murder, came only two years ago last October.

It was away past bedtime, after ten o'clock, but the radio was brand-new then, and we were all sitting up, listening to a fine program given by the Hoot Owls in Portland, Oregon, when the doorbell rang. Sam answered it. Chad stepped in.

He was wearing white corduroy trousers, a long, yellow rubber raincoat, and a straw hat tethered to its buttonhole with a string. He was carrying a ukulele under his arm and a camera in his hand. He took off his hat, displaying a head full of pretty yellow curls. He smiled, displaying a sweet, gentle disposition. (If there is any better index to character than the way a person smiles, I have never found it.)

"How do you do?" he said. "I have come to visit you."

By the time Sam got his pipe picked up, John had got down the forty-feet length of living-room and had Chad by both hands, and was introducing him as the friend he had told us about, the friend he had made at Mather's Field, during the war.

The way of that was, John had saved his life for him down there, and had never since been able to get out from under the responsibility of it. John had found a job for him, after the armistice, and when Chad lost it, John had loaned him money to start out in a vaudeville act.

He did fine with that for three years, and was making good money on the Orpheum circuit, when he got into an automobile accident in Kansas City and was laid up for months in the hospital there. He went back to work sooner than he should have, and spent three months in an Oakland hospital with influenza. John had wired money to him there, and had asked him, again, to come for a visit to the Desert Moon. But, since he had had a standing invitation for years, and since he had sent no word that he was coming, John was as much surprised as any of us that evening.

He had walked over, he explained, from Winnemucca, a distance of a couple of hundred miles. He had had money to buy a ticket no further than Winnemucca. He had had a job there, for a while, dish-washing—a fine job he made of it, I'll warrant—and had used his earnings to get into a solo game, hoping to win enough money to pay for his ticket. He had lost his money, his watch, his coat, vest, and shirt. The landlady at Winnemucca, he said, wanted his trunk worse than he did; and, anyway, he never argued with ladies. She had allowed him to take the raincoat—a raincoat in this part of Nevada being about as much use to anybody as a life preserver to a trout—and the funny straw hat—he had worn both in his vaudeville act— and the ukulele. Who wouldn't be glad to let anyone who wanted to take a ukulele anywhere, take it? The camera he had found on the road between Shoshone and Palisade. He had named it, "Unconscious Sweetness," and called it "Connie" for short, and he was always plum daffy about it, taking expected and unexpected pictures of all of us at all hours and in all places, and pasting them in big albums with jokes and such written underneath.

It is hard to give a fair description of Chad. He was a little, pindling fellow. Around Sam and John and Hubert Hand he looked about as dainty and trifling as the garnish around the platter of the Thanksgiving turkey. He seemed kind of like that, too; like the extra bit of garnishing that makes life's platter prettier and nicer—absolutely useless, maybe, but never cluttery.

Until after he came, I had not realized how little real laughing any of us had done. We had been happy enough, and content; but we had never been much amused. He amused us. He made us laugh. He took the mechanical player off the old grand piano, and played it as we had never before heard it played. He spoke pieces and sang funny songs until we held our sides with laughing. He was a ventriloquist, and a mimic besides. He could imitate all of our voices to a T.

He had been with us about a week before any of us knew that. I was in the kitchen, one day, when I heard someone come into the butler's pantry.

"Mary," Sam's voice called from there, "you are fired. Bounced. You haven't made a cake in two days, nor doughnuts in three. You are getting too lazy and worthless for the Desert Moon—"

I tottered; but, just before I fainted clear away, here came that grinning little ape, dancing and kicking his heels in an airy-fairy dance, but still speaking in that gentle, drawling voice of Sam's.

I laughed until I had to sit down and lean on the table. I begged him, then, not to give it away for a few days; and the fun he and I had, for the next week, would make a book in itself.

Martha adored him. He played with her by the hour. He made two dolls, Mike and Pat, for her, and he would let them sit on her knees while he made them talk for her. He had to treat her as he would treat a child, of course;

but he managed, what the rest of us did not always manage, to treat her as if she were a good, sensible child, not
too young to be polite to. Chad had the nicest manners of
any man I have ever known.

At the end of November, when he began to talk about
leaving, Sam offered him a hundred and fifty a month to
stay on. He said, like Hubert Hand had said, "What for?"

"For living," Sam said.

Chad laughed and shook his head.

"Double it, then," Sam urged. "I wouldn't have you
leave the place, and Martha, for three hundred a month;
so why shouldn't I pay it to have you stay?"

Chad never would take any regular money from Sam.
But he stayed on and got what he needed, such as clothes,
and razor blades and films for Connie, and had them
charged to Sam's accounts. He called himself the "Perpet-
ual Guest—P. G." for short, but some of the others said it
stood for "Pollyanna Gush" and called him "Polly" to twit
him. Pollyanna may not be literature, I don't know; but
a person of that nature is most uncommonly pleasant to
have around the house.

The only time I ever felt any differently about Chad was
right after Sam broke the news to the assembled household
that we were to be visited by a couple of lady twins from
Switzerland. Chad began, then, to practice a new song
about "sleep, little baby," and to permit the most ear-split-
ting sounds to issue from the back of his throat. He called
it yodeling; and said that yodeling was Switzerland's chief
export, and that he was practicing up to make the ladies
feel at home. I declare, it nearly drove me out of my wits.
A disturbing element, they were, you see, from the very
first.

5
The Arrival

The girls got here on Friday, the eighth of May. Sam and I rode down to Rattail in the sedan to meet them, and John took the small truck down to bring up their baggage.

Number Twenty came roaring up, on time, and stopped with a snort of angry protest, as it always does when it has to stop at Rattail, which is not often; not more than a dozen times a year at best, I guess.

Sam and I hurried down the tracks to where the porter's white, rapidly swinging arms were piling up the shining black baggage.

I don't know what there is about riding in a train that turns folks haughty and supercilious; but there is something that does. A person who would be right hearty and human on his own two feet, sits in a car window and looks out at the platform people as if they were something he wanted to be careful not to step in. By the time I had passed fifty or more windows, and had reached where the girls were standing, I was so heated up I couldn't find a word to say but, "Pleased to meet you," which was not the truth.

One of them smiled real sweet, and said, "Mary! Upon my soul you haven't changed at all in sixteen years," and made as if to kiss me; which I did at once.

The other one gave me a jerky nod, and stood there, watching the train pull out, until Sam, who had been poking along behind me, managed to catch up.

"Uncle Sam," she exclaimed, laughing and standing on tiptoe, and putting her hands on his shoulders, and tipping her pointed chin up to him, "you dear, to have us! I had always remembered that you were the biggest man in the world, and now I see that I was right about it."

Sam didn't kiss her, as she had expected him to. He patted her hands, took them down off his shoulders and held them a minute before he dropped them and reached to shake hands with the twin who had kissed me.

"Well, now," he said, "this is sure great. Little girls all grown up to ladies, and coming to see their old uncle." (He had bitten on that uncle bait, though he was no more their uncle than I was.) "Which of you is which, now? Let's get you sorted out, so I can call you by name. I used to get you all mixed up, when you were little tykes—couldn't tell one from the other."

"You won't have that trouble anymore," said the one who had nodded at me. "I am Gabrielle, and that prim little puss is Danielle. People never get confused about us any longer."

Indeed, I should think not. Danielle was dressed pretty and neat in a suit of gray about the shade of a Maltese cat, with a nice little round hat to match, and not more than ten inches of gray silk stocking showing between the edge of her skirt and the tops of her neat gray pumps. Gabrielle had on a floppy coat thing, that looked more like a bathrobe, cut off at the knees, the way it lopped and draped, with nothing but a big buckle on one hip to hold it together at all. It was about two shades darker than good cream tomato soup. Her hat was as near as she could match it, I guess; and, though it was small, it was soft and loppy. Her stockings, sixteen inches of them in sight, if an inch, were a kind of sickly cross between yellow and pink. Her black satin shoes had stilt heels and silver buckles. She wore, also, a pair of earrings, dangling almost to her shoulders, that looked like the spinners the boys use here, in the fall, when they go after the big trout.

The population of Rattail had come running to the depot, of course, when the train stopped; and, at last, swaggering his way among males, females, Indians, cowpunchers, and dogs, here came John.

He doesn't usually trim his walk with that swagger; but, bashful as an overfed coyote, he is hard put to it, at times, to cover up this deficiency of his. So he swings his shoulders, and talks loudly, and boasts around, when a person with a keen ear could hear his knees clicking together.

"La-la!" exclaimed Gabrielle, when she caught sight of him. "Who is this picturesque man thing coming toward us?"

John did look pretty fine, wearing his new corduroy suit, and his shining new leather puttees, and his new sixteen-dollar sombrero. He had even gone so far as to button up the collar of his brown flannel shirt. I was sorry he had not been around, when the train came in, to add tone to Sam and to me.

"He," Sam answered, beaming with pride, "is my boy, John."

"How thrilling!" chirped Gabrielle. "It is like living in a cinema, isn't it, Danny?" And off she went, sort of skipping along the tracks, to meet him.

When they met, John gave her about the same attention that a passenger gives the ticket chopper at the gate, in a city depot, when he sees the train he is trying to catch moving slowly out through the yards. He pulled off his hat with a bow, but he passed her, walking very fast. I thought that he was so flustered that he did not know what he was doing. He knew. He was headed straight for Danny. He

had been in the freight house since long before the train
came in, sizing up from a safe distance the girls' arrival.
Then he had sneaked out the back way, up past the station
house, and around it and back again, to give the appearance of having just that minute got into Rattail.

"John," I said, when he reached Danny and me, and
stopped short, like he had just been lassoed from the rear,
"this is Danielle Canneziano."

John dropped his hat in the alkali dust, his new hat,
and reached out and took both of Danny's hands in his.
Falling on his knees in front of her would not have been
much showier.

"I—" he produced, "I—I heard you laugh."

To me, it barely made sense; but she seemed to find it
interesting and important.

"Really?" she said, and sort of trilled it full of meaning.

Standing there, with my new shoes hurting my corns,
and Sam and Gabrielle completely out of sight around the
corner of the depot, I felt as necessary, useful, and wel-
come as a hair in the soup, and a sight more conspicuous.
Rattail's population was beginning to close in around us.
I pulled at John's sleeve; but I declare, if a freight hadn't
come along, forcing those two to get off the tracks, they
might have been standing there yet, gazing into each other's eyes.

I was halfway home, riding beside Danny in the sedan,
when Gabrielle's laughing out again, at some remark of
Sam's, made me remember that she had been the only one
who had done any laughing when we had met. Danny had
only smiled. So, if that laugh was what had put John clear
off his head, he had picked the wrong twin.

6
The Secret

The first minute I heard that the Canneziano girls were coming to the Desert Moon, I was certain that they were not coming for the peace of the mountains and the deserts. Going on from there, I questioned myself as to what reason any Canneziano had ever had for coming to the ranch, or for writing to the ranch. The answer was, to get money. I tried to think that they would stay a few months, long enough to put themselves in Sam's good graces, ask him for a tidy sum, and leave. But they had not been on the place two days before I knew that, though that might be a minor part of their plan, it was not the major part; that there was something far less simple, something, probably, treacherous and sinister at the root of this visit of theirs to the Desert Moon.

On the evening of their arrival the girls had unpacked their trunks in their bedrooms. The next morning the boys carried their trunks to the attic. Going through the upper hall, later that same morning, I saw one of the empty drawers that had fitted into their new-fangled trunks, lying beside the door to the attic stairway.

I hate clutter. I picked it up and carried it upstairs. I went in all good faith: but I wear rubber-soled shoes around the house, and the stairs are thickly carpeted; so the girls, who were up there, did not hear me coming. Just

before I got to the turn in the stairs, I heard one of them
say:

"I am sure that there is no use in searching the house.
In the first place, he never could have gotten it into the
house without being seen."

"You are too sure of everything, when you are unsure
of anything," the other girl answered, and I thought, since
the voice was louder and, somehow, richer, that it was
Gaby's. "Stop being sure, and try being sensible. We must
find it. We have very little time. How do you know whether he could have brought it into the house or not? There
is a back stairway."

Fool that I was, I kept right on going up the stairs. It
took me a while to develop the poll-prying, eavesdropping, sneaking, and generally despicable character that I
did develop later.

"Did you girls lose something?" I asked, when my head
had poked up to where I could see them.

Danny jumped, from being startled, but Gaby never
turned a hair.

"Only a trinket of Dan's," she said. "Possibly she never
packed it at all."

I gave them the trunk drawer and came back downstairs, wracking my brain with questions.

Who was the "he" who had, or who had not, gotten
something into the house? The something that they must
find, and had very little time in which to find it. And,
land's alive, what was the something?

I resolved to say nothing, but to watch those two girls,
like a hawk, from then on. I did so. But it was three weeks
before I heard anything more at all, though I saw a great
deal.

I saw those girls searching, searching everlastingly, the
entire place. I saw them go to the cabin, and stay inside
of it for hours. I saw them in the barnyards, and in the

barns, searching. I saw them down in the outfit's quarters when the men were all away. I heard them get up late at night, and sneak out of the house, and come back in the early hours of the morning. And, once or twice, I thought that I saw them seeing me, as I watched them, and then I was afraid.

It was during these three weeks that Danny and John announced their engagement. My own opinion is that they got themselves engaged the first five minutes they were alone together; but that they had gumption enough to wait for ten days before telling it.

Sam gave them his blessing. That is to say, he said that any agreement they wanted to make was all right with him, if Danny was sure she would be satisfied to live on the Desert Moon, and if they would wait a year to be married. They agreed to this, the year of waiting, reluctantly. Sam, whose one bad habit, not counting his pipe, is using suitable and unsuitable quotations on all suitable and unsuitable occasions, assured them that a year was as a day on the Desert Moon; but that didn't seem to make them any happier. The only people who were downright pleased with Sam's decision were Gaby and myself. I, for certain reasons of my own. Gaby, because she was choosing to consider herself also in love with John.

I realize that this is crowding pretty fast what the books call "love interest." I realize, too, that I have not given any description of John that would account for two traveled ladies coming to the Desert Moon and, at once, falling in love with him.

He had, as I guess I've signified, a heap more than his share of masculine good looks. Outside of hat and collar advertisements, I don't know that I've ever seen even pictures of men that were any better looking than John was. The way he lived, and dressed, and rode, made him sort of romantic, too, I suppose. A Santa Fe man, who met him once when he was taking cattle back east for Sam, offered him a surprising salary to come to the Grand Canyon and live around there, in order to impress and delight the eastern young lady tourists. John was simple-hearted, and slow spoken; but I guess most women don't mind that in men. Too, he was a good boy, all the way through. And, of course, he had plenty of money, now, and would have a million or more, not counting the ranch, when Sam died.

Gaby made no bones about her feelings for John. I did not do as John did, and set all of her open advances toward him down to sister-in-lawly affection. Still, I didn't believe that she really thought she was in love with John, until I hid in the clothes-closet that evening and heard Danny and her talking together.

The closet arrangement was a fortunate one for my purposes. It was between the girls' rooms, with heavily curtained doorways leading into each room, and a door at the end with a transom for ventilation, leading into the hall. This closet had originally been a part of the hall, going down between the two rooms. But, in 1912, when Sam had had the ranch-house remodeled, inside, they had turned the closet spaces for these rooms into two bathrooms, necessitating the present arrangement of a double closet.

The dozens of gowns and frocks—nothing so ordinary as mere dresses—that the girls had brought with them, hanging on padded hangers from the long rods, made as good a hiding place as anyone could ask for; especially, since I always took care to unscrew the light globe in the closet when I went in, so that it seemed to be all right, but would not light when the wall switches were pressed.

I had gone in there so many evenings, during the past three weeks, and had heard nothing for my pains that it was a wonder I had decided to try it again that evening. It was not luck, though. Gaby's actions, that evening, toward John had been so downright disgusting, sitting on the arm of his chair, and trying to coax him out of the house to see the mountains by moonlight, and hanging herself around his neck when they danced together, and so on, that I had a notion Danny might have a little conversation ready for her when she could get her alone.

I had waited about ten minutes when I heard the door of Gaby's room open. I was so tickled I all but squealed, when I heard that Danny had come in with her, instead of going on down the hall to her own room. Evidently they had begun their conversation in the hall, for Gaby's first words were, "Jealous, my dear Dan?"

"I don't know. But it is silly for you to act as you do. John is in love with me."

"Since you are so certain of that, why do you object to my poor little efforts?"

"I've told you. Because they are silly. And—not kind. Why should you try to take him away from me, when you don't want him yourself?"

"Are you sure of that, too?"

"Yes, I am. His good looks fascinate you, and so does his unsophistication. You'd like the fortune he is to inherit. But you would never be satisfied to marry him and live right here for the remainder of your life."

"No, I would not. I'd marry him, if he didn't have a penny—it is you who are always thinking about his fortune—but I wouldn't allow him to bury himself, and his beauty, and charm in this God-forsaken country. I'd get him out into the world, and have him take his place there. With his ability and energy, and with me to help him, what a place it might be! For you to have him is—waste. Waste. You don't know anything about love. You'll never learn. I—I tell you I can't bear it. It isn't fair—" She began to cry, hollow-sounding sobs, that seemed to catch in her throat and wrench free from it.

"Gaby. Gaby, dear. Please don't. I am sorry—"

"Waste. Waste. Waste. You are not sorry. Don't touch me!"

"I am sorry, Gaby. But what can I do? I couldn't give John to you, if I wished to."

"You could give me a chance."

"No, I couldn't."

"You are a coward."

"Perhaps. I love him. He means to me, too, peace, and security, and decent living—the things I want most for my life. Why should I risk it all?"

"Coward! Coward! Peace and security! He means life to me. All of it; full and complete. Love, and passion, and adventure and attainment, for him and for me, too. Do you think I'll stand by, and allow you to have him, to bury his wonder in your peace, and smother his possibilities with your security and decent living?"

"I think," Danny answered, "that you will have to. John and I love each other; and we are going to keep each other. You, nor anyone, can change that."

"Suppose I should tell John why we came here?"

"You won't do that. You can't harm me without harming yourself. But, if you threaten that, just once more, I will go straight to John and tell him the truth—"

"You promised—"

"I haven't broken my promise. I shan't, if you don't. But you must know that I haven't any interest left in the thing."

"What about your desire for revenge?"

"That desire was yours, not mine. I never considered that side of it at all."

"Coward! Quitter! Stool-pigeon—"

"That isn't fair, Gaby. I'll help if I can. I have been helping, haven't I? I won't hinder in any way. But the time is short now. Remember that."

"Danny—" There was a new tone in Gaby's voice, sweet like, and appealing. I did not trust it for a minute; but I think Danny did, for she answered, gently, "Yes, dear?"

"Forgive me. Let's be twinny again. Friends?" I could hear the treachery in that as plainly as I could hear the words. I think Danny did not hear it, for she answered, "I do want to be friends, Gaby. I do, truly. Only—please, dear, won't you leave my man alone?"

"And you'll help me. And you won't tell him—anything?"

"Of course I won't tell, Gaby. It is really your secret, now; not mine. And I'll help you all I can."

7

Three Rings

Revenge. Out of all that crazy conversation the one word kept pestering me like a leaking faucet. No matter what I was doing, or thinking, that word, revenge, kept drip, drip, dripping, until my mind was fairly drenched with it. I got all mixed up about it. Did people revenge other people, or have revenge on them, or—what? I looked it up in the dictionary. "Malicious injuring in return for an injury or offense received."

I got a piece of paper and wrote it down. "The Canneziano girls want to injure, maliciously, some one on the Desert Moon Ranch, in return for an injury or an offense received." I crossed out "The Canneziano girls," and wrote, "Gabrielle Canneziano," since Danny had said that she had never considered that side of it at all. It did not help any. It did not make sense.

Since Sam and I were the only people on the ranch they had known before they came here this time, it seemed as if they had come to injure, maliciously, one of us. I had never done either of them a mite of harm in my life. Sam had never done anything but good for them. Of course, Sam had not been very gentle with their father. But, as I took pains to discover, neither of them had any kind feelings for their father. Gaby said, straight out, that she hated him. Danny, who was too gentle speaking to use such a

39

word as hate, said that she had never liked him, never
loved him. Both of them laid their mother's death at
Canneziano's door. They thought that his cruelty and his
neglect had killed her. It was senseless to suppose that
they were harboring a grudge against Sam for anything
that he had ever done to Canneziano.

Of course, I see now that all that part of it was as plain
as the Roman nose on Hubert Hand's face. How I missed
seeing it, even then, I don't know. I was, I guess, like a little boy so busy trying to watch all three rings at the circus
at one time that he missed the elephant parade.

The Desert Moon was like that sure enough; like a three
ring circus, during the months of May and June. There
were the girls, everlastingly searching for something: leaving the house shortly after the men left it, each morning;
returning, tired out, just in time for dinner; off again for
the afternoon, and coming home just in time to pretty up
for supper. After a while, I began to lose interest in that;
and, being a woman, I allowed my attention to become
distracted by the center ring where all the love interest
was going on.

Not that Danny and John were interesting. If there is
anything that will make two people duller to all other
people than being engaged to each other, I am sure I don't
know what it is. Gaby's unceasing efforts to win John away
from Danny were interesting enough, I suppose, to folks
who can stand to look at that sort of thing. Personally, I
shut my eyes to it as much as possible. Most of my attention I gave to the clown in the ring—to Chad.

I can not explain it, now or ever; but Chad, from the
very first, was head over heels in love with Gaby. He had
no more chance of winning her, penniless, funny, kind
little fellow that he was, than an amateur has of riding an
outlaw pony. I told him that, once, in those very words.

"I know it, Mary," he said. "But you are wrong about one thing. I'm not riding for a fall. I'm not even mounted. I know I haven't a chance with her. I know I can't pull one of those stars out of the sky up there with a fishhook. I'm not trying. But I can sit here in the dark and look at the stars, can't I? Stars make all the difference—in the dark. And, maybe, sometime I can serve her in someway. That's all I ask. . . ." So on. If it hadn't been Chad, and therefore heartbreaking, it would have been downright funny.

She never gave him two looks. He couldn't even make her laugh with his jokes and his songs, as he could the rest of us. Once she did deign to allow him to try to teach her the trick of his ventriloquism. She could not learn it, and she was furious with him, and said that he did not want her to learn it. But he followed her about, and waited on her. He brought her pony up to the house, instead of allowing one of the outfit to do it. He brought her desert flowers, which she tossed away to wither. If Connie hadn't had a strong constitution he would have worn her out, taking pictures of Gaby. Page after page in his album filled with, "Gaby by the window;" "Gaby on the porch;" "Gaby and Danny starting on a walk;" "Gaby in riding costume;" Gaby here, there, and everywhere. And Martha half mad with jealousy.

Right at first, I think that some of the others thought that Martha's jealousy was something of a joke. I never did think so. Before long we all began to feel that it was more than a little serious. Sam talked to Chad, and to Gaby about it. Chad did the best he could, after that, to be as attentive to Martha as he had been before; but, if he so much as opened a door for Gaby, Martha would go into temper fits, and sulking spells.

As for Gaby, Sam's talk with her made things worse. She had never noticed Chad at all, so she had not noticed that Martha was jealous of him. She welcomed the news as another tool she could use to tease and torment the poor girl. All along she had delighted in teasing and torment- ing Martha, though she had dared not do it when Sam was present.

The very evening after Sam had talked to her in the morning. Gaby went and sat beside Chad and curled his pretty, yellow curls around her finger.

It was a cloudy evening, not chilly; but Sam had light- ed the fire as he always does when he has half an excuse, and Martha was sitting in front of it, pretending to read a magazine. She had been pretending to read that same mag- azine, on the same page, for the last five years. She seemed to get pleasure out of sitting and holding it in her hands. No other magazine would do.

Of a sudden, this evening, she thrust the magazine in the flames for an instant, jerked it out, and rushed at Gaby with the burning torch. No harm was done. John snatched it and tossed it back into the fireplace. But all of us, except Gaby, had the good sense to be thoroughly frightened.

Things weren't ever quite the same for Martha after that. No other magazine, or picture book, would take the place of the one she had burned. She would wander about the house, evenings, quietly, but restless, like a cat who had lost her kittens.

One of Gaby's pleasant little ways was to refer to Mar- tha as an idiot, right before her face.

"La-la!" Gaby exclaimed one evening, when Martha was wandering about. "The idiot gets on my nerves. Can't you make her keep still, Mrs. Ricker?"

"She isn't harming anyone," I said, since Mrs. Rick- er, as usual, said nothing. "You leave her alone, and stop talking like that, Miss."

"I'm not harming anyone, now," Martha piped up. "But someday I might. I'd like to. I won't, though," she walked over close to Gaby, "if you'll give me the gold monkey. I'll be good then, for always."

It was a bracelet charm of Gaby's, a gold monkey, about the size of a large almond, with jade eyes. The minute Martha had seen it she had begun to beg for it. There weren't any monkeys in the jewelry catalogs, but Sam sent off and got her a bear and a turtle. She wouldn't have any truck with them. She wanted that one, particular monkey. Gaby would not give it to her; would not so much as allow her to wear it for a few hours at a time. As usual, this evening, she refused to let Martha touch it.

"Yes, and you'll be sorry," Martha threatened.

She went upstairs and emptied a can of pepper in Gaby's handkerchief box.

She was always playing tricks of the sort on Gaby, if we did not watch her. For my own part, I wouldn't have bothered with watching her but for the fact that, more than often, she got the two girls mixed up and it was Danny whose pretty dress would be tied to the chair to tear, instead of Gaby's; or Danny's hair would receive the contents of Chad's paste-pot; and then Martha, discovering her mistake, would make herself ill with crying and remorse. Just as she had hated Gaby from the start, she had loved Danny; but she could not tell them apart.

It seemed incredible that even Martha could be confused about the two girls; because, if ever girls were opposites, those girls were. Of course, they were the same size, about five feet and two inches tall, I should judge, and the same weight—both of them too skinny to my way of thinking, flat as bread-boards. Their faces, just their faces, did look alike. They both had long brown eyes, straight noses, small mouths—Gaby painted her lips until

they looked much fuller and more curved than Danny's—
pointed chins, and complexions the color of real light car-
amel frosting. Danny's cheeks showed a faint pink, coming
and going. Gaby painted her cheekbones, clear back to her
ears, with a deep orange-pink color. They both had wavy,
dark brown hair, cut just the same in the back, real close
fitting and down to a point. But Gaby brushed her hair
straight back from her forehead, and put varnish stuff on
it till it was as sleek and shining as patent leather. She left
all of her ears showing, and she always wore big earrings,
dangling from them. Danny parted her hair on the side,
and allowed it to wave, loose and soft and pretty. She never wore earrings. Gaby's clothes were all loud colored, or
seemed to be—black turned gaudy when she put it on—
and they were all insecure appearing, too defiant of paper
patterns to be quite moral. Danny's clothes were as neat
and quiet as a pigeon's.

No wonder that these frequent mistakes of Martha's
made me decide that she was losing her eyesight. I spoke
to Sam about it, suggesting that Mrs. Ricker would better
take her to San Francisco to visit an oculist.

According to his usual custom, Sam laughed at me. He
said that he had about concluded that Martha was the only
one on the place who could use her eyes to see deeper than
gee-gaws and fol-de-rols.

"If you are insinuating," I said, "that those two girls
are alike in any respect, inside or outside, you've lost your
senses."

"Why shouldn't they be alike?" Sam questioned. "They
are twin sisters. They were brought up together, they
have had the same friends, the same teaching, the same
environments. Of course they are alike. One of them is
play-acting. I don't know which one. I suspect Danielle,
on account of John."

I may as well state, right here, that all of this remark of Sam's, with the exception of the girls being twin sisters, was a mistake from beginning to end. I didn't, at that time, know much of anything about their past lives. I did know their present characters. I told him so.

He laughed again, and wanted to know what had become of all my theories concerning our modern young girls. Ever since the war, I had been standing up for them, through thick and thin.

"It takes a pretty stout theory," I admitted, "to hear a young lady called a 'damn good sport,' and see her receive it as a choice compliment."

"Who said that to who?" Sam wanted to know.

"Who do you suppose? Hubert Hand to Gaby, of course."

"Hubert Hand," Sam said, "had better behave himself."

Since Hubert Hand was too selfish ever to love anything that his Roman nose wasn't attached to, his carryings on with Gaby should be classed, I think, not in the center ring, but as the main attraction of the third ring. And he almost old enough to be her father, with white coming into his hair at his temples!

To this day I have never understood those two, during those months. Gaby was in love with John. Hubert Hand was in love with Hubert Hand. Yet they hugged and kissed, and seemed to think that calling it "necking" made it respectable. It wasn't a flirtation, with them. It was more like a fight, where each of them was fighting for something they did not want. A perfectly footless, none too wholesome performance.

"You make him behave himself, Sam," I urged.

"He is free, white and twenty-one. And she sure can take care of herself, if ever a girl could. It's none of my put-in."

"What about the rest of us," I said, "forced to watch such goings on?"

"Don't watch. If you watch Belle, and Sadie and Goldie, that is watching enough for one woman."

Belle, Sadie and Goldie were the Indian women I had, at that time, to help me around the place. I suppose they were pretty good girls. They did all the actual work there was to do around the house, except the cooking, with me directing them every step they took. But when I remember how they all deserted me, in the time of our terrible trouble, it makes me so fighting mad that I don't like to give them credit for anything, nor think about them at all, even yet.

8
Atmosphere

The girls had been on the Desert Moon a little better than six weeks when, one evening, Sam came out into my kitchen were I was setting bread. Belle, Sadie and Goldie had gone home, and I had tidied up after them, as usual, and everything in the kitchen was sweet, and clean, and shining. I had the doors tight shut, so I couldn't hear the radio screeching away in the living-room, and the windows open, and the evening breeze fresh from the deserts came in, blowing back my ruffled white curtains and purifying the air.

"Mary," Sam began, real solemn for him, "the ancients used to have cities that they called cities of refuge. No matter what a fellow had done, if he could get inside into one of those cities, he was safe. Your kitchen always kinda seems like that to me—a city of refuge."

"Lands, Sam," I said, "what have you been up to that you are heading this safety first movement?"

To tell the truth, I was a little put out with him for moseying in there when I was setting bread. Like most men I've known, Sam never had any particular hankering for my company unless he thought I could be of some use to him. Generally, I am glad and proud to help Sam, anyway I can; but not when I am setting bread. There is something about setting bread that gives any moral woman

47

a contented, uplifted feeling that she likes to indulge in, undisturbed.

"I haven't been up to anything," Sam answered, "and I don't aim to be. But, Mary, some time ago you came to me with some suspicions. I laughed them off. I am not laughing now. I'm worried. Queer things are going on around here. What I want to know, now, is what do you know?"

"Nothing. What do you know?"

"Nothing."

"What do you suspect, then, Sam?"

"Nothing. What do you?"

"Nothing."

That, I see now, wouldn't have been a bad place for us both to laugh. Neither of us did.

"Have you any idea," Sam questioned, "why the girls go prowling all over the place, afoot and horseback, daytimes, and night-times, too, when they should be in their beds?"

I unfolded a dishtowel and spread it over my pan of bread. It was ready for rising and I had not got a bit of uplift out of it.

"If I told you," I said, "you'd only speak your little memory-gem, about so much good in the worst of us."

"No, I won't, Mary. I'm all set for listening."

"Well, all I know is just what I've known all along. They are hunting for something."

"Sure they are hunting for something. But what?"

"I don't know. But, whatever it is, they are going to use it to get revenge, to injure maliciously somebody."

"Revenge, hell!" Sam said.

"Have it your own way. Only I happened one night to hear Gaby say to Danny that they had come to this ranch for the purpose of revenge."

"Revenge, hell!" Sam repeated himself. "Unless they are sore at me about Canneziano."

"It doesn't make sense. They hate Canneziano. I've about decided that they have come here to get revenge on, maliciously injure, someone who isn't on the place."

"'Brighten the corner where you are,'" Sam scoffed. "But never mind. What else did they say, when you happened to overhear this revenge remark?"

If he was ready, at last, to listen, I was more than ready to tell what little I knew. I told; even to confessing about hiding in the clothes closet.

"Well, well," he drawled, when I had finished my story, "we are probably making a mountain out of a molehill. I wouldn't go pussy-footing around after them, any more, if I were you, Mary. There's a screw loose somewhere, that's sure; but it is not in the Desert Moon's machinery. We've got nothing on our consciences. We don't need to worry."

Don't need to worry! Sam and I, sitting in that peaceful kitchen, talking so smart and frivolous, and deciding that we did not need to worry is a memory I could well be shed of. We didn't need to worry a bit more than if I'd used arsenic in my covered pan of bread; not a bit more than if there had been a den of rattlesnakes in the cupboard under the sink, or gasoline instead of water in the tank on the back of the stove. That is how safe and peaceful we really were, at that minute, if we had had sense enough to know it. When I realize that four weeks from that very evening, three people—

But I guess it would be better to tell things straight along, as they happened. It seems to me a good book can not be hurried, any more than a good cake can. "Mix and sift the dry ingredients," is the way all recipes for cakes begin.

However, since I suspected that I knew a sight more about making a good cake than I did about making a good book, and since the young man from back east—Indiana—

in Nevada for his matrimonial health as are about half
of the population here, happened in just after I had finished writing the above paragraph, I asked him whether
he would, for a consideration, read and correct my manuscript.

He had said, when he had come in from his fishing on
Boulder Creek, that afternoon, and asked to buy a meal,
that he was an author by profession. The looks of him
almost made me decide not to put myself in his class. I
don't know why it is that easterners, coming out here and
buying the same sort of clothes that our men wear, look so
ridiculous in them; but they do. Anyway, I invited him to
stay to supper, and then, as I have said, made the proposition about the manuscript.

He said that he would be only too happy to edit the
yarn, but that it would probably take him several days to
do it efficiently. In other words, though he grandly refused the consideration, he got three full days of board
and rooms and fishing on the Desert Moon in return for
around two hours of work. And I got my clean pages all
marked up with "whoms" and "whichs" and funny do-dad
marks. It took me more than two hours to get them all
erased.

"Now," he said, when he finally had read it, "I am going to be frank with you. You mention dry ingredients. In
my opinion, you have far too many dry ingredients, and
it is taking you much too long to accomplish the mixing
process.

"A book, to be successful, has to move swiftly. This is
particularly true of stories of crime and their detection.
A properly constructed story of this sort, begins with the
murder. The wisest thing for you to do, is to burn all of
this that you have done, and make a fresh beginning, at
the time of the first murder.

"In the new copy, do attempt to get in some atmosphere. You must make your readers feel the setting, as it were. Bring them across the wide and multicolored deserts that lie between here and Telko, to this marvelous farm. Show them the massive mountain ranges surrounding it; let them breathe the rarefied air, drink deeply of the beauty. Give them the changing colors of the mountains, from their jade greens to their rich ruby hues, with the purpling cloud shadows swaying across them. Let them hear the scurrying of the desert rats, the calls of the owls, the howls of the coyotes. Paint for them the slender white trunks of your aspen trees, and the green quivering of their leaves. The harsh, rugged beauty, the color, the wonder of this northeastern Nevada of yours is marvelous beyond description. But for all of it that your manuscript shows, the action might have taken place on a chicken farm in Vermont."

"If the folks who read this story," I said, "are downright pining for Nevada atmosphere, let them come out here and get it. There is plenty for all. A mile and a half of it, statistics show, for each person now in the state. Nobody ever reads the descriptions in a story, anyway. I've decided that authors put them in for the same reason that a cook, when unexpected company comes, makes a double amount of dressing for the chicken, or serves her creamed canned oysters on toast—to fill up, to make enough to go around."

"Well, Mrs. Magin," he said, "I can only remark that as an author you are a most excellent cook."

"When I heard the first variation of that," I said, "years, and years, and years ago, I thought it was a little comical."

"I am sorry," he answered. "I thought that you were the sort of person who would appreciate sincere criticism, even though it might not be wholly complimentary."

"Job wasn't," I told him, "and I don't set up to be any better than he was. What is more, if you can point to any man or woman in history or out of it, who ever did appreciate sincere, uncomplimentary criticism, I'll pepper this story so full of atmosphere that folks will think they are reading booster club's literature about Florida."

He could not do it. Consequently, I continue this story in my own way, stating that if any more atmosphere is in it, it got there by mistake. My plan is to turn it out so that, from now on, not more than a page of it can be skipped at one time and the rest of it make sense.

9

The Cabin

For three days, beginning with the fourth of July, there was to be a big celebration and rodeo at Telko. Trying to keep cowpunchers on the ranch, when there was a celebration of any sort going on within a distance of a couple of hundred miles, would be about as sensible as trying to keep gunpowder in a hot oven. So all the outfit that was on the ranch—never very many in July—were tinkering with their flivvers, and currying their mounts, and building up their boot-heels, and washing and ironing, and making elaborate preparations to attend.

Sam suggested at noon on the second of July, while we were at dinner, that maybe all of us would like to go; all, that is, except Martha and himself. Celebrations were never good for Martha.

I spoke right up and said to count me out. I know the deserts in July. But the boys were enthusiastic about it, and Danny was interested. Gaby, coming in late, greeted the idea with the same enthusiasm with which a woman greets moths in the clothes closet.

"Whence the crave for a fourth of July celebration?" she asked.

"We have never seen a rodeo," Danny answered.

"Go, by all means," Gaby said. "Buy pink lemonade. March in the parade. Ride in the Liberty car. Mrs. Magin would be stunning as the goddess of Liberty, with—"

"Don't let my stunningness stop anything," I said. "I am not going."

"We'll think it over," Danny said. "It would be a long, hot ride. Probably we should all have a pleasanter time, right here at home."

But there was something in the way she had said it, too quickly in answer to a look from Gaby, that made me think there was more to her backing out of the plan than had appeared on the surface.

Gaby had just begun her dinner. The rest of us had finished; so, according to our custom, we excused ourselves and went our ways. Chad tried to stay with Gaby, but Martha fussed and insisted that he come with her.

I had a sure feeling that Danny would return, and that she and Gaby would have something to say to each other. I went into the kitchen and told Belle to clean the stove. Nothing made Belle so angry as to have to clean the stove. The angrier she got, the more she clattered. When I stepped back into the pass-pantry, and opened the pass-window a crack, the kitchen sounded as if half a dozen women were busy in it.

Just as I opened the window I heard John say, "I thought Danny was in here."

"No," Gaby said. "But won't you come in and talk to me?"

"What about?"

"About—this."

I dared not peek, so I did not know what she meant until she said, "Why won't you kiss me?"

"Shall I say, I don't want to pick flowers in Hubert Hand's yard?"

"I hate you!"

"Don't be sore at me, Gaby," John said. "But I'm telling you, that's a lot nearer the truth than—than what you usually say."

John was one of the poorest talkers ever heard. One of those strong, silent men supposed to abound in the west, and who are likewise supposed to make every word that they say count. If John's did, they counted backwards.

"My dear, haven't I proven over and over again that I love you?"

"I don't know how."

"In every way. I have made myself ridiculous, here, because I haven't been able to conceal my feelings for you."

"I think," John said, "that most of that stuff you pull is just to spite Danny. It doesn't spite her, though. She knows she's the only girl in the world for me. I wish you'd cut it out—all of that, Gaby. Won't you, and just be good friends?"

"You'd not want me for an enemy, would you?"

"Getting at anything, going any place, Gaby?"

"Perhaps. If Danny should hear that you have made love to me—"

"I have never made love to you. It would be your word against mine. I think Danny would take mine, if it came to a show-down."

"You'd lie about it?"

"Gosh, no, Gaby. A lot worse than that. I'd tell the truth about it. Listen here, child; don't you try to make trouble between Danny and me."

"Meaning?"

"Nothing. Except that it wouldn't be healthy for anyone who tried it."

"Boo-oo! Dangerous Dan McGrew stuff? Out where men are men? Killer loose to-night—all that, eh, Johnnie?"

"Nothing like that," he said, and his voice was so gentle that if Gaby had been a puncher she would have reached for her six-gun. "But killing would be too good for the imaginary person we are talking about."

A door opened. "John," came in Danny's voice, "uncle is looking everywhere for you."

"What," Danny questioned, when the door had closed behind John, "made you both look so angry, just now?"

"Nothing important. John had just threatened to kill me, but—"

"Don't be silly."

"Never mind. Are you going to that fools' celebration, with only a day or two left, now?"

"I suppose not, if you don't want me to. I'd love going. I know there is no use in staying here."

"In other words, you would sacrifice my future for a rodeo?"

"That is silly."

"Everything is always silly, with you. I more than half believe that you know—"

"That's sil— I mean, what possible object could I have?"

"Many, my dear. Very many. Though I think that getting rid of me would outweigh the others."

"Gaby, I don't want to get rid of you. I wish you would not be so silly, with John. But you know how eager I was to get you away from the continent. I wish I knew that you were going to stay right here for always."

"Is that your game? Listen to me, Danielle Canneziano, if I thought that you were keeping this from me, in order to bury me alive in this God-forsaken hole, and force me to watch you and John—"

"Gaby!"

"I've been a fool! Why can't I learn to take into consideration your damn moralities? Understand this, Dan. Don't fancy for one instant that failure is going to keep me here. Did you think, with a weapon like that in my hands, that I'd stand for anything less than a fifty-fifty proposition? Our original plan would have been better—easier, simpler. But I'll have my share out of this, anyway. So, if you do know—"

"Gaby, I don't know. I'll swear that I don't. How could I? But surely you wouldn't—wouldn't attempt—"

"That is for you to say, darling."

Darling, as she said it then, was as wicked a word as I had ever listened to.

"For me to say?"

"Give John to me. I've changed my mind. If you'll do that, I'll stay right here, and settle down, and do an imitation of a moral, model wife that would satisfy even you."

"Gaby, you speak as if John were a child's toy, to be passed about. I couldn't give him to you, if I were willing to."

"You could, and you know it. You won't. So, that's that. But keep your righteous fingers out of my life; stop your damn preaching, and meddling. I am going to the cabin now. You would better come with me."

"We've searched that cabin a thousand times."

"All the same, it is the one logical place; far removed, and under cover. Too, I must see whether that Indian nailed those floor boards down again, before I pay him."

The cabin is the one Sam built to live in when he first came to the valley. It is up Boulder Creek, about half a mile from the ranch-house, and, built in a big grove of aspen trees, it is one of the prettiest spots on the place. Sam has kept it in repair, inside and out; owing, I think, to sentimental memories, though he declares it is because he dislikes wreckage on the place. The best fishing on the creek begins just above there; so the men, as a rule, leave their fishing paraphernalia in the cabin's kitchen. That is the only use the place has been put to, since John and Martha were little things, and Sam used to hide their Christmas presents up there, under the shelf in the kitchen.

The shelf, about three feet wide, is built across one end of the kitchen. It served Sam for a table, pantry, and sink. Being a man, he built it right handily, like a chest, so that the entire top of it had to be raised to get to the storage place underneath. There was no secret about it. All anyone had to do, was to move everything off the top of it, and lift the lid. But I had read how the hardest problems for detectives always turned out to be something that had been too simple to notice; so my plan was to go up there and raise the lid.

On my way, I met the girls coming home. I imagined that they looked at me with suspicion. I passed a remark about the sweet-smelling clover hay, and hurried right along.

Half an hour later, when I was expecting instant death at any minute, I thought about that sweet clover smell, and how unappreciative I have been of it, and of the blue sky and fresh air, and of the green things, lighted yellow with sunshine, and I took a vow that, if I ever did get a chance to enjoy them again, I would spend the remainder of my life in so doing, and in being grateful to the Creator of them. The same as the last time I had a jumping tooth-ache, I thought that, if that tooth ever did stop aching, nothing could ever make me unhappy again; I was going to be peacefully happy, always, for the reason that I did not have a toothache. Human nature, I have since decid-ed, is never happy because of negatives. At least, I have never known anyone who was happy, for long, because he did not have a toothache, or was not in a hospital, or not hungry, or not—which brings me back to my story—shut up in a chest with packages of explosives.

In the cabin, I went at once to the kitchen; and, remov-ing fish-baskets, fly-books, and reels from the shelf, lifted it back.

I am sure that I had expected to find it empty. Perhaps I had hoped to find a small iron box containing a treasure, or a jewel-casket, or maybe an aged leather case, containing

the missing will, or the plans of some secret fortifica-
tion—any of the simple, ordinary things generally hunted
for and discovered. What I had not expected to find, and
what I certainly had never hoped to find, was what was
there: any number of neatly wrapped packages, addressed
to Mr. Sam Stanley, sent by express, and labeled, various-
ly, "Danger." "Explosives." "Handle with Care."

10

A Conversation

I am not claiming that I possessed one particle of common
sense at that minute, nor for a good many minutes after
that. My actions would give the lie, direct, to any such
assertion on my part. It did not take any common sense to
know, straight off, that, sent to him or not, Sam was not
mixed up in any business that had to do with explosives,
bombs, and Bolshevism. It was easy enough to remember,
then, that Sam had not been to Rattail for the past ten
days; that Hubert Hand had been making the trips down
for the mail, expressage, and supplies.

Just as he came into my mind, I heard his voice. It was
a startling coincidence; but I need a better excuse than
that, for surely no mortal ever did a more foolish thing
than I did then. I climbed into that chest, along with
those packages, and lowered the lid down over me. If I had
any idea, I suppose it must have been a desire not to let
him know that I had discovered his secret—his and Gaby's
together, undoubtedly—but I can't remember having any
thought at all until, just as the lid closed, I remembered
the sad poem about the bride and the mistletoe chest.

I thought, then, that her situation was comfortable
compared to mine. If you have never been packed in a
box with a lot of explosives, as I hope you have not, you
can have no notion of what I went through. I could have

climbed out. But, if you are an elderly woman, of my size
and build, as I hope you are not, and if you have a certain
reputation for dignity to live up to, and a certain reputation for snooping to live down, you can have an idea why
I didn't come springing out of there, like a jack-in-the-
box, or like the immoral ladies who emerge from pies—so
the papers say—at bachelor's parties. I weighed the matter carefully, as I heard, through the thin boards, Hubert
Hand, talking to someone, come into the kitchen. I chose
death by suffocation or combustion.

"My dear woman," were the first words I heard from
him, "you may set your mind at rest. I am not going to
marry the girl. I am not a marrying man, as you know;
and, if I were, she wouldn't have me."

"You leave her alone, then. Understand me. Leave her
alone."

If I believed my ears, that was Mrs. Ricker's voice; that
was Mrs. Ricker, not only talking, but talking like that to
Hubert Hand.

"You flatter me," he said. "Jealous, still, after all these
years?"

"I despise you. But you leave that girl alone. If you
think I'll stand, silent, and allow you to marry her—"

"Hire a hall. I told you that I wouldn't marry her, and
that she wouldn't have me, if I were willing to."

"Wouldn't she, though? Wouldn't she? She is mad about
you. She can't look at you without love in her eyes, nor
speak to you without love in her voice. She tries to hide
it; but she can't hide it from me. I know. She loves you."

I am not sure whether I read it, or whether I figured it
out for myself; but I do know it is a fact that no woman
ever accuses another woman of being in love with a man
unless she could imagine being in love with him herself.

"As to that," Hubert Hand said, in that preeny, offhand
manner that men, who will discuss their love affairs at all,

use when discussing them, "what possible difference could it make to you, Ollie?"

"Only that I would kill her, and you, too, before I would let her have you."

"Easy on there, my girl. Your last attempt at murder—at least I hope that was your last attempt—was not, you may recall, very successful."

"I would be successful another time."

I clamped my teeth to keep them from chattering. I wished that I had some way as easy for muffling the sound made by the pounding of my heart, which was thudding away as loudly as a butter churn in rapid action. Except for that I kept quiet; very quiet. Surrounded, in there by explosives, and out there by people who talked of murder as calmly and as comfortably as if they were discussing moss-roses, very quiet did not seem half quiet enough.

They went into the other room of the cabin and stayed there for a few minutes. I could not hear what they were saying, but I did not budge an inch. After I heard them passing the window, and was sure that they had left the cabin, I remained, very quiet, in the chest for about five minutes longer before climbing out of it.

I was progressing toward home, shivering in every bone, limping, since both my legs had gone to sleep, when Sam, riding his bad-tempered bronco named Wishbone, came up behind me and dismounted.

"Corns bad, Mary?" he questioned. "Must be going to have rain."

"Keep water in the ditches. Both my feet are asleep, from the ankles up."

"Upon my soul! First time in history you ever sat still in one place long enough to have that happen. Well, well. 'Do the thing that's nearest.' Want to climb up on Wishbone and have me lead him?"

"When I go to meet death," I told him, "I shan't go on the back of a nasty tempered bronco."

"Speaking of tempers," Sam grinned, "a person would think I had sung your feet to sleep, Mary."

"Considering," I replied, "that everyone on the Desert Moon is, at this minute, in mortal danger of their lives, all your lighthearted jesting seems pretty much out of place."

I told him, then, about the packages of explosives hidden under the shelf. I had not told him about my climbing in with them; so I was in no way prepared for his actions.

He stopped. He dropped Wishbone's bridle. He put both his hands on his stomach and leaned over and burst into uproarious laughter. "Ho-ho-ho," it rolled out, seeming to fill the entire valley. He leaned to one side; he leaned to the other side, and kept on laughing to deafen the far distant deserts.

"Fireworks," he gasped. "I got them for Martha. Going to surprise her on the fourth. Sent for them months ago. Hid them up there. Ho-ho-ho! I told you to stop pussy-footing around, Mary. Ho-ho-ho! 'Do not look for wrong and evil, you will find them if you do—'"

With as much dignity as a heavy woman, with both of her legs asleep, could muster, I turned and left him. His words and his actions had certainly given me one decision. From this time on, I would tell Sam Stanley nothing.

11

The Letter

When I got back to the house, John was driving up the road in the sedan. He had been to Rattail for supplies and for the mail. He tossed the mailbag out to me, and drove around to the kitchen door to unload.

As a rule the Desert Moon mail is mighty uninteresting, being made up, almost entirely, of bills and advertising matter. Since the girls had come, a few sleazy, foreign-looking letters had livened it up a bit. To a person who has never been farther east than Salt Lake City, a letter from England, or from France, does carry quite a thrill with it. There was a letter for Gaby to-day, postmarked France.

About a month before this, Gaby had received another letter that was a duplicate of this one; the same gray paper, the same sprawling handwriting. Instead of taking it indifferently, as she did other letters, and reading it wherever she happened to be, she had snatched it out of my hand and had run off to her room. All that evening she had seemed to be preoccupied, and worried. The writing looked like a man's writing; but, like a lot of other things, including cigarette smoke, hip pockets and hair cuts, it is not as easy as it used to be to distinguish between male and female in handwriting, at a distance. Sending only two letters in close to two months, it seemed to me that

65

whoever had written them did not write unless he or she had something of importance to say. I was still puzzling over it, when Gaby came into the room.

Sure enough, she snatched it out of my hands, just as she had done with the other letter, and ran straight upstairs with it.

When John and Danny came in, a few minutes later, I went upstairs. Habit stopped me at Gaby's door for a minute, with my ear to the keyhole. Faintly, sounds don't come plainly through our thick doors, I heard the portable typewriter that she had brought with her when she came to the ranch, click, clicking away.

My first judgment was that she was not losing any time in answering that letter; but, as I went down the hall, I had a hazy notion that there had been something queer, different, about the way she had been using the machine. Instead of snapping away on it, lickety-split, as she usually did, she had been touching the keys slowly and carefully, picking them out one at a time, the way I have to do when I try to use Sam's plaguey machine to copy recipes for my card catalog.

I was tuckered and tired. So, after telephoning some instructions to Belle and Sadie in the kitchen, I took plenty of time to tidy myself up. I dawdled in my bath, and I cut my corns, and rubbed hair tonic into my scalp. But, when on my way downstairs again, I stopped for a second at Gaby's door, the typewriter was still going, with its slow click, click. There was nothing to be made out of it, so I went along. It was fortunate that I did, because, before I had reached the top of the stairway, Gaby's door flung open and she called to me, with something in her voice that made me shake in my shoes.

I turned and looked at her. Her face wore an expression that was not human; an expression that would have made any decent woman do as I did, and turn her eyes quickly away.

"Tell Danny to come up here," she said.

I hurried off downstairs, and delivered the message to Danny who was with John in the living-room.

"What's the matter, Mary?" John questioned, when Danny had gone upstairs. "You look as if you had seen a ghost."

"I think," I answered, "that I have—the ghost of Sin."

"Doggone that girl," he said. "I wish she were in Jericho."

"Gaby, you mean?"

"You're darn right. She's causing all the trouble around here."

"What trouble?" I asked, just for a feeler.

"I don't know—exactly. She keeps Danny miserable. But that isn't it, or not all of it. Don't you seem to feel trouble around here, all the time? I thought everyone did. I do, Gosh knows."

"I know," I said. "I feel it, too. I think Sam does, though he won't altogether admit it. Just the same, John, there isn't a thing we can put our fingers on, is there?"

He walked to the window and looked out at the long range of Garnet Mountains, turning blood-red, now, under the sunset.

"I suppose not," he said, at last. "Sometimes, though, when I see Danny looking as she looked when she went upstairs just now, I feel as if it would be a good thing if somebody would put their fingers around that vixen's throat."

"John," I spoke sharply to him, "don't say things like that. You don't mean it. It is wrong to say it."

I was sure that he did not mean it. I was sure that only the voice of one of his rare ugly moods had spoken, and that the wicked thought had died with the wicked words. But, from that day to this, I have never repeated those words to a living soul. Because that was the way that Gaby was murdered: choked to death, with great brutal bruises left on her throat.

12

An Insight

In spite of all my efforts not to do so, I have, again, run on ahead of the story. But, I declare to Goodness, the horror of it, after all these months, is still so strong upon me, that I know the only way to get that written is to write it, with no more dilly-dally, and then to go back and lead up to it properly with the events that immediately preceded it.

That evening, then, the second of July, the two girls came down, late, together. Danny was paler than usual, and her face had a drawn, hurt look, which she explained by saying that she had a severe headache. Gaby was gayer than gay.

I kept watching her, trying to catch her face in repose, to see if any trace remained of that dreadful expression I had seen in the afternoon. Her face, nor one bit of her, was in repose for a minute from the time she came downstairs until she went upstairs again, after twelve o'clock that night.

She put "La Paloma" on the phonograph, and did a Spanish dance, clicking her heels and snapping her fingers until they sounded like firecrackers. She did an Egyptian dance, slinking about, and contortioning. It wasn't decent. She got the whole crowd, including the girls from the kitchen (who had stayed to gape through the door at her dancing, instead of going home as they should have gone), and excluding only Danny, with her headache, Mrs. Ricker and me, to join in a game of follow the leader, and she led them a wild chase all over the house from cellar to attic. Laughing, and jumping, and screaming, and shouting they went, with the radio shrieking out the jazz orchestra in Los Angeles; and me with depression so heavy upon me that it felt real, like indigestion.

Mrs. Ricker was doing some tatting. As I watched her, I decided that, ears or no ears, she was not the woman I had heard talking, that afternoon, up in the cabin. Hubert Hand had said to that woman that she had attempted murder. She could not have been Mrs. Ricker; not our Mrs. Ricker, the thin, silent woman who had lived so decently with us for so long. Those white, bony fingers, darting the shuttle back and forth, making edgings for handkerchiefs, had never held any murderous weapon. Those tight, wrinkled lips had never said, "I would kill her, and you too." John had never said— I shivered. It was fanciful thinking, but it seemed to me that for years the Desert Moon had ridden in our sky, clean and clear, a lucky, fair weather moon, and that now the shadow of the wicked world was slowly creeping over it, inch by inch, with the darkness that was to end in its eclipse. Wicked thoughts and wicked words breed wicked actions, and I knew it then as now.

Martha came crying to Mrs. Ricker. "Gaby hurt Chad," she said. "I wish she would die. We could make her a nice funeral."

Mrs. Ricker's fingers darted faster, back and forth.

Danny spoke, from the davenport. "You shouldn't talk like that, Martha, dear. It is wrong."

Her voice sounded as if it ached. She looked, lying in a huddle over there, as miserable as I felt. I was drawn to her. I went and sat beside her.

"Could I do anything for your headache?" I asked. "Get you some aspirin, maybe."

"No, thank you, Mary." There was so much gratitude in her big dark eyes for nothing but common decency on my part, that I felt downright ashamed of myself.

"Danny," I said, straight out, never caring much about mincing words, "I know that something is troubling you. Why don't you tell John, or Sam, or even me about it? Just tell us the truth. We'd all go far to help you, if we could."

Her eyes filled with tears. "Bless your heart, Mary," she said. "Bless all of your hearts. You are all so good, here—"

I was enough annoyed with John for coming up right then, to have slapped him. I answered his question for Danny.

"There is plenty you could do for her," I said. "You could shut off that screeching radio, for one thing. And you could quiet down, and get the others quieted down. Nobody ever told me that noise like this was a remedy for a splitting headache; did they you?"

"The dickens! By Gollies! It is a wonder you wouldn't have told me before, Mary." Man fashion, putting the blame on me.

Danny wouldn't hear to John's stopping the racket. Everyone was having such a good time. Bed was the place for her. She couldn't hear any noise in her room, with the door shut. And off she went.

I know now that she would not have told me anything that could have helped matters. But I did not know it then, and I was sorely disappointed. For those sudden tears in her eyes, and her voice when she had said, "bless your heart," had convinced me that there was sincerity behind them, and honesty, and good.

In the black days that followed, when all of us were living in the dark shadows of doubts, and confusions, and fears and suspicions, I was thankful, time and again, for those certainties, for that one fleeting but sure insight into Danny's soul.

13
The Quarrel

The morning of the third was biting hot, with that sting-ing, piercing heat that we have, when we have heat at all, in this high altitude. The sixty-mile trip across the deserts to Telko, on a day like this, would be exactly the same as a sixty-mile trip through an oven at the right heat for a roast of beef.

Nevertheless, before seven o'clock that morning, every man-jack of a puncher on the place, with all of his trim-mings and trappings, including wives, squaws, papooses, children and firearms, had set off in flivvers or on horseback, bound for the celebration, leaving the place hole-empty, as Sam said, when he came into my kitchen with a gallon of cream from the dairy.

He pulled the stool out from under the table, perched on it, and remarked, as cheerfully as if he were reading it off a tombstone, "'Sufficient unto the day is the evil thereof.'"

I didn't want him bothering me in the kitchen, when I had everything to do, with Belle, Sadie and Goldie gone gadding; but being a woman, normal I hope, I asked him what he meant by that.

"I'm not going to be surprised," he answered, "if we have another visitor, one of these days."

"Nor me either," I said, though much astonished, because it was as if he had read my mind. At that minute I had been worrying about Sadie. She was expecting her baby, before long, and Land only knew what such a trip as she was off taking now, and the celebration to boot, might precipitate. "That fool girl," I went on. "It wouldn't surprise me a bit if this was the death of her—not a bit."

"Pshaw!" Sam said. "What have you found out, Mary?"

"She told me herself, the last of July."

"Yes? I thought all along that she knew."

Since he seemed as sober as an owl, and as serious, I decided that there was no answer to make, and I made none.

"She's off a few weeks, though. I sent a telegram, and got an answer yesterday. It is the fourth of July."

"Sam," I found breath to retort, "one of us is plumb crazy. I think it is you. Do you think it is me?"

"Not to make any bones about it," Sam said, "I have thought, here lately, that every dang soul on the place was only saved from being in the asylum because of the ignorance of the authorities. But, in this case, I think I am sane and certain. I wired the warden of the penitentiary. He said that Daniel Canneziano was to be released on the morning of the fourth of July. Gaby told you the last of July? Probably some time off, for good behavior."

"I wasn't talking about Canneziano," I snapped. "And how did I know you were? I was talking about Sadie's baby."

I dropped into a chair, feeling sort of weakened from the news about Canneziano, and waited with what patience I could for Sam to stop laughing.

"You mark my words," I said, when the laugh had gone down to a silly giggle, over which I could make myself heard, "all these queer actions around here have something to do with that man's release."

"I'll bet you," Sam said. "But blame my soul if I know what to do, about anything."

"I know what I'd do about Canneziano, if he shows up here," I told him.

"Yes, I know. But he is Danny's father, and Danny is going to marry John. After all, money is not much good unless you take it to market. If I could come to a decent agreement with the fellow—And if he'd take that Gaby with him. I'm dead certain that her hanging around here isn't going to contribute any to John's and Danny's married life—"

"What do you mean by that, Sam?" Gaby asked the question, walking right into the kitchen. I was all taken aback; but Sam didn't seem to be.

"Eavesdroppers, my girl," he said, "hear no good of themselves. I mean that I don't think any girl who wanted to act right would treat her sister's betrothed as you treat John."

"You," she said, very slowly, to make insult baste each word, "are a damned old fool, Sam Stanley."

I shook in my shoes. I had not dreamed that there was a living human being who would dare say that, in that tone of voice, to Sam.

He stood up. He put his hands on her shoulders, gently though, and turned her around.

"You are a bad, wayward girl," he said. "March out of here, now, and get your manners mended before I see you again."

He sobered even her, for a minute. She walked to the door, without another word. There, she whirled around like a crazy thing, and, I declare to Goodness, I don't know what she said. It was the sort of talking I had never heard in my life; my ears were not enough accustomed to the words to take in their meanings. But one thing that she kept screaming, screaming so loudly that she could be heard all over the place, was that Sam had threatened her once too often. Sam stood there, paralyzed, I think, as I was, for perhaps a couple of minutes, before he turned and walked off, into the backyard.

Hubert Hand came rushing in. Gaby threw her arms around his neck, and kept on with the screaming and sobbing. Chad came in through the pantry. Mrs. Ricker opened the door that was at the foot of the back stairway.

She stood there, in the doorway, watching Hubert Hand, with both his arms around Gaby, petting and soothing her. She dampened her tight lips with her tongue; but, without saying a word, she went back up the stairs, closing the door behind her. Hubert Hand led Gaby into the dining-room, and through it into the living-room.

"What in God's name happened?" Chad said to me.

I went and washed my face and took a drink of water. "Chad," I said, "Gabrielle Canneziano has lost her mind. She is insane."

His face went white as lard. "I don't believe it."

"Either that," I said, "or else she is the wickedest, the—"

"Stop it," he shouted at me. "You, nor anyone, can talk to me like that about the girl I love."

"Love! Love your foot!" I snapped at him. The idea of mooning about love to me, at a time like that.

"None of you understands her," he said, "nor tries to. She is in some sort of trouble—terrible trouble. Anyone can see that. I'd give my soul to help her— To serve her—"

"If you are so crazy about serving her," I said, "you might go into the dining-room and set the table, and help me serve her, and the rest of you, some breakfast."

He went into the yard. Like a lot of men, I thought, who want to give their souls and so on to women, he didn't care to be bothered with smaller details, such as feeding them.

I wronged him. Whether or not a man has the giving of his soul, in his own hands, I do not know. A man can give his life. That is what Chad gave.

14
Two Departures

After dinner, which we didn't have until nearly one o'clock on the fourth of July, owing to Chad's not getting the ice-cream frozen on time, John surprised us all by saying that he was going to take the sedan and drive down to Rattail for the mail.

I suspicioned, right then, that he was up to something. He could not fool me into thinking that he would take a fifty-mile trip—twenty-five miles each way—through the desert heat for no other reason than to get the mail. He couldn't do any trading, since all of Rattail would be off to the Telko celebration. When Danny seemed hurt and troubled about him going, and when he went riding right off, anyway, I decided that Sam must have sent him, expecting some word concerning Canneziano. I was wrong.

We had had a stiff breeze, with a promising sprinkle of rain in the morning; but it had died down about noon and, at two o'clock, it was too tarnation hot to do anything but try to keep cool. I stacked the dinner dishes, to wash in the evening, and joined the others, sitting around in the living-room with the electric fans going full blast.

Sam, chess board in hand, stopped long enough by my chair to say in an undertone, "What did I tell you, Mary? 'It is always darkest, just before the dawn.'"

That piece of optimism from him was due, in part, to
the extra good holiday dinner he had just eaten; and in
part to a sense of quiet, edging close to peace, that had
pervaded the place since morning. I had noticed it, too,
with thankfulness, and had accounted for it with the sup-
position that Gaby had spent all of her energy in meanness
the day before, and was obliged to rest up for a spell.

"That's a nice little piece," I answered Sam. "There is
another one, though, isn't there, about a lull before the
storm?"

That was not pure contrariness on my part. I was expecting, every minute, to see Gaby break out again. She
didn't. She yawned around, and fussed about, and then
went and sat beside Danny, who was looking at the pictures in *The Ladies Home Journal,* and put her arm around
her, and petted her up a little—a most unusual performance for her.

When Chad, who had been monkeying with the radio,
got a rip-roaring patriotic program from Salt Lake, the
two girls went upstairs together.

A few minutes later I had an errand upstairs—a real
one, I wouldn't have taken myself up in that heat to satisfy
any curiosity—so, out of habit, I stopped at Gaby's door
to listen. I heard the girls giggling in there; and, knowing
no great harm is afoot when girls giggle, I went on, got
my scrap of pongee silk to mend Sam's shirt, and came
downstairs again.

Sam and Hubert Hand were deep in their chess game.
Mrs. Ricker was tatting. Chad and Martha were playing
dots and crosses. In spite of the noise from the radio,
there was a comfortable feeling about the room that made
me lonesome for the days we had all had together before
the Canneziano girls had come.

The radio program, which was to last from two until
four o'clock, had just that minute stopped. Martha, who

when she didn't forget it, usually fed her rabbits about
that time of day, had gone out to do it. Gaby came downstairs, humming a tune.

She had on the tomato soup colored wrap that she had
worn on the train, and the hat to match the wrap. She
was carrying a beaded bag. She never dressed up like that,
to go walking around the place; a wrap, even such a light
one, in the heat of that day, was downright ridiculous.

Chad said, "All dressed up and no place to go?"

She tossed her head at him, and hurried straight down
the room and out through the glass doors. Chad followed
her. They stopped together on the porch. She stood with
her back to me. Chad faced me. In a minute, I saw his
mouth bend up into a grin of bliss. Nothing would have
surprised me more. For this reason.

As that girl had walked through the room, I had seen
that she walked in mortal fear. In spite of her humming,
in spite of her attempted swagger, fear was in her widened
eyes, in her drawn in chin, in the contraction of her shoulders. Wherever it was that she was going, she was afraid to
go. But where could she go? John had the sedan. Except for
the trucks, which she couldn't drive, and her pony—she
surely would not be dressed like that to ride horseback—
there was no way for her to get off the place. It must be,
then, that someone was coming to the place, and that she
was going out alone to meet them. Who? Canneziano? Not
unless Sam had been mistaken about the time when he was
to be released from prison. Usually, when people think at
all, they think quickly. All this had gone through my mind
while she had walked the forty feet to the door. Before
Chad smiled, I had spoken to Mrs. Ricker.

"That girl," I said, "is afraid of something."

Mrs. Ricker darted her tatting shuttle back and forth.
She moistened her lips, with her tongue; but changed her
mind and said nothing.

Gaby and Chad stood on the porch talking for two or three minutes—a very short time, at any rate. Then she went down the steps, and Chad, still smiling, came back into the room.

As he came in, Danny called down from the top of the stairway. "Gaby—oh, Gaby?"

She knows where Gaby is going, and whom she is going to meet, and she, too, is afraid, I decided, because of the queer, strained quality of her voice.

"Gaby has gone out," I called, in answer. And then, since I could still see Gaby, walking down the path, "Do you want her, Danny? We could fetch her back."

"No," Danny answered. "Don't bother. I'll come down."

I had to reverse my first decision about Danny's being frightened. At least, her voice was natural enough, now; I fancied, perhaps, a note of relief in it.

It couldn't have been more than ten minutes after that, when Martha came running into the house, laughing and dancing, and wearing the gold bracelet with the monkey clasp. Gaby, she said, had given it to her, just now, out by the rabbit hutch.

While we were all still exclaiming over the monkey, and praising it up, to please Martha, Danny came downstairs. She was freshly dressed, and sweet smelling with the nice, quiet flower scent she used, but she looked really ill. She said her headache was worse again, and she drew the curtains at the windows beside the big davenport, to ease the glare of the light, before she curled up on it.

I thought it was a good time to continue the conversation we had begun the other evening.

"Danny," I said, as I sat down beside her, "if you just could tell John, or Sam, or me what is troubling you, I am pretty sure that we could find some way out."

"Bless your hearts," she repeated. "You are all too good. I am afraid I can't tell you what has been troubling me.

But I can tell you, honestly, that I think now the worst of the troubles are over. They never were really mine, you see; they were Gaby's. And now Gaby has decided to—well, stop being troubled.

"We had a good long talk this afternoon. She has made me some promises. She is going to try to act differently, to be good—as she used to say when we were little. She had a dreadful disappointment day before yesterday. It made her act very badly—at first. She has decided now to make the best of it, for there is a best of it to make. You've noticed how much better she acted last evening and all of to-day? She is making a fresh start. You see, she has even given Martha her precious monkey. I am sure we shall all be much happier, from now on."

"Do you know where she was going this afternoon?" I asked.

"For a little walk."

"Why did she wear her wrap, and carry her beaded bag, just to go out for a little walk?"

Danny sat up straight, pressing her hands to her aching head. "Her wrap—to-day? Her beaded bag? Surely not."

"That's just what she did. Didn't you see her before she left?"

"I was lying down. She came to my door and said that she was going for a walk, and asked me if I cared to go with her. I said that my headache was too severe. She went into her room, and from there downstairs. I felt guilty about refusing to go with her, after our talk. I thought that I should; so I called after her. But, when you said she had gone, I was afraid she would be annoyed at being called back. I had gotten up; so, since John will surely be home before long, now, I came down. I can't understand her wearing a wrap. It is so silly, on a day like this."

It sounded all right, but I was not quite satisfied.

"I thought," I said, "that, when you called after her, you were frightened, or worried, or—something."

"Frightened? No, Mary, I had nothing to be frightened about."

"Gaby was frightened," I said.

"Gaby! She couldn't have been. She was all right this afternoon. Nothing could have happened since then."

"I don't know. Something was the matter with her when she walked through this room. I'll go bond that, wherever it was she was going, she was afraid to go."

"Mary, it must be that you are imagining this. Unless— Oh, it couldn't be that Gaby has not told me the truth about—about anything. I am sure she was honest with me this afternoon. I am sure— And yet— Dear me, I wonder where she went for her walk?"

"She talked to Chad, just before she left. Maybe she told him where she was going."

Danny called the question across the room to Chad, who was improvising cheerful, happy music on the piano.

"Not a word," Chad spoke above his music, "except that she was going for a walk and didn't want my company."

"Gaby told me," Martha piped up, from where she was sitting on the arm of Sam's chair, "that she was going to the cabin. She was in a big hurry. She ran."

"Up toward the cabin?" Danny questioned, though we all knew we could not put a mite of trust in anything Martha said.

"Yes. Chad loves me better'n he loves her. Don't you, Chad?"

"You are positive," Danny insisted, and I couldn't see why, for a minute, "that she went to the cabin, or toward it? You aren't fibbing, are you, Martha dear? Are you sure that she didn't go around the house toward the road?"

When she asked about the road, her meaning was clear to me. Danny was afraid that Gaby had gone to meet John, who should have been back from Rattail before this. But, if she had hoped to get anything out of Martha, she had made a mistake in her questioning. For anyone to accuse Martha of a fib, was to make her stick to it like a waffle to an ungreased pan.

"She told me she was going to the cabin," Martha answered. "She ran. She was in a hurry."

Danny stood up. "I think I shall walk up to the cabin and see whether I can find her. You'll come with me, Mary?"

I said not in the heat. Besides, it would soon be five o'clock, and time to be starting supper. She asked Mrs. Ricker to go with her. Mrs. Ricker refused. I wondered why, when neither of us would go, Danny did not go by herself. She did not. Had she, perhaps, guessed at the cause of Gaby's fear? Did she share it? Was she afraid to go to the cabin alone?

15
One Return

At five o'clock the men put up the chess board. Chad stopped playing the piano, and the three of them went to the barns together.

I went into the kitchen to get supper. Danny, in spite of her headache, insisted upon helping me. She did the best she could. She managed to get the table set, in between times when she was not running to the window to see whether John was coming.

At six o'clock, though neither John nor Gaby had returned, we sat down to supper. Danny was too nervous to touch a bit of food. She kept looking out of the windows, and at her watch, and out of the windows again.

"Don't worry, Danny," Sam said. "John has had tire trouble, on account of the heat. They'll come riding up the road any minute now."

"They?" she questioned.

"Gaby togged up and went down the road to meet John, didn't she?"

"No," Danny's voice curled into a wail. "No, Uncle Sam, she didn't. Martha saw her going to the cabin. Didn't you, Martha?"

"Martha," Mrs. Ricker astonished us all by saying, "doesn't know where Gaby went. She knows only where Gaby told her she was going."

"But why should Gaby tell her a fib about it?" Danny asked.

"And why," I questioned, "should Gaby go around the house to get to the road, instead of going right out the front way?"

Again Mrs. Ricker shocked us by speaking. "She would not go out the front way, if she wanted to keep her trip to the road a secret."

"Mrs. Ricker," Danny's voice trembled, "What are you hinting? What is it that you know?"

"I know," said Mrs. Ricker, "that there is not a man living who is not as false as sin."

Sam growled, "Come down to facts, Mrs. Ricker, if you have any."

I think it was the first time Sam had ever spoken unpleasantly to her. He betrayed his own anxiety by so doing. It was easy to see that she was cut to the quick.

"I have no facts," she said, "except, that right after dinner to-day John and Gaby had a private conversation, and he decided, very suddenly, to go for the mail."

At that minute we heard a sound for sore ears—the car coming up the driveway. Danny jumped up and ran to look out of the living-room window. "He has gone all the way around to the kitchen," she said, when she came back. If it had not been sort of pathetic, showing how worried she had been, her impatience at having to wait another minute or so to see him, would have been funny.

She ran into the kitchen. She and John came to the door of the butler's pantry. John was gray with dust. His brows were knitted, as they are whenever he is troubled about anything.

"He hasn't seen Gaby," Danny announced, with an exultation that showed plainly what she had been most anxious about. "He brought up the rock-salt. That's why he drove to the kitchen. Come and see, Mary?"

"I'd rather see you two come and eat your suppers," I said.

"Goodnight!" John answered. "I've got to go and get rid of a few tons of dirt before I can come to the table."

"No," Danny insisted. "Never mind the dirt, dear. Supper is all cold now. Please come and eat—"

John patted her on the shoulder, and smiled at her, and, manlike, did as he pleased. He went through the kitchen and upstairs the back way. Danny called after him, asking him to hurry. He didn't.

When he finally did come, all slicked up, and bathed and shaved, he said it was too hot to eat, and would have nothing but some ice-cream.

Sam asked him what had kept him so long, on the trip. John said tire trouble; and that he had met Leo Saule, two miles this side of Rattail, with his flivver broken down. John had stopped to help him, and, at last, had been forced to tow him the six miles north to his place.

John has a way, when he is worried, of shutting and opening his eyes, and of tossing his head back and to the side with a quick little jerk, as if he were trying to get shed of something that was in it. All the while he was eating and talking, he kept doing this. I asked him whether his head ached.

"No," he said. "But I think I'm sort of loco from being out in the sun."

"Gaby kept you waiting quite a while?" Hubert Hand stated and asked.

"What do you mean?" John questioned.

"Waited for her down the road, didn't you, and took her to Rattail in time to catch the train for Reno, or 'Frisco?"

I thought John would fly into a temper. He has a handy temper. But he only looked around at all of us, with a bewildered expression, and, "Say, are you fellows trying to put something over on me, or what?" he asked.

"Then you don't deny—" Hubert Hand began.

Sam, who has enough dander for John and himself both, when necessary, broke in.

"John doesn't have to deny anything. Marcus will be in the office now, waiting for Twenty-one. 'Phone down. 'Phone's handy. Ask him whether he flagged Twenty, to-day, for a passenger, or whether he is going to flag Twenty-one."

Hubert went straight to the telephone. From his end of the conversation, we could tell that Twenty had not stopped, and that no one was waiting for Twenty-one. He looked foolish, when he turned from the telephone, and said, "Take it all back, John. My mistake."

Sam looked mighty serious. "Well," he drawled, "I don't know but what as good a plan as any would be for us all to go out and have a look around for her—"

"Oh!" Danny exclaimed, sharply. "Uncle Sam, you do think that she has met with some mishap?"

"I think," Sam said, "that she has met with another machine and ridden off in it. But, better safe than sorry; then we'll be fine and fit for the fireworks. Eh, Martha?"

Martha, who had been drowsy all during supper, was half asleep on the davenport, and did not answer.

16

The Murder

Sam's first plan, after he and Hubert had made a quick ride to the cabin and back with no sight of Gaby, was for the two of us to go down the road in the sedan. Fortunately, he decided at the last minute to have John come with us to drive. Danny came along with John. Chad and Hubert Hand were to scout around the place on their ponies. Mrs. Ricker stayed at home with Martha.

As soon as we had started, Sam said, in a cocksure, overbearing way he never has except when he is not as certain of himself as he'd like to be, "We'll not have to go far. Not more than a mile, I reckon, to find the fresh tire tracks of the machine that came up here to meet her. After the breeze and the shower this morning, the fresh tracks will show up like mud on a new fence. Whoa! What did I tell you? See there."

Tire tracks, sure enough; but they were the tracks made by the sedan, patterned like a snake's back, and showing, plain as print, on top of the dim tracks made by the outfit's departure for Telko the morning before. We rode along, watching the four long trails; two for John's trip to town, and two for his trip back to the ranch. The only breaks were the spots where, as it was plain to be seen, John had twice had tire trouble.

Our road—and it is that, since Sam had it graded himself, and pays for having it kept up—runs north, straight as a string, with Sam's fields and fences on one side of it and sagebrush covered deserts on the other side of it, for ten miles to where it joins the Victory Highway. Sam has a sign at the junction with the highway; so no one has any reason for using this road unless he has business with the Desert Moon Ranch.

We drove to the highway before we turned around. We had come back about a mile, when the wind, that always ushers in a storm in these parts, came howling up, blowing the sand and dust in thick clouds, jerking and snapping the sage and the greasewood, chasing and bouncing the tumbleweed balls. The sky turned black. The thunder growled, mean as a threat, in the distance.

John drove fast; but we barely made the ranch before the storm broke. When we came out of the garage doors, the first drops of rain, big as butter cookies, had begun to fall; and, just as we reached the front porch, the rain came pouring down as if all the sky were the nozzle of a big faucet and someone had turned it on, full force.

"This will bring her in," Sam said, as we ran up the steps. "She'll be there, high and dry, when we get in."

She was not. Chad and Hubert Hand had come in, and they acted as if, since we had set out to get news of Gaby, it was a wonder we had not done it. Martha was awake, and sobbing because she could not have the fireworks. Mrs. Ricker was showing a little last minute sense by hurrying around and getting the house closed against the storm. She should have done it when the wind first came up.

Sam went and touched a match to the fire, ready to be started, in the fireplace. I ran upstairs and closed the bedroom windows, and turned the fans off. I don't care for buzzing fans during one of our electrical storms. I had come downstairs, ready to take my rest, when I remembered the attic, with all its windows wide to the drenching rain.

My corns had been hurting me all day; so, Chad being handy, I asked him to go and close the attic. He went up the stairs, and almost at once came back to the head of them to call down that the attic door was locked.

One of my principles is, that if you ask a man to do anything about the house for you, you do it twice yourself. I thought, again, how true that was, as I went on my aching feet up the stairs to prove to him that the door was not locked, never had been locked, and, likely, never would be.

It was locked. Chad stood by, pleased as Punch, when it would not give to my shaking and pulling. He walked off, saying that he would see whether someone downstairs had locked it and had the key, or, if not, whether he could find another key to fit it.

I stood there waiting. I put my hand in my pocket for my handkerchief. There was a key. It fitted the lock. I opened the door.

About half way up the steps, Gaby was lying in a huddle of pink wrap. Her hat had fallen off. I thought that she was asleep. I spoke to her. She did not answer. I ran up the steps and put an arm around her, trying to lift her. Her head rolled to one side. I saw her throat. It was saffron color, with great blue-black bruises at its base. I touched her swollen face. It was cold.

For an instant, my only sensation was one of violent nausea. I tried to scream. My throat had closed. I must have shut my eyes, for I remember thinking that, if I did not open them, the dizziness would sweep me off into unconsciousness. I opened them. I saw, there on the red carpet of the steps, something that shocked my reeling senses into sanity. Dropped all over the bright beaded bag, lying there, were the burned tobacco and the ashes from Sam's pipe.

All of my horror concentrated into a frantic desire to get those ashes cleared away so that no one else could see them. I shook them from the bag to the carpet. I brushed them from the carpet into my handkerchief. Just as I got to my feet from my knees. Chad came up.

"Call the others," I said. "Gaby is here—murdered."

I stuffed the handkerchief filled with ashes into my pocket, and, for the first and last time in my life, I fainted dead away.

17
Suicide

The next thing that I knew I was lying on my back listening to someone screaming, above the voices of Sam and Mrs. Ricker. I realized that those awful sounds were coming from my own throat. I tried to stop them; but I could not. I put my hands to my throat to make it stop the noise. Sam's voice came, clear and strong then—real, like a light in the dark.

I sat straight up. The screams ceased. "What," I managed, "is the matter?"

"Everything on God's earth, that could be," Sam answered. "But here, Mary. Drink this. Get some sleep. Nothing to be done, now. We'll need you, to-morrow. Some water, Mrs. Ricker—"

He shook a powder into my mouth. Mrs. Ricker held a glass of water to my lips.

When I opened my eyes again, it was gray dawn. I saw that I was in Mrs. Ricker's room. She was sitting by the window tatting. Yes, tatting; darting the shuttle back and forth, back and forth, with her long, white fingers. I watched her for a full minute before memory seized me, and I cried out with the pain of it.

"Sh-h-h," she warned me, in a whisper. "You'll wake Martha. She is asleep here on the couch."

I got out of bed, shook my skirts down and fastened my corsets under my dress. I felt in my pocket. The ball of handkerchief was still there. I went into the hall bathroom, washed my face and hands, and drained the last crumb of tobacco down with the water out of the washbowl. I washed the handkerchief, scoured the bowl, and went back to Mrs. Ricker's room.

As I opened the door, she again warned me against waking Martha.

"Was the shock too much for her?" I asked, going and standing beside Mrs. Ricker so that we might talk in whispers. She stopped to pick a knot out of her thread before she answered me.

"I didn't allow her to go upstairs. She followed Chad out of the house and saw him shoot himself. He died within ten minutes. It was terrible for Martha. I had to hold her, while Sam gave her the narcotic—"

"No, no," I protested. "What—what are you saying? Not Chad? What was it you said about Chad—"

"He walked out and shot himself, through the head." She pulled the thread looser on her shuttle.

I rushed out of the room, away from her. I staggered down the stairs into the kitchen.

Sam, Hubert Hand, and John all jumped up from their chairs and started toward me. John reached me first, and put an arm around me.

"Chad—" I began, but I couldn't get any further.

"There, there, Mary. Pour her some coffee, dad. Quick! Here, sit here. Turn on that fan, Hand. Get some water—"

"No, no. Tell me. Mrs. Ricker said— It isn't true. It—it can't be true. Not our Chad—"

Sam answered, gruffly, to keep the choke out of his voice. "It is a damn shame, Mary; but, it is true. The boy shot himself, not fifteen minutes after we found her. Wait," he went on quickly, "before you think *anything*. I want to tell you what I have told the others. It is God's truth. That poor boy is as innocent of any connection with the murder as I am."

"Sam!" I managed, and hid my ugly, twisted old face down in my arms.

I will say that the men did pretty well, just sitting quiet, and leaving me alone, and letting me have my cry out. It seemed to me I never was going to be able to stop; but they didn't bother me with contorting, they let me get clear through to the sniffling and swallowing stage. I was the first one to speak.

"What," I said, "are we going to *do?*"

"We are going to do a lot, Mary," Sam said. "We are going to keep Chad's name clean. Sure," in answer to my protest, "we all know. But, just the same, I'm mighty thankful that I have his alibis for him, myself. A suicide looks bad, you know. That is, it would until we find Canneziano. This is his work—"

"But, Sam," I said, "if he wasn't let out of San Quentin until yesterday morning, he couldn't possibly have got 'way up here that same evening."

"We've told Sam that, a thousand times," Hubert Hand said.

"All right, all right," Sam said. "But if I ever get that long-distance call through, you'll find that Canneziano was released a day or two early. She met him yesterday—"

"How'd he get up here, Sam?" I questioned. "You remember there were no tracks on the road except the sedan tracks—"

Hubert Hand snapped me short. "Did you have a passenger up from Rattail, yesterday, John?"

Sam spoke, before John could answer. "Son," he said, "did you, by any chance, as a favor to one of the girls, bring that skunk here yesterday?"

"I did not, dad."

"He got here, then, as I've said all along. Horseback, across the deserts. And he murdered the girl. By God, he'll hang for it, if it takes my last dollar. He killed Chad, too, as much as if he'd shot him down. We aren't overlooking a couple of murders, not here on the Desert Moon. Not right yet. She went out to meet him yesterday, I tell you. She brought him into the house, for some purpose; through the back way and up into the attic."

"Without anybody seeing or hearing them?" Hubert Hand questioned.

"Nobody was looking nor listening, as I remember. You know damn well that, with the doors shut, nothing can be heard from room to room in this house—let alone upstairs to downstairs. I tell you, he killed her there on the stairs, and he made his get-away—"

"If you think that," I said. "Why aren't you out hunting him?"

"Hell!" Sam exploded. "Why ain't I out hunting last night's lightning? The girl had been dead anyway two or three hours—more likely longer, when we found her. He had that head start on us. And he could ride. God, how that skunk could ride; no mercy for a horse! He's gone. He went straight across the deserts, hell bent for Sunday. He'll need food. He'll need water, worse. I've telegraphed to every town within two hundred miles of here. They are watching. I've 'phoned every ranch. I've kept that 'phone hot for six solid hours. I've got posses at every water-hole—"

"Listen, Sam," I said. "You shouldn't have doped me up with that sleeping powder. Because, unless after he murdered her, he walked downstairs, with none of us seeing or hearing him, and into the living-room or the kitchen, and put the key in my pocket, Canneziano is not the guilty man."

Sam's pipe fell out of his mouth. I shivered. During all of his talk, I had clear forgotten about those pipe ashes, dropped all over the beaded bag.

It was Hubert Hand who put the question to me about the key. He made me feel guilty. My explanation to them that the key had been in the pocket of my dress, the dress I had been wearing since morning, yesterday, had the feeling of a confession.

"Still," Hubert Hand said, when I had finished, "that does not, necessarily, disprove Sam's theory. If Canneziano was let out of prison in time to get here yesterday, he could have murdered her, as Sam insists, and he could have given the key to some one of us to put in your pocket. Chad, for instance, or—"

"No!" Sam thundered. "That boy, I tell you, is as innocent as I am."

The telephone bell rang.

Hubert Hand and John followed Sam into the living-room. I stayed where I was. I had to have a minute to think. The ashes on the bag? The key in my pocket? Sam?

"Mary Magin," I told myself, "for twenty-five years, ever since Sam Stanley took you, a sniveling, pride-broken, deserted bride, into his house, and gave you a chance to make a life for yourself, you have never seen him do a mean trick to man, woman, child, or beast. You never even heard of a questionable nor an unkind action of his. And you never will, for the simple reason that the ingredients for anything but honor and decency aren't in him. If they were, he would not be Sam Stanley, any more than bean soup would be bean soup if it was made out of gooseberries and ginger. That being the one certainty you have, at this minute, you had better hang on to it tight; stop thinking and guessing; keep your mouth shut; and you won't go far wrong. Good resolutions are easy to make. So is lemon meringue. Both are almost impossible to keep."

I went right on thinking. If Sam, I thought, had found it necessary to murder Gabrielle Canneziano, he had probably done it to keep something worse from happening. Sickened at myself, for that thought, I found another way of thinking, not much better.

It did seem to me, remembering the pipe ashes on top of the bag, that Sam must have been there on the stairs at some time after she had been murdered and before I had found her. He must, then, be keeping some secret concerning the murder. It did look as if, considering his talk, he must be shielding the murderer, with every ounce of his horse-sense and ingenuity, both of which he had in plenty. But who would he shield to that extent? Chad, alive or dead? No. Martha? Yes. But Martha could not have done it. John? Not unless there was something to it than one of us dreamed of. Hubert Hand, or Mrs. Ricker? No. Danny? I thought not. Myself? I couldn't be sure.

The men came back into the kitchen. Sam looked ten years older than he had looked ten minutes before.

"It was San Quentin," he said to me. "Canneziano was positively not released from there until nine o'clock yesterday morning."

"That," I said, "lets him out."

"And," Hubert Hand said, "lets every man-jack of us here on the place, in."

Habit was too strong for Sam. "'Well in,'" he quoted, with a groan.

18

Clarence Pette

The sheriff, the coroner, the undertaker, a newspaper reporter, and another man that the coroner had brought along for a juryman, drove up to the ranch at five o'clock that morning. It had been past midnight before Sam had been able to get hold of one of them at Telko, on account of them all being out taking in the celebration there.

Sam and the sheriff had been friends for thirty years. Sam's money had paid for the coroner's medical education. They, and the others, were mighty sorry to have to bother us at all, and their sole aim was to make as little trouble as possible.

They interviewed each one of us, alone, but pleasantly and informally, in the dining-room; each one, that is, but Danny—the coroner, visiting her as a doctor, said it would never do to pester her, in the state she was in—and Martha, who was still asleep, and whom they said it was no use to wake. They kept each of us about ten minutes. They brought in the verdict of died by his own hand, for Chad; and, murdered by person or persons unknown for Gaby. They left, on tiptoe, holding their hats in their hands clear to the end of the driveway. The coroner and the sheriff both came, I think, with the conviction that Chad was the guilty person; but Sam was so right down violent about Chad's innocence, that they let that drop at once.

The sheriff left, I am all but certain, with the strong conviction that I had committed the murder, and with the resolution that he would not do Sam an ill turn by depriving him of a good cook. The coroner, and the others, except the reporter, were sure, I think, that one of us was guilty; but were thankful to goodness that they had not found out which one.

The undertaker did not leave with the others. He was preparing the bodies to take them to Telko; there to await the instructions that we could not give until after we had gotten in touch, if possible, with Chad's people, and had come to a decision about Gaby's burial place.

The reporter, whose name—not that it matters except for its fitness—was Clarence Pette, waited to return to town with the undertaker. While waiting, he went snooping about the place, looking for footprints—there could not have been any, after the deluge of rain the night before—cocking his head to one side and the other, writing in a notebook, making knowing, humming sounds between his tightly closed lips. He had been bothering me, like a fly on the ceiling, all morning. Finally, when he came poking right into my kitchen, and opened the door to the back stairway, I turned on him.

"What's the matter with you?" I asked. "If you have any business, why don't you go about it?"

"Yes, yes," he said. "Precisely. Now, my good woman, if you can spare me a few moments—"

Sam came ambling into the kitchen and threw himself into a chair.

"Ah, Mr. Stanley," Clarence said. "I was just telling your cook here that, if she could spare me a few moments of her time, I probably could be of much service here, under these unfortunate circumstances. You see, we reporters are, necessarily, detectives, in a smaller or greater degree. Until I came to Nevada, I was on one of the large San

Francisco dailies. Not taking undo credit to myself, I will say that, while serving there, I was instrumental in getting to the bottom of numerous crimes. Have I your attention, Mr. Stanley?"

Sam looked at him as he would look at some snapping puppy that was pestering around his heels.

I don't know what Clarence thought. What he said, was, "Precisely. By mere observation. Trained observation, that is, coupled with a naturally analytical and deductive mind, and imagination. Observation, first. As an example: since entering this kitchen, I have observed that your cook—"

"If you mean Mrs. Magin," Sam interrupted, "say so."

"Precisely. I have observed that Mrs. Magin has been but recently divorced. She was married to a man of some property. Of this she received a share, at the time of her divorce, in lieu of further alimony. She has come here, recently, from Chicago, where she lived in comfort, but not in luxury. She did not keep a servant. Her daughters were dutiful girls. All of her children, at the time of the divorce, however, sided with their father."

I glanced at Sam. He was resting his head in his hands, elbows on the table. He had not, I could tell, heard one word that Clarence had said. To my own discredit, at an hour like that, I was curious to find out how a man could make so many mistakes in so short a time. "But how—" I began.

He was too eager to explain to allow me to finish the question. "Very simple, for a trained observer. You no longer wear a wedding ring; but the mark of one, worn for years, shows plainly on your finger." (My wedding ring is set around with garnets; so I always take it off when I cook, and hang it on a nail for that purpose, over the sink. It was hanging there in plain sight, right then.) "If you were a widow, you would continue to wear your ring.

Your clothes, your wrist watch, your silk stockings, show
that you have been accustomed to a comfortable living.
Since you came to Nevada, it was you who got the divorce.
Hence—alimony. Had you received a lump sum of money,
or monthly payments, you would not have taken a position
as a cook. You undoubtedly received property, on which
you can not at once realize. Your kitchen apron, here on
the hook, and like the one you are wearing, has the label
of a Chicago firm in its waistband, and is of excellent
material. Had you been poor, you could not have afforded
such an apron—more than likely you would have made
your own aprons. Had you been wealthy, you would not
have owned a kitchen apron. It is easy to tell, from watching you, that you have been accustomed to having help in
your work—hence, your daughters. If your children had
been in sympathy with you, at the time of the divorce, you
undoubtedly would have returned to make your home with
one of them, instead of remaining as a cook in Nevada—"

Sam, who had shifted his position, stretched, and
crossed one leg over the other, interrupted. "Oh, dry up,
young fellow," he said, as if the sound of Clarence's voice
had tuckered him clear out.

Clarence tittered; embarrassment, I think, made him do it.

"And take yourself and your laughing out of here," Sam
said. "If you need to be told that this isn't a place for
laughing, this morning, I'm telling you, now."

"But, Mr. Stanley, I assure you—"

"Never mind. Just get on out of here. That's all."

"As you say. I shall report to my paper, shall I, that the
millionaire owner of the Desert Moon Ranch is, apparently, undesirous of having the murderer discovered?"

"Report what you damn please to your paper," Sam answered. "But get out of here."

That was all right for the Nevada papers, where Sam
was known; but, if the other papers copied the news, I

didn't care to have that impression of Sam strewn all over the country. It never did do any harm, I reckoned, to have the press on your side.

So, with Sam glaring at me, I cozied Clarence up a bit. Told him to sit down, and have some pie and coffee. While he ate, I flattered his vanity by asking whether he had formed any opinions concerning the murder.

"Opinions—no," he said, pulling back his chin for dignity. "Theories—yes. Theories, I may say, that I have arrived at quite independently, since the testimony at the inquest was without value. Observation, trained observation, and a certain instinct that might almost be described as clairvoyance.

"For instance: the contents of the bead bag, carried by the victim. Apparently, rather damning evidence, there, against Mr. Hand. Also, apparently, other valuable clues. Pouff—" He made a gesture of blowing the beaded bag and its contents off the palm of his white hands. Since this was the first I had heard of the bag's contents, I was sorry to have them dismissed so airily. I let it pass, not wishing to question him. "Even the coroner, and the other members of the jury, untrained as they were, realized, I am sure, that all that was too obvious. A murderer, my good woman, leaves clues—but not obvious ones. The contents of that bag were probably arranged by the murderer, after the murder had been committed. By someone, moreover, who had access to the victim's personal belongings.

"Regard this, please, as a suggestion, merely. Does it occur to you that it is peculiar that a young woman who was unable to meet the coroner's jury, should, in the next hour, be able to arise and assist the undertaker?"

"Is Danny up?" I questioned Sam.

"Teetering around like a sick little ghost. Mrs. Ricker went to ask her about what dress to put on Gaby, and nothing would do Danny but that she get right up and help to lay Gaby out."

"You see nothing extraordinary in that?" Clarence persisted.

Sam made another profane request concerning Clarence's drying up.

"Well," I said, "she is her twin sister, you know. And she is a loving-hearted, unselfish little thing. I reckon she thought it would be the last service—"

"True. True. But! The victim was last seen at the side of the house near the rabbit hutch. Suppose that, as soon as she had gotten rid of the child by giving her the bracelet, the victim had at once re-entered the house, through the back way, and had gone, at once, up these back stairs. Miss Danielle Canneziano was upstairs at the time, was she not? Alone?"

I remembered Danny, coming downstairs, not more than fifteen minutes after Gaby had gone through the room. I remembered how fresh and sweet she had been, and how untroubled, except for her headache. A dozen defenses for Danny, who needed none, flashed through my mind. I should not have deigned to use one of them, to Clarence, but unthinkingly, I did.

"If you are hinting at Danny," I said, "she had neither the time nor the strength. If she'd had a year, she wouldn't have done it, and couldn't have, with those frail little hands of hers."

"In my opinion," Clarence returned, "that job took science, rather than strength. It took fingers that knew how to find the windpipe and the carotid artery at the same instant. The Japs understand that grip, perfectly. An Occidental might stumble onto it by accident. But, granted your objection, that strength was required. The young woman might have had an accomplice. One who, filled with remorse, killed himself. Or one who, in tense excitement, dropped the key into her own pocket—"

I gasped. Sam rose. He took hold of Clarence at the back of his collar, and at the back of his trousers, and began pushing him toward the door.

Sam's first remark won't do to repeat. His second was, "And now, you blithering fool, if you publish one of your filthy, lying insinuations, against that little, grief-stricken sister, or against our dead boy, or against Mrs. Magin, just one, in that rotten dirty sheet of yours, you won't be in Nevada long enough to get your divorce." Sam boosted him out through the doors.

All the Nevada newspaper accounts made much of the fact that the fiend, who had committed the terrible murder on the Desert Moon Ranch, had made a complete escape, without leaving any clues of any sort.

19

The Note

No clues! Land's alive! The place was positively cluttered with clues; and most of them about as useful, in the end, as clutter generally is. I am not saying that none of them were of value. I am saying that a person, out in a grove of aspen trees, all bending and bowing to a high wind, would be sort of simple to go hunting a straw to find which way the wind was blowing. That was about how sensible I was, when I asked Sam, after he had got shed of Clarence, about the contents of Gaby's beaded bag.

"It is all on the table in her room," he said, "where I put it for the coroner's jury. You can go and see. But, first, read this. It was tucked inside her dress. The undertaker found it, and gave it to me. I dread giving it to Danny."

He handed me a folded sheet of paper. I opened it, and read:

"Danny dear: If you ever read this, I shall be dead—murdered. Don't have me buried here in this God-forsaken country. Take me to San Francisco and have my body cremated. I love a flame. I hate the cold earth.

"You have had much trouble on my account, old dear. Don't blame me for having kept the fear and the dread of this thing, which I felt certain was going to happen, from you. You, nor no living person, but one, could have saved me.

107

"Remember, Dan, that in spite of all the distress I have caused you, and may still be causing you, I have always, in my own way, loved you. Gaby."

"Sam," I said, "I knew she was afraid, yesterday. Oh, why didn't she tell us? Of course you men could have saved her. Why did she go out alone to meet that fiend?"

Sam's only answer was a slow shaking of his bowed head, and a deep sigh.

"Mary," he said, then, "will you give this note to Danny, and explain to her how it is?"

"'How what is?"

"I mean—Well, she can't leave the Desert Moon, now, to take the body to 'Frisco. Until we find out who murdered that girl, not a man-jack of us is going to leave this place, for any reason."

"Sam Stanley!" I gasped. "You can't refuse. That's all. Own twin sisters! And Danny as innocent as a new born babe—"

"Don't talk like a book, Mary. Danny may be as innocent as she seems to be, and—she may not. She, nor anyone else, can leave this place until we have gotten to the very bottom of this thing. That goes."

"To think you paid attention to that fool reporter!"

"Don't be a fool yourself," Sam urged. "This note, in Gaby's handwriting, clears Danny of the crime, if all the other evidence didn't, which it does. We know that she did not kill her sister. But, of all the people in this house, she is in the best position to know who did do it. Of course, if she is involved in this she is involved innocently. If she put the key in your pocket, while we were out in the car, she did it with no idea of what she was doing. Just the same, I want her right here on the Desert Moon, for a while. Mary, you take the note to her, and explain, in your nice way—"

"I'll give her the note, Sam," I said. "But you'll have to do the explaining yourself. I'll tell you why. It isn't right for you to try to protect anyone, not even Martha, to the extent of refusing to allow one sister to carry out the dying request of another sister."

Sam dropped his pipe. As I saw the tobacco and the ashes scatter, I was more certain than ever that I was acting as a decent women should.

The door opened, and Danny came in. She was so pale that her cheeks had sort of a greenish tinge to them. Great dark circles spread far down under her eyes that were red and swollen from crying.

I hurried to her, and put my arms around her. She clung to me, and hid her head on my shoulder, and said my name over and over. Sam turned away, as if he could not bear to look at us.

I took her into the living-room, and sat down in a big chair and held her in my lap.

"If only," she kept saying, "if only she could have left us in her beauty. She was so beautiful, Mary. And now—"

Remembering what I had seen the night before, I knew that I must get her mind into other channels if her reason was to be saved. I thanked my stars, when I remembered the note.

After she had read it, she cried harder than ever; but I knew that it was crying of a saner sort.

"Will you go with me, Mary?" she questioned, when she had quieted some. "To San Francisco?"

"We'll have to talk to Sam about that, dear," I said. It was the habit of helping him, not any kindly impulse, that made me continue. "I am afraid that Sam wants us all to stay here, for a while. There, there, dear. You see how it is, don't you? Sam thinks that the duty of each one of us, right now, is to stay here and help try to find the guilty person."

"Does Uncle Sam think we will find him here?" she questioned.

I tried to tell myself that I had been mistaken; that she had not emphasized Sam's name in a hard, pointed way, as she had seemed to do.

"There isn't anywhere else to try to find him," I said. "Did you know about the key in my pocket?"

She nodded. "I knew about that," she said.

"What else did you know about?" I asked, a mite sharply, for there was no mistaking her emphasis this time.

"Nothing," she said, hurriedly. "Nothing. But, Mary, doesn't it seem possible to you that someone, clear from the outside, did it? And gave the key to Chad, and asked him to put it in your pocket? And that, for some reason we probably never shall discover, Chad could not, dared not, tell on the person who gave it to him? And that that is why he shot himself?"

"And we hadn't thought of that!" I gasped. "I do believe it. It is as clear as day."

Her sudden, definite silence talked as plainly as any words she could have spoken.

"Danny," I questioned, "you thought of that, but in your heart you don't believe it. Do you?"

"I—I want to believe it," she evaded.

"But you don't?" I persisted.

She was silent.

"Danny," I pleaded, "tell me about it. Just tell me, dear. I'll never breathe it to a soul, if you say for me not to. What is it that you know, or think that you know?"

She waited so long before answering me that I thought surely she was finding the words with which to take me into her confidence. I was so disappointed I could have cried with her, when she hid her face on my shoulder, again, and moaned, "Mary—I can't. I dare not tell. I tell you—I dare not."

She jumped up out of my lap, and ran upstairs as if wicked, dangerous things were running after her.

20
A Confession

John came into the room. "The outfit is back, or most of it," he said. "Darn their souls! Curiosity, nothing else. But for this, they wouldn't have shown up for two days yet. I think the women went into the kitchen just now, Mary."

There they were, Belle, Sadie and Goldie, all huddled up together like a bunch of something, near the back door. As I came into the room, they jumped and screeched. The only thing that makes me madder than being scared myself is to scare somebody else. I spoke to them right sharply.

I told them that I expected them to go about their work, and to act like sensible girls while so doing. I told them that we had enough to put up with, just now, without adding a parcel of jumping, squealing girls to our load.

Sadie, the sauciest of the lot, on account of imagining that being married made her more independent than the other girls, spoke up.

"We haven't decided yet that we want'a go workin' in a house where a murderer, and maybe moren' one, is livin'."

"If that's the way you feel about it," I said, "the sooner you leave the better. It is an honor to work in the Desert Moon ranch-house, and you know it."

"Maybe 'tis. Maybe 'tain't." Sadie sauced back. "You'll not get girls as easy to-day as you would of yesterday.

Murders and suicides—if it was a suicide—don't do much in makin' a ranch pop'lar for help."

"Very well," I said. "If you are going, go now. If not, put on your aprons and get to work."

I could scarcely believe my eyes. The three of them skedaddled out through the door. I felt sort of sick, watching them go. Not because I'd have to teach new girls the work and my ways, but because their leaving gave me my first realization that the Desert Moon Ranch was darkened by the shadow of sin, that the eclipse I had feared was upon us.

When I telephoned to Sam, down in his office in the outfit's quarters, I tried to keep the truth from him; saying, only that the girls and I had had a spat, and asking him to find some new girls for me.

He came up, in about half an hour, with an Indian girl, not more than fifteen years old, trailing along behind him. Answering his nod, I went with him into the living-room.

"She is the only one I could get," he said. "We'll have to send to Reno or Salt Lake. None of the outfit want their women folks working here. I don't blame them. The Desert Moon Ranch is disgraced—" He stopped short.

I thought that it was because he could not bear to go on with what he had begun to say; until, following his eyes, I saw that he was looking at a piece of paper on the writing desk just in front of him. It had been propped up against a vase; but it had slithered down into a curve. He reached for it; read it, and handed it to me.

"I killed her. Chadwick Caufield. P. S. Sorry to put you to the trouble of disposing of me. Make it cheap and snappy. I haven't a relative in the world. P. G."

"A lie," Sam said.

"I think so."

"I know damn well it is. I tell you, she had been dead two or three hours, anyway—probably longer—when we found her. Listen, Mary. Between four and five o'clock—

we all saw her alive at four—Chad sat right there at that piano, and he never left it once. Did he?"

"No, he didn't. I kept thinking he would, to join Gaby. But he didn't."

"Between five and six o'clock," Sam went on, "he was with me, every minute of the time, down in the barn, and coming up to the house. Never out of my sight. Between six and seven he was with us all at supper. If he'd been gone all afternoon, I'd know that note was a lie; know it just as well as I know it now—"

"But, why did he shoot himself, then, Sam?"

"God knows. He thought he loved her."

"But this note! A confession! Why would he die in disgrace, when we know he was innocent?"

"God knows. To shield someone else, I reckon."

"Who?"

Sam dropped his pipe.

I heard him stamping the sparks out. I did not look down. I did not want to look down.

21

A Summons

"It might be," Sam said, as he refilled his pipe, "that Chad did not write this. I'll send it, with some of his other writing, to one of these handwriting experts I've read about."

"He wrote it," I said. "The writing is his. So is the wording. You know it."

I looked at him, straight. I felt something tighten around my heart as if it had been roped by a professional. I guess I was too sentimental. But I couldn't bear to see Sam's good old face all aching with worry.

"Sam," I wheedled, "have sense. We've a confession here that will satisfy the world. He killed her; and, when the body was found, he shot himself. Nothing could be more reasonable. No one would doubt it. We can send this to the papers—he has no relatives to be disgraced, or to sorrow over it—and the Desert Moon will be cleared of crime. One of your favorite sayings, Sam, is to let well enough alone."

Sam drew himself up to the top of his six feet and five inches and looked down, from there, at me; away down—as far, say as if I had suddenly dropped into a dirty old cistern. "There is no question of well enough," he shouted, so that I could hear him in my depths, "until the Desert Moon is cleaned, clean, Mary Magin. Cleaned and fumigated, or destroyed. It is not going to be whitewashed.

There is someone on this ranch who is as guilty as hell; who knows who committed the murder; who aided and abetted it. We are going to find that person. Then we will find the murderer. They'll be hung together. After that, we can leave well enough alone."

"Suppose," I suggested, "that Chad was the accomplice."

"I reckon," he said, growing suddenly kind, "that you've been through too much, Mary. That's it. You aren't quite responsible to-day. I don't wonder. But reason with me, Mary.

"Somebody suggested, already to-day, that it was Chad who put the key in your pocket. When did he get the key to put it there? Well, say that he got it between seven and eight o'clock, when he was out scouting by himself. Did he meet some entire stranger, then, who asked him to dispose of the key? Did he agree to do it, as a favor to said stranger? Did he, later, shoot himself and leave a lying confession to shield the stranger? The stranger, that is, who had killed the girl Chad loved? Chad did carry some secret to the grave with him, Mary. I am sure of that. But not a secret that we can't discover. We are going to discover it."

To doubt Sam, standing there before me talking so earnestly to me, to doubt his honesty of purpose and his goodness, was more than a question of doubting my eyes, my ears, my senses, for the moment. It would have been to doubt the things that had made up my life for the past twenty-five years; it would have swept away all of my accumulated certainties, all of my conclusions, all of my standards, as a wind sweeps trash from the desert. It would have uprooted me, and it would have left me as aimless and as wind-tossed as tumbleweeds.

"Sam," I began, resolved to tell him, then and there, about those pipe ashes of his on the beaded bag. I had waited too long. Mrs. Ricker was coming down the stairs.

"I think," she said, "that Martha should not sleep so late. I fear that she is sleeping too heavily."

"It is a blessing that she can sleep," Sam said. "She is all right. Those sleeping powders are as powerful as all get-out. I got them from a doctor in 'Frisco, when I was down there last year, and they made me sleep when I had neuralgia. I'm going up, though, I'll have a look at her.

"By the way," he added, from the stairway, "I want you two ladies to be here in this room, at promptly three o'clock this afternoon."

"Upon my soul!" I said, when Sam was out of sight. "What do you suppose that means?"

I might have spared my breath. She did not answer. But she did something downright unusual for Mrs. Ricker. She looked at me; and, as I met her look, it seemed to me that there was a pleading expression in her face, as if, were she able to talk, she'd like to ask me to do something for her. I have seen dogs look like that, at times.

"What is it, Mrs. Ricker?" I questioned.

She shook her head, and walked to the windows and turned her back on me.

I looked at the straight, gaunt back, and at her long arms hanging at her sides. She seemed frail. And yet, she could hold Martha still, when Martha was in one of her tantrums, and that was more than I, a much stouter woman, could do. She, with no one but Martha who did not count, had been alone in the house for an hour the evening before, while the others of us had been out hunting for Gaby.

Sam insisted that Gaby had been dead two or three hours when we found her. But was he certain of that? How did he know? Might he be mistaken? Mrs. Ricker had hated Gaby, as only a jealous woman can hate.

22
The Pact

All the while I was getting a make-shift dinner ready, that last thought of mine kept bothering me like the smell of something burning. So, as soon as dinner was over (I need not have bothered with it; everyone straggled in and straggled out again, without doing any justice to good food. Mrs. Ricker and Martha did not even come down.), I told the Indian girl, whose name was Zinnia, to manage the dishes the best she could, and I went off up to my room.

I took up some dinner on a tray with me, for Mrs. Ricker and for Martha. When Mrs. Ricker opened her door, I managed to get the information that Martha was awake, at last, and that Mrs. Ricker had just been helping her with her bath.

"Is she all right, now?" I questioned.

"I—suppose so." She edged the door shut, in my face.

I went into my room and combed my hair. I can always think better when I am doing some absolutely unimportant thing like that. But, to-day, it was as if someone had put an egg-beater into my mind, and was beating it to best time. My thoughts whirred, and tossed, and foamed.

Sam's pipe ashes. The key in my pocket. Chad's suicide. Chad's note of confession. Gaby's fear. Mrs. Ricker alone in the house. What it was that Danny knew and dared not tell? Not all plainly, and separately, as they look in writing;

but all jumbled, and each one seething with its own details
and complications.

Sam's pipe ashes— Lands alive! What had been the matter with me? Sam was the only member of our household
who smoked a pipe, but he was not the only man in cre-
ation who did; nor was his the only pipe, I supposed, that
had ever dropped and spilled its contents. A very nice and
comforting thought, if I could have fooled myself into
believing it.

Try as I might, I couldn't keep from thinking that part
of Sam's talk was bluff—that is, soon as I got away from
him I thought that. Did it mean that he was trying to
shield Chad? No. It could not mean that. Besides, Chad
himself had surely been trying to shield someone. Sam?
Gaby had feared someone, when she had left the house. No
woman had ever feared Sam.

Mrs. Ricker had hated Gaby. But, so had John hated
Gaby. Mrs. Ricker had said— John had said—

I jumped to my feet, holding my head in my hands. It
seemed to me that the only decent thing I could do, since
it held my brainpan, was to wrench the disloyal thing off
and sling it away. How dared I think such thoughts of
people with whom I had spent the best part of my life?
They were the only friends I had in the world. I had never
seen one of them do an unkind thing. Never. Mrs. Ricker
was as queer as Dick's hatband, but she had always been
gentle and patient. She had always been the first to spread
crumbs on the snow for the birds in winter. Though, of
course, she had said to Hubert Hand— I was off again.

I could not endure the thinking of such thoughts. I
must stop it. I must find work to do; someone to talk to. I
ran across my room and pulled open the door, just in time
to see Hubert Hand straighten from where he had been
stooping to my keyhole.

He brazened it out. "Sorry, Mary. But I guess it will be dog kill dog around here, from now on."

"Hubert Hand," I said, "what I want to know is, why are you listening at my keyhole?"

"I wasn't listening. I was looking, or trying to. This keyhole peering is the bunk, Mary. You might as well cut it out yourself." With that he turned and walked on down the hall.

I stood watching him, trying to account for an odd sense of relief that had come to me. In a minute I understood. Since he had been at my keyhole, he must have had some suspicion of me, for something. Possibly he had a good reason for that suspicion. As good a reason as I had, for suspicioning Sam, and John, and Mrs. Ricker. He was clear off the track with his suspicion. Probably, I was just as far off with mine.

He turned, quickly, and came back to me. He looked up and down the hall. He lowered his voice to just above a whisper. "Mary," he said, "I've gone at this all wrong. I'm off my nut to-day—that's all. I've discovered that I— Well, I guess I cared a lot more for the girl than I thought I did. By God, I believe I loved her. It is hell—having her clear gone. But my hanging for her murder isn't going to do her any good; not now."

Horrified, I backed away from him. For one wild moment I thought that the man was confessing to me.

"No!" he said. "Not that! I swear to God I'm innocent. But they are going to try to pin it on me, and they may not have much trouble doing it. I want to make a bargain with you. You'll get the best of it, for I know damn well that I'm innocent, and I don't think that you are—entirely. It is this. If you'll keep your mouth shut, I'll keep mine shut. Fifty-fifty. Will you do it?"

"Hubert Hand," I said, "I don't know one solitary thing about you that would be of any importance if I told it to the world. Anything that you think you know about me, I'm glad and willing to have you broadcast, or publish in the papers."

"Sure of that? Sure you are willing to have me broadcast that you found the body; that you didn't scream; that you stayed there, quiet and alone with it for ten minutes, before you gave the alarm?"

Fool that I was, I said, "It wasn't nearly ten minutes. It wasn't more than four or five."

He smiled. I saw what I had done. "It took me that long to discover the truth. I thought she was asleep. I had to run up the steps—"

Double fool, to try to explain.

"Say it took you a minute to run up a few steps. Another minute to discover that she was dead. Should it take you three or four minutes to run down again, and give the alarm?"

"I was sick, stunned, dizzy with horror."

"Probably any jury would believe that, all right. Just the same, I'll bet it would save you a lot of trouble, now and later, if no one knew anything about your lonesome five minutes, or longer. I'll tell you how I know. I came out of my room at the minute you opened the attic door. I saw you leave the hall to run up the steps. I went on downstairs. Chad was kidding around down there, collecting keys. I didn't know what he wanted with them, fortunately for you, or I'd have said you'd gotten the door open—"

I interrupted with a new, and it seemed to me a clever idea. "What you are forgetting," I said, "is that I fainted dead away."

"Gosh, Mary, but you are a rotten liar. Don't try it. Sam and I both saw you totter and go down, just as we got to the top of the stairs, after Chad had shrieked the news down at us. That was close to fifteen minutes after I'd seen you open the door."

"And—and," I couldn't keep my teeth from chattering, "you think I killed her, then?"

"Rot! She had been dead for hours. Rigor was complete. No, all I think is that you were—trying to cover someone, maybe. All that I know is, that you know more than you are telling."

"I did tell you. I was frozen, stiff, with horror."

"All right. Tell the jury. Tell them, too, why you came rushing out of your room, as you did just now, white and trembling. Don't like your thoughts, all by your lonesome, do you? Come on, Mary. Be a sport. We are both innocent. But—Fifty-fifty? Shut mouth for shut mouth?"

His talk about telling a jury scared me. I had heard of third degrees. I knew that if I ever told anyone but Sam himself, about those pipe ashes, the words would choke the life out of me, as I would want them to do.

"Dog kill dog, then?" he asked.

"Hubert Hand, I'm going to be honest with you. I don't know what it is you want me to keep my mouth shut about."

"Don't? Well, I want you to keep still about that conversation you overheard between Ollie Ricker and me in the cabin. She went back to get her parasol and saw you coming out. We knew you had been hiding there in the closet, listening."

With the sense I had been showing, it is a wonder I didn't speak right up and tell him that I had not been in the closet, but in the chest. I did not.

"Lands alive!" I said. "I'd had no idea of telling that, anyway. It was none of my business."

"Fine! I didn't have any idea of telling anything, either. It was none of my business. Shake on it."

I let him take my hand. I said yes, when he made me promise. I felt like I'd been associating with a sidewinder.

I went on down the hall, wracking my brain to remember exactly what I had heard in the cabin. Mrs. Ricker's threat. That would incriminate her, not him. And, though the threat had proven, of itself, that she was in love with him, I had certainly come away with no idea that he was in love with her. His mention of a previous attempt at murder, made by her. Again, that was nothing against him. No; what he was afraid of having told, must have been said in the room with the closet. I found slight, but some comfort in realizing that, though I had probably been a fool to make the promise to him, he had probably been a worse fool when he made the one to me.

23

An Omen

As I was trying to hurry past Gaby's door, Danny opened it, and asked me if I would come in and sit with her for a while.

I should have been there, long before. I went right in, apologizing, and trying to explain. But, when I saw that she meant for us to sit in Gaby's room, I suggested that we go somewhere else.

"No, please Mary," she said. "I don't want to be alone; but I do want to sit here. I feel as if here, with all her things around me, I might—get in touch—I mean—something might come to me. They say, you know, that people who have died—violent deaths, do not leave the earth sphere at once. I don't know whether I believe that or not. But, it could be true. If she is still on earth, she would come here. Wouldn't she? And she would try, I am sure, to give me a sign. Something to help me—to help all of us. If it should come, I want to be here to receive it."

"It won't come, Danny, dear," I said.

"No. I suppose not." She leaned back in her chair and sighed, and her arms dropped straight down over the chair's arms—a position that showed how tuckered she was. The engagement ring that John had given her slipped from her finger and came rolling over toward me. I scrambled to pick it up. When I rose from the floor she had jumped to her feet. She was ashy, shaking and trembling as if she had a chill.

"Mary! Promise me that you'll never tell that, not to anyone. It didn't—It couldn't mean anything."

"It means," I said, handing her the ring, "that you are wasting away. You'd better let me go down and bring you up some good, hot soup; or an eggnog."

She clung to me. "Don't leave me, Mary. I am afraid. I am dreadfully afraid. Promise that you won't tell about the ring. It—didn't mean anything."

I will admit that I did not like it any too well myself. There, just as she was asking for a sign, the ring, which had fitted snugly enough, I had thought, had dropped off. But, of course I had to put up a brave front to her.

"Nonsense," I said. "I won't tell anybody, because it is nothing to tell. All that it means is that the ring is too large for you."

"It is too large," she agreed. "I've been losing weight, lately. I have meant to ask John to send it to have it cut down—but I hated to be without it. Still—just as I was asking for a sign. Though it has dropped off several times before this. I shouldn't think it meant anything, this particular time, should I?"

"Of course not, dear," I said, relieved to hear that it had dropped off before. "You had your hands hanging straight down, that's all. You are all overstrung, and no wonder. Anyway, what could it have meant?"

How a person will babble, along, seemingly for no reason. I had paid no attention to what I was saying; but, the minute I had said it, the question needed an answer.

It could have meant that Gaby did not want Danny to marry John. Or, since nothing in the house could have signified John's name as plainly as that ring could, it might have meant—I refused to go on with it.

Danny must have been answering the question to her-self, as I had been doing. She sat down in a deep chair, opposite me, her hands clasped on her knees, and leaned forward, and looked into my eyes.

"Definite things, Mary," she said, "are always so wise. A definite answer to your definite question proves, as nothing else might have, that this was a silly, futile little accident. The ring has dropped off, I suppose, half a dozen times this week. Gaby's last note to me was all affection. Living, if Gaby could have taken John away from me, for herself, she would have done it. Dead—she wants us to marry. I know that. As for any other implication—" As I had done, and in spite of her talk about definite things, she refused that. "If only Uncle Sam were not so heart-less," she finished.

"Heartless!" I spoke sharply in spite of myself. "If the Creator ever made a man with a bigger heart than Sam Stanley's, nobody ever saw him."

"He has been good to you," she said. "But you give him his own way about everything."

"Well, after all," I said, "he does own the Desert Moon."

"And everyone on it, body and soul," she said. "Some-times I think he owns everyone in this county."

I did not want to know what she meant by that; so I only reminded her that Sam was John's father.

Her voice, when she spoke next, came muffled from where she had hidden her face in her curved arm on the back of the chair. "Uncle Sam is not John's father," she said.

"What do you mean by that?"

"John is uncle's adopted son. They are so different, so utterly different, they could not be father and son."

"Maybe not," I said, trying to keep pleasant, for I did not want to be snapping at the poor child on this day, "but

no real son ever loved his father better than John loves
Sam. He all but worships him, and he has ever since he
was a little fellow."

"I know. I know. Sometimes I think John cares more
for uncle than he does for me. Mary, tell me, honestly. Do
you think John loves me as much as he loves Uncle Sam?"

It is hard to explain; but, ever since we had begun to
speak of Sam, I had had a fighting feeling, as if I were
warding off danger; so I was right down relieved to have
the conversation take this silly turn.

"Love," I told her, "though, mercy knows, I know little
enough about it, can't be measured with a pint cup like
flour. But John is a good, normal boy. That means that his
sweetheart comes first with him; first and last."

"I—don't know," she answered. "I should hate to have
John have to choose between uncle and me."

"That is foolish talk. Why should John ever have to
choose between you and Sam?"

She sighed, and shook her head. A sudden certainty
came to me. Whatever it was that Danny had refused that
morning to tell me, whatever it was that she had said that
she dared not tell, had had something, somehow, to do
with Sam.

I did not urge her again to tell me what it was. I did
not wish to know. I sat there, dumb, trying to think of
some decent excuse that would take me away from her and
from that room, and from the need of fighting; fighting,
not in a fog, but the fog itself, trying to fell nothingness
with a blow, trying to catch smoke in a trap. My dull wits
worked too slowly. She began, again, to speak.

24
Clues

"What I can not understand," she said, "is, that Gaby knew that she might be killed. And yet, so far as anyone knows, she did not do one thing to save herself. If only, only she had confided in me! Surely I could have found some way to help her—to save her."

"You know, dear," I said, "I think that Gaby was not— well, at least not doing any clear thinking, those last few days."

"I know. I thought it was only her disappointment. But now— Who could be quite sane with such a fear confronting her? Yet—she left all of her things in order; as if, deliberately, she prepared for death. She burned her papers and letters. See-—" Danny pointed to the fireplace.

I crossed the room and looked into it. Papers had recently been burned there. I took the poker and stirred in the fluttering, black bits; but nothing had escaped the flames. I hung the poker back in the rack with shovel and tongs and bellows. It did not catch on its hook. As I bent to fix it, I saw a little white circle, down in the corner of the stand. I stooped and picked it up. It was a tiny round of celluloid, with the letter "Q" printed on it.

"It is one of the caps for her typewriter keys," Danny replied to my question. "She put them on over the keys;

softer for her finger tips, or saved her finger nails—something of the sort."

"I wonder why she burned them?" I said.

"Do you think that she did?"

"Well, this one being here on the hearth—"

"It probably rolled there, sometime, when she was taking them off her machine."

"Why did she take them off, if she always used them?"

"I don't know."

"Shall we," I suggested, "look and see whether the others are where she kept them?"

Danny opened the desk drawer. "They aren't here, at any rate," she said, and came back to me, and reached out her hand for the little cap, and turned it over in her fingers. "It could mean only," she said, "what we knew before. That she expected death. That she tried to leave everything tidy and in order."

"I don't know," I objected. "It seems more than orderly, to have taken these off the machine and burned them. It seems right down queer."

She smiled a little pitying smile at me, and patted my shoulder. "Poor Mary," she said.

"Well," I tried to defend myself, "in all the mystery stories that I ever read it was always some stray, meaningless little thing that solved the mystery in the end. A criminal never was discovered without any clues, was he?"

"I believe," she said, "that you are the only one in the house who hasn't looked at what Gaby had in her bag—"

She walked to the table by the window. I followed her. I dreaded seeing that bag again; but I was curious about its contents. It was lying limp on the table.

She picked it up, brushed it flickeringly with the tips of her fingers, and blew on it, as if she were trying to blow something off of it. "Everything," she explained, "sticks to the little pointed beads."

I took it from her and looked at it closely; but I could see no speck of ash, no minute particle of tobacco, nor of dust on its pattern of parrots, tree branches, and flowers.

"It is a beautiful thing," I said.

"Gaby got it in Vienna."

"I've wondered," I said, "why it was that Gaby had all the beautiful, expensive things, such as this. Your clothes are pretty and tasty, but they aren't near the quality of Gaby's."

She hesitated a moment before answering. "I have been in England for the past eight years, while Gaby has been on the continent, where beautiful things are more plentiful, and cheaper."

"Lands alive! I thought you girls had lived together, all these years."

"No," she said, and picked up Gaby's cigarette case, and handed it to me.

It was made of a dull gold, with her monogram, "G. C." set in tiny black opals, with green and blue lights flickering in them as if they were alive.

I opened the case. It was full of cigarettes, except for a space at one side, where about two of the pesky little things would have fitted in.

"And, see," Danny said, opening the gold match-box that was like the cigarette case, "it is quite empty. It doesn't seem reasonable that she would start out with an empty match-box. I believe that she used the matches to smoke the cigarettes."

"She wouldn't have used a box of matches to light two cigarettes."

"She may have shared her matches with another person, who was smoking."

"Likely she had only a few of these short matches," I said. (Sam would use about as many matches as that box would hold to get rid of one pipeful of tobacco.)

I picked up another little gold box. It had powder, rouge, lipstick, and a mirror in it. I had seen it often enough before. I put it back on the table, and took up a beaded coin purse that matched the large bag. It was entirely empty.

"Isn't it queer that that should be empty?" Danny asked. "And her bill-fold is missing. She surely would not start to go anywhere with not a cent of money. Doesn't it look as if she had been robbed?"

"Only," I said, "if anyone had robbed her, why would he have left the valuable gold cigarette case, and vanity case, and match-box?"

"He might have thought they would be hard to dispose of."

I stood silent, thinking and shaking my head.

"Mary," Danny's voice, always low, grew lower still with her intensity, "there is one thing that no one has thought of. Daniel Canneziano could have reached here from California in a few hours, by aeroplane."

"I had thought of that. But, Danny, no aeroplane ever came within twenty miles of the ranch without every man-jack of us hearing it, and rushing out with our heads tipped back to gape at it. Aeroplanes aren't stealthy things, you know, that people can slip up in, and slip off again."

"But, on the third of July, two aeroplanes passed over, going to the Telko celebration."

"On the third," I reminded her, "as advertised. And you know how much noise they made. And how we all went out and watched them, from tiny specks in the south until they were tiny specks and lost in the north again."

She shook her head, and drooped her shoulders with a sigh.

I picked up a little red handkerchief. It was crumpled in a ball; if ever I saw a handkerchief that had been cried into, and turned to a dry spot, and squeezed, and cried into again, it was that little red wad. It was dry now, of course; exposed to the air in this altitude. I wondered whether it had been dry when it had come out of the bag. It was a question not to be asked; so I dropped the handkerchief on the table, certain, only, that the fastidious Gabrielle had never started out with a handkerchief in that condition in her Vienna bag, and picked up the carved ivory cigarette holder. It fell to pieces in my fingers.

"Was this broken in her bag?" I questioned.

"Yes. Snapped in two. And she loved it."

I fitted the pieces together again, on the table, and took up a folded sheet of paper, and opened it, and read:

"Glorious Gaby: Be a good sport. Be a darling. Be game—that is, be Gaby, and meet me this afternoon, around four thirty, in the cabin. H. H."

"Well!" I said.

"Yes, I know," Danny answered, "but Hubert Hand swears that he wrote that note several weeks ago. Too, we know that he was playing chess with Uncle Sam at half-past four."

"He could have gone to the cabin later, when the men went to do the chores. Or was he right with Sam and Chad all the time?"

"I suppose so. He must have satisfied the coroner's jury, at the inquest, of his innocence. Mary," her voice went all tense again, "does it seem to you that the jury was very readily satisfied?"

Perhaps this would be as good a place as any to explain that this tale is not being written to prove that Mary Magin was, or is, a wise, clever, or smart woman. As I have said before, and will say again, from the beginning to the very end I was a fool. I made mistakes, over and over; and, as will be told, I made a disastrous mistake in the end. If I had been blind, deaf and dumb, I could not have been as big a fool; for then, all the time, I should not have been imagining that I saw things, which I did not see; heard things, which I did not hear; and I should have been obliged to keep my clattery old tongue quiet. The only virtue I can claim, concerning this story, is that if I were a vain or a conceited person, I should never have written it.

I spoke sharply, too sharply to her in answer to what I had imagined I had seen in her attitude. "Never mind about the jury being easily satisfied. Sam is not going to be. He told me this morning that he would find the murderer if it took every dollar he had in the world to do it. Sam is going to get to the bottom of this. Be sure of that."

"I—wonder," she said.

"What do you wonder?"

"Mary!" she exclaimed, close to a reproach, "I merely wonder whether or not Uncle Sam will succeed."

I looked at her brown eyes, all red and swollen from tears, and at the deep, dark circles under them, and I was ashamed.

25
More Clues

I put my arm around her shoulders and drew her close to me. "Honey," I said, "forgive your old Mary. We are all over-strung, overwrought. I didn't mean to speak so sharply."

"There is nothing to forgive, dear," she said. "But—I don't understand. What did I say, or do, that made you feel like being cross to me?"

"Nothing," I told her. "I'm all on edge—that's all."

"I know. Were you looking for something else, on the table? There was nothing else in her bag."

"I was wondering," I said, "about that foreign looking letter she got on the second of July. Did she burn it, with the other things?"

"Oddly, she didn't. I found it in her desk; or, rather, beneath her typewriter. Either she forgot about it; or knew that none of us could read it."

"It was written in a foreign language?"

"No. In code. Here it is."

Code, indeed! When I took it from its envelope, this is what met my eyes.

"Paexzazlytp! f-y nyx ogrgrago, rn fgao atf jan j-asn, ahzgo zkg c-. ahhalo, vkgt nyx clplzgf rg zkg kypulzae, zkaz nyx palf, vlzk nyxo lrlzazgf r-yta e-lpa prleg, "p-yoon, yef fgao, l-rafg—"

135

I have copied only the first lines on the first page. There were four sleazy pages, all closely typewritten. Not a scratch of handwriting on it. What I judged to be the signature, was, "Slrsl."

"Do you know who wrote this?" I asked.

"I am sure, if I dare be sure of anything, that it was written by a man named Lewis Bauermont."

I counted the letters of "Lewis" on my fingers. Five. The number of letters in the signature, "Slrsl."

"If he signed his name Lewis," I said, "then 'S' would be, 'L,' and 'l' would be 'e' and so on. Get a pencil, dear. Let's see if we can work it out."

She came and looked over my shoulder at the jumbled letters.

"No," she said, "you see, the letter 's' comes twice in the last word, and there are no duplicate letters in Lewis. I am sure it will be more difficult than any substitution of letters. I don't know anything about codes; but I have a notion that the letters are mere symbols of something else—numbers perhaps, that work out with a key quotation."

"I'm going to have a try at my idea, anyway," I insisted.

I went and sat at the desk. She sat beside me, and handed me a pencil.

"Perhaps," I suggested, "the man who wrote this, signed some nickname. Did he have one?"

"Men called him 'Mexico,' and 'Mexie.' Gaby never used either of those names for him."

"What name did she use?" I insisted, though I felt like a brute.

"None, except 'Lewis,' that I know of. She didn't read the signature, when she read the letter to me. At least I don't remember—"

"She read it to you!" I exclaimed.

"I thought that she did. Now—I don't know. I can't be sure of anything. She read to me what she said was a copy of the letter; that is, the worked out code. She may have left out entire paragraphs. She may have changed it, in any way, in order to keep her terrible secret from me."

"Yes, but what did she tell you the letter contained?"

Danny looked at her wrist-watch. "It is too long even to begin to tell, now. And—I don't want to tell it again; not to-day. I have told John all about it, you see. Later, of course— Or you may ask John to tell you. It—it was an insult from beginning to end. An insult to her. I can't bear thinking of it, any more; not to-day.

"Mary," her voice changed suddenly as did her manner, "do you know why Uncle Sam asked me—almost commanded me to be in the living-room at three o'clock to-day?"

"No, Danny, I don't. But he told Mrs. Ricker and me to be there, too. I guess he just wants to talk to all of us, together."

"Oh—talk! What good is talk going to do? Talk, in a place like this, now, where there is not one true, certain thing to get hold of, anywhere; where not one of us can believe in another—"

She put a quick hand to her lips; her eyes widened; she turned, and hastily pushing aside the heavy curtain, went through the clothes closet into her own room.

I sat still, at the desk. The paper before me, and the sharp pencil in my hand, tempted me to make a list, as they always do in books, of the clues, to date. I wrote:

"Locked door.

"Key in my pocket.

"T. A. (I put only the initials of tobacco ashes.)

"Chad's suicide.

"Chad's note. What person was he trying to shield?

"What did Hubert Hand think that I had overheard in the cabin?

"Mrs. Ricker's threat.

"'Q' cap for typewriter key.
"Contents of the beaded bag.
  "1. Two cigs missing from full case.
  "2. Empty match-box.
  "3. Empty purse. Missing bill-fold. (Robbery?)
  "4. Crumpled handkerchief. (Tears? Pleading?)
  "5. Broken cig. holder.
  "6. Hubert Hand's note.
"The code letter.
"Gabrielle's note to Danny."

This, I submit as the world's worst list of clues. It is the best example I have ever seen of the saying that a person could not see the forest for the trees. The forest was there, right enough. All I would have needed to do, was to back off far enough away from the trees to look at it.

My face burns, even yet, when I realize that, at half-past two o'clock on the afternoon of the fifth of July, if I had been possessed of just one lick of sense, I could, instead of writing that list of clues, have written another one; a list that, step by step, just as sure as straight ahead, would have led to the guilty person.

Why did I not take into consideration the fact that, for two months, the Canneziano girls had been searching for something on the Desert Moon; something which I was all but certain they had not found?

Why did I not give a thought to the fact that John, after a secret conversation with Gaby—according to Mrs. Ricker—had been clean and clear away off the place since early afternoon until evening?

Why did I not include in my list the fact that Gaby had given the gold monkey to Martha?

Why, instead of trying to puzzle out the code letter, did I not read between the lines of Gabrielle's last note to Danny?

However, at the time, since it was of my own making, I was quite well satisfied with my list. I took it to the table to check over the items. Sam had put the key, with which I had opened the attic door, alongside the other things there.

I picked it up, now, and looked at it for the first time. I had not looked at it, I had merely used it, the night before. My heart jumped up in my throat. It was not the key to the attic door. It was a rusty old pass key that had hung on a nail in the broom closet, off the kitchen, for more years than I could remember.

Whoever had put this key in my pocket, must have been well acquainted with the Desert Moon kitchen, to have found that old key, under the brooms, and mops, and dust-rags, and chamois skins, and the rest, that hung around it and over it in the broom-closet.

What had become of the key to the attic door?

26
The Session

When I went down to the living-room, at five minutes before three, Danny, John, Mrs. Ricker and Martha were all there. Danny and John were sitting at the far end of the room. Mrs. Ricker was in a chair near the window, tatting. Martha was on the biggest davenport, playing with the monkey charm. I went and sat beside her.

"I feel sleepy," she answered my question. "But I am happy, now. I am very happy."

"That's nice," I told her. "But, if I were you, I wouldn't talk much about being happy; that is, not to-day."

"I don't care. Gaby was hateful and mean, even if she did give me the monkey. She was good, then; but she wasn't good long enough for me to like her. I'm sorry because Chad died, though. I was awfully sorry, until I happened to remember about heaven. He is happy there now. When I die, I'll go to heaven and be happy, too. He'll love me then, won't he? I know he will."

"Of course, Martha," I said. "And he loved you here, too."

"Only like a little girl. I wanted him to love me like a lady. He would have, I guess, if he hadn't shot himself. I am sorry he did that. But I'm happy, anyway, 'cause we are going to have the fireworks to-night."

"Tut, tut," I said. "We won't be having any fireworks to-night."

Her lower lip curled out. "Daddy promised," she whimpered. "Yesterday, when it looked like rain, he said never to mind, that we'd have them the very first night it didn't rain. To-night is the first night. Daddy promised."

To my shame, I never, in all the years, had gotten used to Martha. She looked like a big, healthy, strapping girl. And when, as now, I realized that a smart five-year-old child would have had a better mind, it shocked me all over.

Sam and Hubert Hand came into the room together. Sam looked around, counting noses.

"All here," he said, and locked the door he and Hubert had come through, and dropped the key in his pocket. He went all around the room, closing and locking the doors and windows. He moved a chair to the foot of the stairway, pulled a small table over beside it, took his six-gun out of his back pocket, put it on the table, and sat down in the chair.

No one had moved nor had said a word. I know that I was frightened. I was not afraid of Sam, and I was not afraid of that six-gun. It did not make me a mite more uneasy than a bouquet of flowers would have; that is, if Sam had carried the bouquet in and put it on the table with the same manner with which he had carried and placed the gun. Mostly, I guess, I was afraid of being made afraid; partly, I was afraid of myself.

Hubert Hand spoke first. "Cannon, ugh?" he sneered.

"That's all right, Hand," Sam answered. "This is here, mostly I think, for ornamental purposes."

"Daddy," Martha piped up, "aren't we going to have the fireworks to-night?"

Sam frowned at her. "Not to-night, daughter."

She opened her mouth and began making those dreadful noises she always made whenever she was crossed in anything.

Sam rapped on the table, "Shut that up, here and now," he said. "Not another whimper out of you. Hear me, Martha?"

She closed her mouth with a snap. I thought those immense eyes of hers would pop out of her head. I am sure that the others of us all felt the way she looked. In all the years we had lived together on the Desert Moon, it was the first time any one of us had ever heard Sam speak impatiently to Martha. As for scolding her, being stern with her, up to this minute it had never been in the book.

"John," Sam said, "you and Danny come out of that corner, up here nearer the rest of us, and where it is light."

I tell you they came, straight, and sat on the small davenport beside Hubert Hand.

"I reckon," Sam began, "that all of you in here know that anyone could walk up to any man or woman in here and call him or her a murderer, and that not one of us could give him the lie, right now.

"I reckon that you know, too, as everyone in the country knows that, at this hour, the Desert Moon Ranch is rotten with the muck of crime and suspicion. Maybe you don't know that it is not going to stay that way for many more hours.

"We have called the law in, as was right and proper. And the law has been real polite, and blinked its eyes, and departed. 'Folded its tents like the Arabs, and silently stole away.' Well, that's all right. I didn't much care about having those fellows mix into my private business; anyway, not until I had found out that I couldn't attend to it myself. I am not going to find that out. I can attend to it. I am going to, right here and now. Later on, when we need the law again, we'll call on it. The innocent in this room will have their names cleared. The Desert Moon will be a fit place for a white man to live on.

"Now this gun here may look like I felt violent or something. I don't. And I'm not going to act violent. This gun is here for just one purpose, and I'm dead certain it won't be used for that. A word to the wise, though. No person, barring none and including the ladies, is to leave this room until I give the word. No innocent person in here will try to leave. Any guilty person in here—and, before God, there is a guilty person here; guilty, at least, of aiding and abetting—is going to have too much sense to try to make a break. That is why I won't need the gun. Not, I mean, until we find the guilty person. When we have found him, it may be of some use until the sheriff can get here. That is all of that. Except that we are going to stay here, one and all, right here in this room, until we are ready to 'phone for the sheriff.

"If everyone does as I am going to tell them to do, we should be through with this session by supper time. But, if we don't get through until midnight, or until next week, we'll stay here until we do. All I'm asking, of everybody here, is that you all tell the truth. You'll have to, sooner or later. Better make it sooner."

During this speech my dander had been rising. It had got up pretty good and high by this time. "Sam Stanley," I spoke out, "you ought to know that you can't force truth out of anybody at the point of a gun, nor by keeping them locked up. We'll get hungry. We'll get thirsty. And when we do we'll eat and drink and go about our affairs. At least I will—unless you shoot me. I'm not fixed to put up with this kind of foolishness."

"Mary," Sam roared at me. "That's enough out of you. You be quiet. You are going to do as you are told. So are the others."

Sam had never spoken like that to me before. It left me limp as a drained jelly bag. Before I could get my breath for an answer, Hubert Hand was talking.

"Changed your mind since morning, haven't you, Sam? You were dead sure this morning that no one on the place had had anything to do with the murder; that Mary had locked the attic door herself, earlier in the day, and, absent-mindedly, dropped the key in her pocket."

"Never mind about my morning's opinions, Hand. You are right. Dead right. I've changed my mind. Now, since you are already going pretty good, I'll begin with you and work around the room, taking each one in turn. I want you to tell everything you know, and everything you suspect concerning the murder."

"Sorry," Hubert Hand said, "but I don't know a damn thing except that, apparently, she was strangled to death sometime between four o'clock yesterday afternoon and eight o'clock yesterday evening. We saw her alive at four. We found her dead at eight. That's the extent of my knowledge."

"All right. Now go ahead with what you suspect."

"I can't see," Hubert Hand objected, "that suspicions have any place here. Beyond stirring up a rumpus and hard feelings, they wouldn't get any of us any place."

"That is for me to decide," Sam said. "You were mighty busy for a while this morning, throwing out hints and slurs. If this session doesn't do anything else, it can anyway clear out all this whispering that is going around. Just now, everybody here is busy suspecting everybody else here. Suspicions usually have some reasoning behind them. 'Where there's smoke there's fire.' It is only fair to give everyone here a chance to examine everyone else's suspicions, and disprove them, if they can. If you think that I did the killing, I want to know it. I want a chance to prove you wrong. Come on now, Hand. Come clean."

"Suppose I refuse?"

"That is up to you," Sam drawled. "As the sheriff's against you, a sight harder. If I knew you had no suspicions, I wouldn't try to force you to invent some, just to be sociable. But you were pretty free with your hints this morning. All right. Talk."

Hubert lowered his Roman nose and pulled at his moustache for a minute. It was easy to see he was busy with a decision of some sort. He settled back in his chair more comfortably and, still pulling at his moustache, he began.

27
Hubert Hand Talks

"Well," he said, "I can talk all right. But I want to start with this understanding. I don't know any facts that amount to a damn. You're right that I have suspicions. If you weren't forcing them out of me, I'd have sense enough to keep my mouth shut, from now on, at least until airing them might do some good. But, since you are determined to have them now, at the point of a gun, I'll say that I think John did it, and that somebody else in the house is shielding him."

Danny gave a thin, sick little shriek and threw her arm around John in a protecting way. John straightened. Under his tan I could see the color seeping out of his face. Gently, he removed Danny's arm.

Sam lowered his white eyebrows until his eyes looked like two slits of blue light, glinting out from away behind his face. When he spoke his voice was iron.

"Why do you think John killed her?"

"In the first place, John is the only one here who hasn't a water-tight alibi—"

"Not by a damn sight he isn't," Sam interrupted. "But never mind. Go on."

"At four o'clock Gaby came down through the room. While she was still in sight, Danny called down, trying to get her to come back. Now this is just another suspicion, I don't know whether anyone here will back me up in it or

not—probably not,"—he added the last in a hateful, slur-
ring way—"but I noticed that her voice sounded strange,
like she was excited, maybe, or else afraid."

Sam asked, "Did anyone else here notice anything of
that kind?"

I had decided, right at first, to keep my mouth shut
about everything; so I did.

"I thought not," Hubert Hand said, as if he had known
from the start that he was the only honest one in the
crowd.

Mrs. Ricker spoke. "I noticed it," she said.

Hubert bowed at her, in a sort of mocking way. Knowing what I knew, I thought that her corroboration would
do Hubert Hand more harm than good. But, of course, the
others did not know what I knew. Nor were they going to
know it, since Hubert Hand was keeping his part of our
bargain. Right or wrong, I was thankful, just then, that we
had made that bargain.

"Let me see," Hubert Hand continued, "where was I?
Gaby, after going through the room, stopped on the porch
for a minute to talk to Chad. He came into the house in
a fine humor. Gaby then went around the house to the
rabbit hutch, and for some reason, gave her bracelet to
Martha. When Martha's turn comes, in this inquisition, I
suggest that she be questioned rather closely."

Sam banged his fist on the table. "Never mind your
suggestions. You are accusing John now. Stick to that."

"You bet," Hubert Hand accepted, "especially since
Martha was in the house again within five or ten minutes, with every last one of us. Danny had come down by
that time. From four to five, then, you and I were playing
chess. Chad was at the piano. Danny and Mary were over
there, talking together. Mrs. Ricker was tatting, where she
is now, by the window. Martha was bothering us, part of
the time, and part of the time she was just fooling around

the room. I'm pretty certain not one of us left this room during that hour. You might check up on that, Sam."

Sam asked Mrs. Ricker, and Danny, and me, if we remembered anyone's leaving the room during that hour. We all said we did not. Danny added that she might not have noticed. I wished, seeing Hubert Hand smile, she had let well enough alone and not bothered to add that.

"At five," Hubert Hand resumed, "we three men went together to let the cows in and to milk. Mary, I believe, was in the kitchen alone, getting supper, during that time. Mrs. Ricker, Danny and Martha remained here in the living-room. Is that right?"

"Maybe it is, and maybe it isn't," Sam said. "There is the hour in there, before supper, that we'll all have to account for, right accurately, before any of us has that water-tight alibi you were talking about, Hand. And," Sam added, with his own sort of emphasis, "we won't have it then."

"All right," Hubert Hand agreed. "You and Chad and I went down to the barns together. We let the cows in. We milked them. At least, you and I did. Chad stayed with you and was kidding around down in your end of the barn. I heard you laughing and talking down there, together, the whole time. Is that right?"

"Practically," Sam answered. "All but, I couldn't swear that you were in the barn during the entire time."

"No? Well, I'll admit that I hadn't thought of that. If I'd thought of it, I'd probably have known that you—how is it?—couldn't swear that I was in the barn during the entire time."

"Meaning?" Sam demanded.

"That if John is guilty, you'll shield him with your last lie."

Sam's fist knotted at his side. His voice was not iron, now; it was tempered steel. "We'll settle about my last lie later, Hand."

"You're begging for this," Hubert Hand reminded him. "Get on!"

"I milked four cows. Not very good, for the time—about forty minutes; but as good work as you did. And I will swear that you were in the barn the entire time. Anyway, that is easy settled. Mary, did I, or did anyone of the three of us, come through the kitchen and go upstairs during that hour?"

"No," I answered.

"Weren't you," Sam questioned, "going back and forth between the kitchen and the dining-room?"

"No. Danny set the table for me. I didn't step foot out of the kitchen."

"Mrs. Ricker," Hubert Hand questioned, "did any one of us men come in, and go upstairs through the living-room, during that hour?"

"No," she said.

"Mrs. Ricker," Sam asked, "were you right there, alone, in the living-room during that entire hour?"

"I was not alone. Martha was with me. And, several times during the hour, five or six times at least, Danny came in from the dining-room to see whether she could see John coming up the road."

"Danny," Sam spoke to her, "were Mrs. Ricker and Martha in the living-room every time you went in there?"

"I—think so."

"Only think so, eh?" Hubert Hand half sneered it.

"I mean," Danny explained, "that I am sure Mrs. Ricker was here. She was sitting right by the window. I did not particularly notice Martha."

"I can vouch for Martha," Mrs. Ricker snapped.

"All right," Hubert Hand went on, "so far, so good. The ladies, I think, especially if you remember the glass doors between the living-room and the dining-room, have established alibis that would satisfy any jury.

"Now for you and Chad and me, again. We walked together, carrying the milk, to the dairy. There we took off
the barn coveralls, and, at your suggestion, washed up in
the dairy kitchen to save time. We came back to the house
together. Mary said that supper was on the table. We all
sat down to the table together. All present, you see, except
John.

"Would it have been possible for you, or for me, or
for Chad, to have gone down to the barn (you and I each
milked four cows, remember), come back to the house and
through it, with not one of these ladies seeing us, committed the murder, got back to the barn, and then to the
house again, all in an hour? I think, Sam, the wisest thing
you can do, is to grant us all our alibis for that hour, anyway, and then work on from there, if you're bound to."

I felt reasonably certain that, if Hubert Hand had gone
through the living-room, between five and six o'clock,
Mrs. Ricker would not tell of it. But I was more certain
that Danny, on the watch out for John, would have seen
anyone who had come in through the front door.

"The alibi hour sounds fine, Hand," Sam said, "but you
are making a mistake. You are assuming that I think that
someone here committed the murder. I don't think that.
I do think that someone in this room, right now, knows
who did it. Where any one of us was, or was not, at the
particular hour you're making such a stew about, probably
doesn't cut any ice."

"I think it does. I began this, you know, by saying that
I thought John—"

"You said that once," Sam interrupted. "Once is plenty.
Go ahead with it now, if you can. Give your proofs."

"There you go. I told you I didn't have any proofs,
didn't I, when you made me talk? But I have got some
pretty solid bases for my suspicions. John decided, all of
a sudden, to go to Rattail for the mail—or something.

The kidding he came in for, right then, shows whether he usually went for the mail on a holiday afternoon. He was gone four hours instead of the two—two and a half, anyway—that he could have made it in. He had two bum excuses. First, tire trouble. That would be a better excuse, if the car wasn't standing in the garage right now with the same tires on it that he started out with."

"I know you said you had no proof of anything," Sam broke in. "I reckon, of course, you can prove that, though?"

John spoke. "I don't think he could prove it, dad, since the spare was a Truetread, same as the others. But he's right. I changed tires twice, that's all. The spare was rotten. When I had the second blow-out, I patched the first tire and put it back on. The patch is there, to prove that."

"And the rotten spare?" Hubert Hand questioned.

"It wasn't worth bothering to put on the rack. I rolled it off across the desert."

"My mistake," Hubert Hand said. "Maybe. Two hours is a long time to change tires, even twice. The second excuse was, that he had met Leo Saule and had given him a tow. Saule is a rotten little half-breed, who could be bought for a half dollar. Also, he lives alone, away off the main road—"

John jumped to his feet. "Get this, Hand—"

Sam had jumped too. He got to John and put his hands on his shoulders. "Keep your shirt on, son. I am to blame for this. Your turn is coming. Wait for it. Go on, Hand."

John hesitated, and sat down again. Sam went back to his chair by the table.

"Sorry," Hubert Hand apologized, "I don't like this a damn bit better than John does; but it seems to be up to me. Well, then, he came in two hours late. He came through the kitchen; and, instead of leaving the car in the garage, he left it in the back entrance. He went straight upstairs. It took him half an hour, or more, to get shaved and change his clothes. When he came down he acted like a man in a daze. He couldn't eat. He offered being out in the sun as an excuse. He is out in the sun every day.

"I think that he had met Gaby, as they had planned, right after dinner when he started for Rattail. Maybe she had promised him to leave the place. He was crazy to get her off the ranch. I know that. He told me so, just the other day—said she was making trouble here, and so on. She may have had something on him, that she was threatening to tell Danny, or Sam. I don't know about that, either. I don't know a damn thing about whatever they might have had between them. But I think that he killed her, out on the desert some place.

"I don't think that he had planned to do it. I think he must have threatened her, off and on, though; her note to Danny, and other things, show that she was afraid for her life. All the same, I think he started it, yesterday, as a bluff. But the desire was back of the bluff—that's pretty certain.

"I don't know why he brought her body back and hid it in the house. I don't give him credit for figuring out what a smart thing that was to do. He may have been afraid of footprints in the road, or on the desert, if he carried the body away and tried to hide it out there. He didn't know that the storm was coming, to cover up his traces. I think, though, that it was pure funk that made him come driving home with the body hidden in the car—covered with the sacks of rock salt.

"I didn't like to think that it was Danny who helped him out, after that. It didn't seem like her. I couldn't think of anyone else, though, who would help him. In the last few minutes, I've managed to think of someone else. It is a lucky thing for John. You are a damn sight stronger ally, Sam, than Danny or any one else would have been. For instance—this present magnificent bluff of yours."

"All right," Sam said. "All through?"

"I'm satisfied, if you are," Hubert Hand answered.

"I'm not," Sam drawled. "Because, like the caterpillar said, 'It's all wrong from beginning to end.' It is a queer thing, though, the way quotations always come to me. Most of the time you were talking, Hand, I kept thinking of this one: 'Give a guilty man enough rope and he will hang himself.'"

28
John Talks

"You mean me, dad," John spoke right up, and I'd given a pretty penny to have had him say something else, for, of course, Sam had not meant him, "I'm not worried. They don't hang innocent men in Nevada, no matter how much rope their friends present them with."

"Asa matter of fact," Hubert Hand said, "I guess they don't hang any men in Nevada, now, do they? Lethal chamber, isn't it?"

Sam growled at him to shut up; and told John that it was his turn to talk, and to go ahead and to try to talk sense, if possible.

"I don't know where to begin," John said. "I've got nothing to talk about."

"Begin at the beginning. What did Gaby say to you, after dinner, that made you decide, right off, to go to Rattail?"

"I've told you that already. I've got no changes to make in it. Gaby told me, after dinner, that Danny's headache was getting worse. She said that Danny had sent to Salt Lake for a certain kind of headache medicine, the only kind that ever did her any good. She said it should have come in the morning's mail. She said that Danny would be peeved at her for telling me about it asking me to go, that is. So, if I didn't want a fuss, and wanted to be allowed to go, I'd better make a sneak of it, with no explanations. I did. Here is something I haven't told, though, for Danny just told me, when we came in here at three. She hadn't sent for any headache medicine to Salt Lake, nor anywhere. That certainly looks as if Gaby wanted to get either me, or the sedan, off the job and out of the way, yesterday afternoon. She must have had some reason for sending me on a fool's errand like that."

"Well, well, go on, son," Sam said, after we had all sat in dead silence for about a minute.

"Go on where?" John asked. "I've got nothing more to say. Hand's told the rest of it, hasn't he?"

"Answer him, you fool," Sam roared. "You've got answers, haven't you? Use 'em. Sitting there like a dummy! Did anyone see you towing Saule to his place?"

"Not that I know of. I towed him all right; but I can't prove it. Hand was right when he said he could be bought for a half dollar. He might come cheaper. I'd try him with a quarter, first, Hand."

"Good God!" Sam shouted. "What are you trying to do? Pry your way into the lethal chamber? Can you give a reason for driving to the back door, instead of leaving the car in the garage?"

"Only two hundred-pound sacks of rock salt. They'd dumped them on the platform for us this morning from Eighteen. I could give a reason for bringing them up, instead of leaving them there until we went down with the truck. Sure, I'm full of reasons. Got a good reason for taking half an hour to bathe and dress. It would be hard to find a guy with more reasons than I can produce for everything—all, but murdering the twin sister of the girl I love."

"Son," Sam said, "I don't blame you a damn bit for being sore clear to the bone. But, come to that, we haven't any right to blame Hand, here, either; not if he is honest in his suspicions, and, maybe, he is. I forced them out of him. Can't you swallow your pride, for a while, and—"

"I've swallowed it already," John said, "if that's what you want. Swallowed it till I'm choked with it."

"I know, I know. But it is like this, John—and this goes for all you folks, too—a person can't get to the bottom of anything without going down. In this case, it looks like we were going to have to go pretty low down—a trip to hell for most of us, I reckon. But it will be a round trip. Most of us will come up clean, to a clean Desert Moon. Can't we go down, then, like a lot of reasonable human beings, and not like a kennel of yapping dogs?"

"It won't hold, dad," John answered. "Not this round trip to hell stuff, as human beings. If I hadn't stopped being a human being; that is, a man, I wouldn't have sat still here and let Hand have his say out. And I wouldn't have done it, not to save my own neck. But I know how you feel about the ranch. I've gone through with it for that reason, and—for Danny, though I know that all of this is a rotten mistake on your part. I know that; but it is no use telling you, now that you've started. I'll go on with it, the best I can. I guess the others will, too. But none of us will come up clean, as you say. Don't look for that—not after this muck. All right. Hop to it, dad. What's your next question?"

I was relieved when Sam asked, "Do you suspect, with reason, anyone in this room?" I had thought, following right along with Hubert Hand's accusations, as Sam had been doing, that his next question would be about what was troubling and bothering John when he came in. Why he had acted so queerly that he had had to explain it by saying he was loco from the sun.

"I do not." John answered Sam's question, straight. "But it seems darn queer to me the way everyone is leaving Chad's suicide out of this. Hold on, dad! I'm not saying that I think Chad killed her. I know he didn't. But I know just as well that he didn't walk out and shoot himself simply because he had loved Gaby. Chad was a queer bird, all right. I guess none of us understood him very well. He was as emotional as the deuce, too— I'll grant that. But he was not, ever, a damn fool."

"John!" Danny interrupted. "Do you think that a man who kills himself, when he finds that the girl he loves has been cruelly murdered, needs to be a fool?"

"Yes," John answered. "A man might not care much about living, after that, but if he killed himself he'd be a fool. I mean— It is like this. Regular fellows, and Chad sure was one, don't walk out and kill themselves, when they find the girl they love is dead. It takes more than death to make a real man kill himself. Sounds like a book, I know; but, loss of honor is a reason, and shame—maybe that's the same thing—is another reason. Or, a fellow might kill himself to save the honor of his girl—or to save a friend's life, if he owed the friend a lot—"

Danny interrupted again. "Absolute despair should be a reason—"

"Sure, I know how you mean. But Chad had despaired of Gaby's love long ago. Dozens of times I've seen her treat him so rottenly that, if he had been the suicidal sort, he would have killed himself right then. No sir. I tell you Chad did not shoot himself because Gaby was dead. Sure, that was a part of it; but not the main part.

"Chad was a darn good guy. Good all the way through. We all know that he didn't kill her. We'd know it, if dad didn't have his alibis for him. But what I'm getting at is, that, someway or other, and not meaning to at all, he got himself mixed up in it. When he saw what had happened, and realized that he had been involved— There's your reason, all right. I think that, if we can find out why Chad shot himself, we'll find out most of the other things we want to know. I'm through, dad. I've said all I've got to say, and more too."

Sam hesitated a minute. I was relieved to see him take Chad's note out of his pocket. "Chad says that he killed her," he said, and read the note aloud. Everyone but me, to whom it was no surprise, and Martha, who was almost asleep again, squeaked, or gasped, or otherwise showed their horrified astonishment.

John spoke first. "I'll bet four dollars he never wrote it."

Sam passed the paper to him. "It looks like his writing. It sounds like him too. Soon as I can get track of one of these what-you-may-call-em's, handwriting experts, I'm going to send it to him. I reckon it will match up all right. I wish there was an expert of some kind that we could send it to, to find out why he wrote it."

"Uncle Sam," Danny said, and I could see that the note had upset her pretty badly, "there is something no one has thought of. We haven't had time to think. But, where was Chad during the hour we were hunting for Gaby? You, and John, and Mary and I were in the sedan. But where were the others, during that time; between seven and eight o'clock, wasn't it?"

"I reckon," Sam spoke real gently to her, "that we have all had time to do some tall thinking about that hour, little girl. But there couldn't be any doubt that Gaby had been dead a sight longer than an hour, when we found her."

"But can you know that, for a certainty?" Danny insisted.

"Just as certain as I know that she was dead, Danny. I— Well, in the early days here— Never mind that, though. I've had experience with deaths, kind of on that order. I know. The coroner and the sheriff knew. But, she might have been brought into the house during that hour. Hand let loose on his alibi business a little too early—"

"I'm no fool," Hubert Hand interrupted. "You admit that she could not have been murdered during the hour between six and seven. Every one of us, except John, can account for every minute of our time from four o'clock, when we saw Gaby alive, up to seven."

"All right. All right," Sam said. "Have it your own way. But you've had your say, and plenty of time to say it in. You'll maybe have another turn later. Now, keep still. We are going to hear from the others.

"It is your turn next, Danny, I'm sorry. You understand, we haven't any time to lose. Take it easy, though. Do you suspect, with reason, anyone in this room of being connected with the murder?"

29
Danny

"I think," Danny said, "that Chad did it."

Sam lowered his brows, and turned those blue searchlights of his on her. "That is a bad beginning, my girl," he said, kindly enough, though. "You don't think that. Not for a minute. Better start over again."

"Uncle Sam," she pleaded, "listen. You spoke about clearing everyone's name, and about the honor of the Desert Moon. Chad's confession does that—does all of it. Why not let well enough alone?"

My own words; but I had not expected to hear them from Danny. The only reason for them seemed to be that Hubert Hand had frightened her with his case against John. Was she the sort of girl who would keep on loving John, and marry him, if she thought that he had killed her sister? I did not believe it.

John said, "Danny!" And, knowing as little as I do about being loved, I knew that I should hate to have my sweetheart pronounce my name with a pinch of horror, and a pinch of anger, and a big dash of bewilderment, as John had pronounced hers.

Sam said, "Somebody else suggested that to-day, Danny. I told them that there was no question of well enough while the man who had murdered your sister was going about alive, and while his helper was keeping his secret on the Desert Moon."

"You said that?" Danny questioned, and gave us all another severe shock by accenting the pronoun.

"I said that, yes." Sam showed signs of rising dander. "And I thought that you, if anyone, more than anyone, would agree with me."

"Only," she answered, "I should rather let a guilty person go free, escape, than to persecute an innocent person."

"No innocent person is going to be persecuted on the Desert Moon," Sam said, "and no guilty one is going to escape, either. You're going to be a good, sensible girl, too, and answer a few questions I want to ask you.

"First thing I want to know is, what was it that you girls were hunting for, all the time, here on the ranch?"

"We had been told," Danny answered, "that there was a very large sum of money hidden here on this place. We came to get it. That is—Gaby did. I mean—before we left the continent I knew that I wanted to stay here, for a long time. I cared much more about staying here, and keeping Gaby here, than I cared about finding the money. Really, I—I hoped not to find the money. The people with whom I had been living in England had broken up their home there. I had no home. That is how I happened to be in Switzerland, with Gaby. I—"

She broke down, and hid her face in her hands. We all sat, quietly, and waited.

With her face still covered she appealed to Sam. "Uncle, I can't tell all this, to-day, I can't. I loved Gaby. I did love her. If she were alive—But she isn't. Please, please don't force me to go on with this."

"You've got me wrong, Danny," Sam said, "I didn't expect you to tell about all of your past lives, and that. But this stuff now about money hidden here. Could it have any bearing on the murder?"

She shook her head. "I think not. Not possibly. There was no money here, anyway, as it turned out. That is—if

Gaby told me the truth about anything. I thought that she did. But now—she spoke of keeping fear and dread from me, in her last note to me. I—I can't talk of this, to-day, I tell you!"

"See here, dad," John spoke up, "Danny isn't fit to go through with this to-day. I think she has told me everything she has to tell. She told me most of it this morning. I've got it straight. How about allowing me to go on with it?"

"Do you think any of it might have a bearing on the murder?"

"Yes, I think it might."

Sam banged on the table with his fist. "By God," he roared, "what kind of people have I got to deal with? Not five minutes ago, you sat right there and swore that you had told everything you know. Couldn't even begin. Couldn't think of a thing to say. No suspicion. No hints of any kind; except a slur at a dead boy. Now you come out with this. By the Lord, Hand, you may be a better man than I think you are—"

Danny's voice cut in like scissors slithering through taffeta silk. "Be careful, there," she said. I remembered the way she had brushed the beaded bag. Something cold went trailing down my backbone. It was time, and past, I thought, for me to take a hand.

"Sam," I said, "what's become of all your fine talk about us not acting like yelping dogs, and swallowing our pride, and helping out, and so on? I told you, when you started this, that it was a fool piece of business. You, nor nobody, can force truth out of folks. You're kind of back on your quotations, or you'd remember the one about leading a horse to water. How do you think anyone is ever going to get any place with you pounding and shouting and blaspheming around all the while? If you think the fact that John wouldn't betray Danny's confidence to satisfy a crazy whim of yours makes him out a murderer, you've got less

sense at sixty-five than you had when you were born. The
best thing you can do, is to follow your advice to me, and
be quiet. John's ready to talk now, if you'll keep still and
give him half a chance."

I have never yet seen the man who wouldn't quiet down,
mild as mush, when a sensible woman took it on herself
to give him a good scolding. The strongest man will drop
before a good, strong volley of woman's words, the same as
he would before a shooting squad.

"Go on, John," I said, seeing that Sam had dropped,
and wanting John to get a start before Sam had had time
to pick himself up, and dust off, and ask Danny what she
had meant by hissing at him to be careful.

"Shall I, Danny?" John asked. She nodded.

"It isn't any too pleasant, even for me," John began,
"but the straight of it is, that while Danny, for years, was
a companion to this lady in England, Gaby was running
around over Europe with a darned rotten lot of associates.
On the face of things, she was an actress; leading lady with
a company that traveled all over the country—over several
countries—giving plays. That seemed to be mostly a blind,
though, for her real occupation, which was leading lady
with a crew of blackmailers. Danny doesn't admit it, but
I think there is no doubt but that she had a lover named
Lewis Bauermont—something like that. He was leading
man in the theatrical company, manager of it, and also of
the blackmailing gang.

"About six months before Danny wrote here, the lady,
whom Danny had been serving as a companion, died. It
left Danny at loose ends. She had stayed there more for
love than for money. She had next to no money saved.
Gaby wrote that she could give her a small part in her
company. Danny joined her in France. She had been there
a couple of weeks, when the company went on the rocks.

Danny thought it was done purposely, since one of their blackmail victims was making it too hot for them.

"Gabrielle and Danny went to Switzerland. This Lewis what's-his-name—"

"Bauermont."

"Bauermont, showed up there in a few days and hung around. He and Gaby got to quarreling all the time. Gaby, who had always had plenty of money, began to be short of funds.

"Danny was as miserable as—well, as Danny would be in a mess like that. She remembered this place, and begged Gaby to come here, and rest a while, and get rid of this Bauermont, and the other hangers-on, and get ready to make a fresh start. You know, a clean start. Dan says Gaby had real ability as an actress; and that she could have easily found a position in some stock company in the United States. Gaby wouldn't listen to Danny's plan of coming here. But, once or twice, she used the idea as a threat to make this Bauermont bird come to terms. He wouldn't come. Later, Gaby began to give him some of his own blackmailing medicine. I guess he was pretty keen to get rid of her. And her having talked about the Desert Moon gave him his idea.

"He showed up one night with a letter from Canneziano, written from San Quentin. Bauermont was old enough, by the way, to have been Gaby's father. He and Canneziano had been pals here in the United States, and had gotten together again, three years ago, when Bauermont had been over here for six months. The letter, which had been forwarded all over this country and half of Europe, said only that he was to leave prison on the fourth of July, and wanted to know where he could meet Bauermont shortly after that date. Probably all Canneziano wanted was to renew his old connections; but the letter was cryptic enough for Bauermont to make his story out of it.

"A cock-and-bull yarn about how he and Canneziano had held up that Tonopah mail train, three years ago—the train that was carrying a big shipment of currency for the federal reserve bank. A hundred thousand dollars, wasn't it? We all remember it, I guess. The robbers got away. Well, this Bauermont bird told the girls that he and Canneziano had been the robbers.

"It seems he made a pretty fair story out of it—how he and Canneziano had decided that every bank in the country would have the numbers of the bills by morning, and how they'd agreed to cache them in some safe place for a rather long time. They'd thought it best, too, to part company. So Bauermont went on to Salt Lake, and Canneziano, since we were handy, came and hid the money here on the ranch."

Sam interrupted. "Like hell he did!"

"No, of course he didn't, dad. I'm giving you Bauermont's story, that's all. According to him Canneziano hid the money here. He was to have joined Bauermont in Salt Lake, but he got scared and went south instead, to 'Frisco. He'd been there only a few weeks, when he got pinched for running a gambling hall and sent up for three years.

"Bauermont went to see him after he was in prison. He told Bauermont that he had hidden the money here, all right; but he would not tell him where. He said it was safe, that no one could find it—not in a thousand years. That was all Bauermont could get out of him, except a promise to meet him, when he got out of prison, and come here with him to get the money.

"You, anyone, can see that the whole story is as full of holes as a sieve. I don't understand how Gaby ever fell for it. Danny will believe most anything anyone tells her. She is so honest herself, she thinks everyone else is honest. You can imagine how this plan, of coming here to get the money, went against the grain with her. But she was so desperate about Gaby, and the rottenness there, that she was willing to accept any plan to get Gaby away from it."

"I thought we could not find the money," Danny supplemented. "Though John says I believe anything, someway I never did fully believe that story. I never took it, on the principle, you know, of solving one problem at a time."

"Well," John said, "that's that. The letter Gaby got, a few days ago, was from this Bauermont. Danny could not read the code, but she has every reason to think that the copy Gaby read to her was genuine. In it he said that the whole thing, from start to finish, had been a put up job on Gaby. He and Canneziano had been in Denver at the time, had read all the accounts of the train robbery in the papers, and had kicked themselves to think that they hadn't been smart enough to have pulled it off themselves. But they had not; had had no connection with the affair. The point of it was, that he had found another girl, was tired of Gaby, and wanted to ship her out of the way. Danny says the whole thing was an insult, from beginning to end; and that it seemed to have been written with no other motive than a desire to humiliate Gaby, twit her—laugh in her face."

"Sounds fishy to me," Sam mused. "If this fellow wanted to be shed of her, seems as if the best thing he could have done was to keep his mouth shut, and keep her here, hunting the hidden treasure until the end of time."

"I think," Danny answered, "that he thought Gaby might grow tired of searching, and return to him. Lewis knew that father was to be released, and that he and Gaby might meet at any time, and Gaby would then learn the truth. Lewis is mean and cruel. He wanted the zest—if you can possibly understand—of writing that cruel, wicked letter."

"See here," Sam said. "Suppose, after writing it, he got scared of what he had done. Gaby, you know, was—well, she was a pretty violent girl. He might have thought it over, and decided that it would be a lot safer to have her clear out of the way. Or, more likely, before he ever wrote that letter, he might have made arrangements with some one of his gang over here to come up and put her out of the way, shortly after she'd got the letter—"

"I move," Hubert Hand interrupted, "that we all adjourn, and go to hunt for the secret staircase and the concealed passage-way."

"Trying to be funny?" Sam asked, with a bright blue glare.

"Not at all. But the secret staircase is all that is lacking, isn't it? We've begun with the buried treasure, we've got the motive, and the international band of organized criminals. Slick. All there. Romantic and thrilling as you please. Only, it is a long way from Switzerland to Nevada and the key in Mary's pocket."

30

An Accusation

"Damn the key in Mary's pocket!" Sam exploded. "I'm beginning to think I was right, at first, when I said that Mary locked the door, absent mindedly, and dropped the key in her pocket herself."

I judged that I could wait until my turn came to mention that the key in my pocket was the old pass-key, and not the key to the attic door. In the next minute I wished that I had not waited, but had told it so that Sam might have busied his mind with that.

"Well, John," he said, "does that finish up the part of the story Danny couldn't tell?"

"I think so, dad."

"All right. Now, Danny, what did you mean, a few minutes ago, when you warned me to be careful, like you did?"

"I—" Danny stammered, "—wanted you to be careful about what you said, in anger."

"In other words, you wanted me to be careful about saying anything that would seem to implicate John?"

She did not answer.

"If John was guilty," Sam insisted, "would you want him to go scot free?"

"John is not guilty."

"How do you know that?"

"I know it in the same way that you all seem to know that Chad was not guilty. I know John."

"That's all right. But you can't know John's innocence like we know Chad's; because, from the time Gaby came downstairs, until we all set out to look for her, Chad was not out of my sight. He was at the piano. He walked to the barn with me. He stayed in the barn with me. He walked back to the house with me. He was with us all during supper."

"You," said Danny, "say that Chad was in the barn with you during all of that hour. I wonder whether Chad, if he were alive, could swear that you were in the barn with him, during all of that hour?"

"What do you mean by that, my girl?" Sam questioned.

Danny sat and stared at him, her eyes wide, her lips bitten tight; sat and looked as if she were frightened plumb out of her senses, and did not say one word.

"You meant something when you said that," Sam insisted. "Now what was it? Come, speak up."

It was no way for him to talk to her, feeling as she felt, and her sister not yet in her grave. I was downright ashamed for him. I guess the others felt as I did, for Hubert Hand said, "Never mind. Lay off that, Sam. What do you expect to get from an hysterical girl. You don't deserve it; you let me down flat; but, just to prove that I'm a white man, I'll say that I know you were in the barn all the time. Of course, if I wasn't there, my testimony for you wouldn't amount to much. But you know damn well I was there; and I know damn well that you were. So let up on the little lady. Mary's turn, next, isn't it?"

"Hold on!" Sam said. "Since Danny's gone this far, she shouldn't grudge an extra word or two. Come, now, Danny. I don't aim to treat you mean, and you know I'm sorry for you, and feel for you in your trouble. But what is it you have on your mind?"

She sat there, still as a mouse; her big eyes growing bigger from fright.

I guess there is some of the brute in every man. I had never before suspected that Sam Stanley had his share.

"You'll have to talk when this case comes to court," he said. "It will come to court—don't forget that. Just now, it looks as if John were going to have to come up for trial. Your silence does him a sight more harm than good; you should know that."

"Oh!" she exclaimed, short and sharp, as if it hurt her. "It isn't John I am trying to shield. I am—I am trying to save his happiness for him, that's all. His happiness, and my own."

"Just now," John said, gently, "isn't the time to be thinking about our happiness, Danny. If you have anything to say—please say it."

"You won't blame me?" she pleaded. "You won't blame me, afterwards?"

"Could I blame you for telling what you think is the truth?"

"Hubert," she spoke suddenly, and very sharply, for her, "did you see Uncle Sam, all that time, in the barn? Could you see him, all the time, while you were milking the cows? He says he could not see you."

"No—" Hubert hesitated. "No—I guess I didn't see him, all the time. He was at one end of the barn, and I was at the other. But I heard him talking to Chad all the time. They were kidding back and forth. Sam baiting Chad along; you know how they do—did. Sam was right there all the time, Danny. No getting away from that."

"But there is," she said. "You all seem to have forgotten it, but Chad was a mimic and a ventriloquist. He could have stayed there in the barn alone, and with no trouble at all, made you think that Uncle Sam was there, too, and that they were talking together."

I stopped breathing. I think the others stopped breathing. Their breaths would have sounded noisy in that silence. John spoke first.

"Four cows got milked. Chad couldn't milk. He never milked a cow in his life."

"How do you know?" Danny said, and I was surprised that she should oppose John like that. "You know only that Chad said he could not milk. We all know that he was lazy. He was raised on a farm—"

"How do you know that?" John echoed her own words.

"I don't know it. He told me that he was."

John said: "He told me that he was born and reared in Chicago."

"Shut up, John," Sam commanded. "Go on, Danny."

"That's all," she said. "Except, that if Chad could milk, that would have given Uncle Sam nearly all of that hour—"

"Dan!" John's voice sounded as if he were talking to one of his meanest broncos. "Stop it! Sitting here and accusing dad, with no evidence—nothing but a crazy, wild idea—"

"That is not true. I have evidence. I picked up Gaby's bag from the steps yesterday evening. Tobacco and pipe ashes were sticking to it. Only a few. I think someone had tried to brush them off, hurriedly, as a man might, and had made a poor job of it. No one else on this place smokes a pipe. No one else, anywhere, drops his pipe whenever he is excited." She turned to me. "That is what I told you I dared not tell—" She hid her face in her hands.

Sam's pipe fell from his mouth.

31

The Session Ends

It seemed to me that, when Sam's pipe hit the floor, it made a noise like doom cracking. We all sat still as stones. I suppose it could not have been more than a minute, but it seemed a long time before John left Danny's side and went and picked up the pipe and handed it to Sam.

"It's all right, dad," he said.

"Not by a damn sight, it's not all right," Sam came back to his senses vigorously. "But it is interesting—this thing. It is getting interesting, anyway. Let me see— If I had got Chad to help me—and I could have, by telling him it was some joke or other I had on hand—I could have sneaked out of the barn, met her and killed her, during that hour. When could I have got the body upstairs, though? That's the first missing link. My reason for killing her would be another, but—"

"Say! See here, dad," John cut in.

"You shut up, son. We are waiting to hear the rest of what Danny has to say. Come, Danny, can you supply either of those missing links?"

"No," she said, and sighed. It was easy to see that she was plumb tuckered out. "No, of course I can't."

"If," Sam went on, seemingly talking entirely to himself, "if I'd hurried like blazes, I might have done the deed,

173

and carried her into the house during the time I was absent from the barn. I'd have had to pass Mary in the kitchen—I'd have been bound to sneak in the back way—but, if I asked her not to, more than likely Mary wouldn't tell on me. Or, I might have had a hireling (that's what they call them, isn't it? There's another word, something like—marmot—no, never mind.) on the outside, who would have toted the body in for me, while we were at supper."

Written out, that sounds as if Sam had been trying to be comical. He was not at all. He was sitting there, speaking his thoughts for all to hear, making out a case against himself, cool as Christmas. For my part, I had heard enough of it.

"Sam, you look here—" I began.

"You shut up, too, Mary," Sam said.

Mrs. Ricker spoke. She had her say out. Nobody, not even Sam, would any more think of telling Mrs. Ricker to shut up, than they would think of telling any other dumb object, that suddenly started to talk, to shut up. Leading a life of silence, I thought, certainly did have its advantages, at times.

"I think," Mrs. Ricker said, "that the girl herself probably killed her sister. If Sam's pipe ashes were on the bag, she put them there, afterwards, to make trouble for him."

Sam said, "Shucks!"

I thought John would be the first to speak. I was mistaken.

It was Danny herself who said, "Make her talk, now, Uncle Sam. Don't wait for her turn. I—can't bear it. Make her talk now, and give her reasons for saying such a cruel, wicked, lying thing."

"Mrs. Ricker," Sam put the question very solemnly, "have you any reasons for making this accusation?"

"My only reason is, that I believe it."

"Don't beat around the bush. Why do you believe it?"

"I have a feeling that she is guilty."

"This," Sam said, sternly, "is no time for feeling, nor for quibbling. You made a serious accusation—straight out. I want your reason, or reasons, for making it, and I want them just as straight."

"I have no reasons," Mrs. Ricker said. "That is why I suspect her."

"Ah-ah-ah! Women!" Sam said; and the way he said it, it was the blackest oath he had used that day.

I looked at Danny. I had not been feeling any too kindly toward her, for the past few minutes; but, just the same, seeing her there, white and pitiful, with her hands caught up to her throat, and with the echo of Sam's last blasphemy still in my ears, I had a woman feeling toward her. I knew then, as I know now, that Danielle Canneziano could no more have killed Gaby than she could have created her.

"I think," I said, talking fast to keep Sam from shutting me up before I could get anything said, "that if, in suspicioning an innocent girl like Danny, Mrs. Ricker is simply drawing on her woman's instinct, she'd better pass it up, for the present, and listen to some plain sexless sense.

"Gaby came downstairs at four. Danny called after her, right then; so Danny was in the house right then. Gaby went to the rabbit hutch and stopped long enough to give Martha the bracelet. Almost as soon as Martha was in the house with the bracelet, Danny was downstairs with us, cool, collected, and undisturbed. Now suppose, as an idiot suggested this morning, that Gaby had come straight back into the house. I guess everyone Would agree that it would take her five minutes to get back upstairs. That would leave Danny not more than ten minutes to kill her, and to come downstairs, as I've said, collected and undisturbed. Come to think of it, Gaby could not have talked to Martha and got to the attic stairway in any five minutes. At the widest figuring, that leaves Danny about five minutes—"

As I had been fearing he would, Sam stopped me. "That's all right, too, Mary. But there is no need to draw so long a bow. No need to count minutes on Danny. The note in Gaby's bag fixes her innocence better than all the minutes on the clock could."

"No, it does not," Mrs. Ricker said. "Gaby knew that she had reason to fear an enemy. She probably found that out from the code letter. She may never have suspected that the enemy was her own sister."

"I wish I knew," Sam said, giving Mrs. Ricker a long look, "what you are getting at, Mrs. Ricker. I'd give that," Sam dangled out his right hand, "to know what any one of you was getting at. You, for instance, know that Danny did not kill her sister. I think that Hand knows that John didn't do it—maybe not. I'm beginning to suspect him of honesty in this; but a damn mistaken honesty, at that. I think that John knows that Chad is as innocent as—as—a new born babe, as Mary says. I think Danny would have to be pretty hard put to it, before she'd invent that story about my pipe ashes—"

"Dad," John said, and high time he was saying something, "Dan didn't invent any story. I know that she was clear off about the pipe ashes, and I think she shouldn't have made such a mistake. Since they couldn't have been there, she couldn't have seen them. But Danny doesn't lie. She thought she saw the ashes there, or she would not have said so."

"All right, son," Sam conceded. "I'd a heap rather think that than not. But, see here, did anyone else think they saw my pipe ashes around there?"

I looked into my own blue voile lap. I imagined I could feel Hubert Hand's eyes boring into me. My face burned. I could feel the waves of red going up into my scalp and spreading out around my ears. I prayed a quick, private prayer to the Lord. But I have learned, through the years, that trying to instruct the Lord, through the pretense of prayer, is a supreme impudence that he usually punishes pretty promptly. My face burned hotter than ever. I raised my eyes. Sam was staring straight at me.

"Mary," he said, "you found the body. Did you see pipe ashes there, then?"

My only excuse is, that it takes longer than a minute or two minutes to betray a person who has been your best friend for twenty-five years.

I said, "No."

"I am going to ask you to swear to that. Somebody get the Bible."

Nobody moved.

"You haven't made any of the others swear to anything," I said.

"I haven't caught any of the others in what I was sure was a direct and deliberate lie."

I felt weaker than filtered water. It is one thing to tell a lie, offhand into the free air. I haven't much use for a person who can't do that, when absolutely necessary. It is another thing to put your hand on the Good Book and swear to a lie. I knew that I could not do it.

"Martha," Sam said, "run and get the Bible for dad."

Martha seemed to be sound asleep again. I did not notice anything queer about her appearance. Mrs. Ricker must have noticed something queer. She jumped to her feet and dashed across the room to where Martha was lying. A shriek went piercing through the house, splintering the air into quivering bits of agony.

Everyone has wakened from sleep, cold with the sweating terror of some hideous nightmare, but with only the vaguest impressions of its detail. So it is with me, and that nightmare hour. I can not reconstruct it. It remains, yet, in my mind as nothing but a horror of confusions.

We all ran about. I know that there was telephoning. That some of us made desperate attempts with restoratives. I remember Sam's crying, with his face uncovered, like a child. I can hear him saying that he had given her the sleeping powder, had forced it upon her. I can hear, plainest of all, Mrs. Ricker's voice, with all the pent up passions of years breaking forth in torrents of heartbreak.

"My baby. My baby girl. My darling. Mother's life. Mother's heart. Speak to mother. My lamb. My baby . . ."

Her voice again, but cruel now, as she shrieks at Hubert Hand. "Stand there, you beast! Stand there, dry eyed and look at your dead daughter. The child you deserted. The child you ignored—"

I remember the feeling of the fresh air as I walked beside Sam, who was carrying Martha, out of the house. I think that it was John who explained to me that the doctor, who had left Telko, was going to meet us on the road, in order to save time. We must have walked slowly, but I can not rid myself of the impression of Mrs. Ricker, running beside us. I remember her scream, when—futile, unnecessary horror—Sam stumbled with his burden as he went to step into the sedan.

As the car went dashing away, I remember looking out of its windows at the house—the great structure, with its wide expanses and its towers; and it seemed to me that it looked like some monster, crouching there in the green; some grim, horrible monster, waiting for its victims. Three of us had been caught in its clutches. Were any of us to escape?

32

A Part of the Past

The doctor, who was younger and more cruel than even a doctor has a right to be, said that Martha had died from a stoppage of the heart, undoubtedly induced by the strong drug in the sleeping powder that had been administered. In other words, Sam had killed her. He loved her. How deeply he had loved her, none of us had ever had sense enough to realize.

We had her funeral, and Chad's, two days later. They were buried in the second grove of aspen trees, two miles beyond the cabin. All the people in the valley came. At first, I thought that they had come to honor the dead, and Sam. But, as I stood by the graves, and watched the faces about me, faces that held suspicion, horror, curiosity; sly faces, cruel faces, eager faces, I did not care to think why most of them had come.

Sam noticed it, too. For, though I had not said a word to him, as we walked home from the graves, he said to me, "Don't blame them, Mary. What else could we expect? Decency breeds decency, and—filth draws filth."

There were only four of us around the table that evening. Mrs. Ricker had gone straight to her room, after the funeral. Danny, with no protest from Sam, had left the day before to take Gaby's body to San Francisco. It had seemed heartless to allow her to go alone; but I could not be spared, and there was no one else to go with her. John might have gone; but Danny refused to allow him to, saying, unselfishly, that Sam needed John more than she needed him.

"You people," Hubert Hand spoke suddenly, to John and Sam and me, as we sat there, looking at a supper that nobody pretended to eat, "have been awfully decent about not asking questions since the other afternoon."

"I'm done with questions," Sam said. "Through. Finished."

"Just the same," Hubert Hand replied, "there are a lot of answers that are going to have to be given, sooner or later. You heard Mrs. Ricker say that I was Martha's father—"

"Never mind that, now, Hand," Sam interrupted. "I've known, since the first week you came to the ranch, that there was, or had been, something between you two. You'd been her lover, I suppose. Well—men do. That's all. I never went around thinking you, nor any man, was a plaster saint. I reckon you deserted her, eh? And treated her like hell, generally. And she found a refuge here. And, later, probably, heard that you were in trouble, and sent you a letter and told you to come here. Put you wise about the chess racket. Helped you. Made a refuge for you. Women do.

"I suppose she slipped poor Martha in, in place of the child she'd got from the orphanage—used the same papers. Well—to keep on repeating myself, mothers do. You and she have both lived straight and acted decent for the years you've been here. If the two of you want to keep on living in this hell-hole, and keep on straight and acting decent, you'll get the same treatment from me you've always got. If you are Martha's parents, that's more reason, not less, for my not wanting to break up our family here, or make trouble for either one of you."

Hubert Hand pushed back his chair, got up, and walked to the window. "By God, but you're a white man, Sam!"

he said. "You're so damn white that you make every one around you look yellow as sulphur by contrast.

"You've got it doped out right about Ollie Ricker and me. She was twelve years older than I was—I always felt like that was kind of an excuse for me. Guess not, though. She was a good enough girl until I came along, just out of prison, and as rotten as two years in prison can make a kid. That's pretty damn rotten. I shouldn't have been sent up, that time. Nothing but a kid's trick—grand row in a dump down on Barbary Coast.

"My mother was dead. My dad was a high-hatter. He went back on me, cold, after that. Found my room locked when I went home. I went back to Ollie. She kept me pretty straight for a while. I ought to have married her, and I know it, before the kid was born. But she was so jealous that she made life a living hell for me. I—well, I wouldn't marry her.

"It was her fault that I got sent up the second time. She talked to a girl friend of hers, and the girl snitched. Up to that time, I think that Ollie Ricker talked more than any living woman. She took a vow, the day they got me, that she'd never speak an unnecessary word again in her life. I'll say she's kept that vow pretty well. I wish to God I'd taken the same vow, before I shot my mouth off about John, the other day."

"You don't think that I did it, then?" I wished John could have seemed less eager.

"On the square," Hubert answered, "I don't see who else could have done it. That makes no never minds. I wish I'd kept my mouth shut, on account of Sam—"

"Leave me out of it," Sam growled, "and forget it. Forget the whole damn thing, if you can. I'm through. If I hadn't been so busy playing the fool while Martha was dying, we could likely have saved her. We'll never get any place with this thing. Nobody will. Look at us, messing around with a lot of damn fool clues, and suspicions, telling one lie to cover another—like a batch of gossiping old grannies, while Martha was lying there, dying. And me growling and snarling at her all afternoon. I'm a fool. I'm a damn sight worse—I'm an old fool. A girl got killed on the Desert Moon Ranch. A boy killed himself for love of her. The killer got clean away. So far as I'm concerned, it is going to rest there. I'm closing the book. Soon as I can, I'll sell out the damn place, lock, stock and barrel."

"That doesn't go for me, dad," John said. "And I think you'll change your mind. I'm not willing to go on the rest of my life with half a dozen people thinking that I killed Gabrielle. No sir, not with one person thinking it. Hubert Hand seems to be in a sort of sentimental mood, right now. How long's he going to stay that way? When he gets over it, what's he going to do with the club he has in his hand? Nothing? Maybe. Depends on how much he might need some cash, sometime in the future."

Hubert said, "I'm no damn blackmailer."

"What did you serve your second term in prison for?"

"None of your business."

"All right."

"No. Hold on, I'll tell you. It's up to me to tell things to-day, and I'm telling them. It was forgery, all right; but, just the same, I don't feel, yet, like I was much to blame. I'd gotten in with a rotten crowd, and—"

"Never mind. Let it go at that. Here's another thing, dad. Danny honestly believes that, someway or other, you are mixed up in this thing. We can't marry, with a thing like that between us. I guess it doesn't make any difference in the way we feel toward each other; but it makes a barrier, just the same, that will have to come down before we marry. I haven't talked it over, exactly, with Dan, but I'm dead certain she feels the same way I do about it."

"You think Danny is coming back here, then?" Hubert questioned.

"How do you mean?"

"I'm not looking for her to come back—that's all."

"You're crazy with the heat. They read a telegram to me, not an hour ago, saying that she'd get in on number Twenty-one Friday afternoon."

"I'll bet she's not on it."

"Say, Hand—"

"Keep your shirt on, John. We all know that Danny is innocent of the crime, and that she is a good little scout—a lot better than Gaby was, if not half as charming and attractive. But—she knows more than she wishes to know. She knows more than she's going to tell. Maybe more than she can tell, in safety. For the love of Mike, folks— couldn't you see that she had some reason for working up that case against Sam? Cutting it out of whole cloth. If she'd been trying to shield John, do you think she'd have used Sam for that purpose? Not on your life she wouldn't have, she'd have pinned it on me, or Mrs. Ricker, or even on Mary. She did try to pin it on Chad—"

Mrs. Ricker came tottering into the room. Sam jumped to meet her, and helped her over to his own big chair at the head of the table.

She leaned forward, her long black-sleeved arms stretched straight in front of her over the white cloth, her hands clenched into fists.

"For hours," she said, "I have been trying to reach a decision. I have reached it. I have come here to confess."

33

Another Confession

"Before I came to the Desert Moon—" she began, but Hubert Hand stopped her.

"Never mind, Ollie. No need confessing, as you say, any of that. Sam knows all about us. He'd guessed it, or most of it, years ago. I've just now told him the rest. It is all right with him. I mean—he realizes it's all long past. He thinks, as I do, that the best thing we can do is to forget it; and, as he says, keep on living straight and decent."

"Do you know all of our story?" Mrs. Ricker lifted her faded eyes to Sam.

"Enough," Sam sort of sighed it. "I don't care about details. All but—I was kind of wondering what became of the brown-eyed baby, named Vera, who the papers from the orphanage were made out for."

"I found her a home with the mother and father of one of the nurses in the hospital. They thought that she was my own child. They loved her, and were kind to her. Until she died, during the influenza epidemic in San Francisco, in 1918, I sent half of my salary to them, for her, each month."

"I always knew you were a good woman," Sam said. "Now what do you say we forget it, let bygones be bygones?"

"No," said Mrs. Ricker. "Martha did not kill Gaby, as
you think she did, Sam. I killed her."

Sam dropped his pipe.

There was another one of those dead, awful silences.

"The guilt," Mrs. Ricker went on, "is entirely mine. All
of my life I have been cursed with an abnormal jealousy,
and with the violent temper that usually accompanies such
jealousy. Martha, you all know, possessed both of these
traits—a heritage from her mother—without the balanc-
ing power of an adult mind." She turned to Hubert Hand.
"Have you told about Nina Ziegelman?"

"No," he spoke sharply. "I wouldn't, Ollie. No need—"

"But I would," she said, and continued, more rapidly. "About four months before Martha was born a woman
named Nina Ziegelman betrayed us—Hubert and me. I had
given her a confidence, and she betrayed it. When I found
what she had done I went to her hotel room and tried to
kill her. I did not succeed. I shot her; but she recovered.
For many reasons, of their own, she and her friends prof-
fered no charges against me. I went free. But I had marked
Martha for murder. She was powerless against it; as powerless as she would have been against any evil physical in-
heritance. She can't be blamed. No one could dare blame
her for that. It was I, who planted those seeds of violence,
jealousy, hatred, and murderous intent, who killed Gabrielle. Martha was only the helpless instrument."

I was sorry that there was eagerness, mixed with the
pity in John's voice, as he asked, "Did Martha tell you that
she committed the murder?"

"No. Other parental heritages of hers were a lying
tongue, and slyness. She persisted in her denials, to me.
But it is all so evident.

"Gabrielle joined Martha at the rabbit hutch. You know
how one sits down on one's heels to peer in at the rabbits
in the low hutch. I think Gaby must have been squatting,

so, when Martha jumped at her and overpowered her. Martha was strong, you know. Her hands were very strong. You remember, Mary, how she could open fruit jars that neither you nor I could budge? She had hated Gaby ever since Gaby had come. Martha had said to me, dozens of times, that someday she thought she would kill Gaby.

"The marks on her throat, I thought, and so did the coroner, looked as if she had been caught by someone who had been standing behind her. Seized unawares, it would not take long to strangle a person. Martha must have done it in two or three minutes. She took the bracelet then, rolled the body under the clump of berry bushes, right there, and came straight into the house.

"She showed no feeling of guilt, because she had none. At that moment, we should all have suspected something. We should have known that girl would not, suddenly, have given Martha the bracelet. Later, she told you about it, didn't she, Sam? And you left Chad in the barn, to hoodwink Hubert, and came up and hid the body for her?"

"By God, I did not," Sam said.

"No need to deny it, now, Sam," she said. "It was the deed of a good man. Martha was never responsible—but courts might not have understood. Now we will all shield her—keep her secret. Chad's confession will satisfy the world. Danny must know, I suppose; but no one else need ever know—"

"But I tell you—" Sam shouted.

I don't know how, without raising her voice, she made it sound through his shouting, and silence it, but she did. "Sam—don't. Why can't we be honest, now, among ourselves? You see, I know that both you and Martha were on those stairs when the body was put there—"

My thoughts jumped out into words. "Chad must have known it, too. He must have decided that he'd rather die than betray either Sam or Martha."

"He might have thought it," Sam said, with a lack of emphasis that edged stupidity. "He could not have known it. It is not true."

"Mrs. Ricker," John questioned, "what makes you think that dad and Martha had both been on the stairs?"

"Sam's pipe ashes were strewn about. And there was an old tatting shuttle, with which I had been trying to teach Martha to tat, that morning. She had it in her pocket. It must have dropped out. I think that Mary tried to clean the pipe ashes away. They were gone when I saw the body the second time. I should have tried to do it, but I didn't think. I had no time. I was frantic with fear.

"Wait," she answered our looks and our exclamations of astonishment. "I will explain. Martha and I, as you know, were alone here in the house while the rest of you were out looking for Gaby. Martha was sleepy. I was worried about her sleeping so much, and tried all sorts of ways to keep her awake until bed time. I kept sending her out to look at the sky, to see whether a storm was coming to spoil her fireworks. She would run out, and right in again, to curl on the davenport and try to sleep. Finally, though, she stayed outside, for a long time. But for Sam's pipe ashes, I would think that then she had managed to drag the body upstairs by herself. Still though I believe that she did have strength enough to move the body, I do not believe that she would have had wits enough.

"When the wind rose, I looked first for Martha. I called her several times before she answered. Finally she came around the house from the direction of the rabbit hutch, again. Surely, you must have noticed, as I did, that she had seemed strangely excited during all the late afternoon and early evening. At the time, I thought it was because she had been given the monkey charm, and because she was to have the fireworks.

"But, when we were alone, she talked very foolishly— even for her. She began with it again, when she had answered my call. She kept insisting that soon we were all going to be surprised about something; something very nice, that had to do with Chad—but she would never, never tell what it was. As a rule, I should not have paid any attention to such talk. But, for some reason, her excitement, and her insistence about a surprise, disturbed me. I spent some minutes quizzing her. I even tried to bribe her. I could get nothing from her but further talk about the nice surprise.

"At last I gave it up, and ran upstairs to begin closing the house against the storm. I thought I'd begin with the attic, and come down through the house. I tried the attic door. It was locked, and the key was missing. I was alarmed. Possibly, because we were all disturbed concerning Gaby's absence; and possibly, because inside doors are so seldom locked here. I remembered the old skeleton key hanging in the broom closet. I ran down and got it.

"I opened the door. I saw the body. I touched it—and knew, even before I saw the tatting shuttle there, and the beaded bag, covered with Sam's pipe ashes. I snatched the shuttle and hid it in my dress. At that instant, through the open window at the end of the hall, I heard your voices, as you ran up the road from the garage to escape the rain. I shut the door, locked it, and ran downstairs. Do you know, when I met you, I had that key in my hand?

"Mary came up to me to help me close the French windows. I did not think. I had a wild desire to rid myself of that key. I was determined to protect Martha, at any cost. Mary's pocket was hanging like an open bag, right below me. I dropped the key into it. It was a frightful mistake. If I had kept it, and thrown it away, everyone in the house would have been exonerated. It was, as you know, the one

link that connected this household with the crime. That
is, after Mary had cleaned away the pipe ashes. The little
fleck or two of them, which Danny saw, might have fallen
there days before—"

"Mary," Sam questioned, "were my pipe ashes on the
bag? Did you stop to clean them off, before you gave the
alarm?"

"Yes, they were, Sam. Yes, I did."

"Then," Sam said, "whoever put the body there, put the
pipe ashes there to throw suspicion on me; and whoever
it was, knew my habits, too. He must have put the tatting
shuttle there, as well, for good measure. Does anyone of
you think that Martha would have had the wits to save
ashes out of my pipe and put them on the bag? I tell you,
that would take an amount of logic, of reasoning, that
Martha could no more have managed than a kitten could."

"Chad!" John almost sang it, in his eagerness. "He was
wise enough, and fool enough. His one idea was to protect
Martha. He helped her get the body up there, between
seven and eight o'clock, and he put the ashes there to
shield her. I said fool enough. But, come to think of it, he
knew what he was doing. He was protecting her with the
one person in the house who could not have done it; with
the one person that no Nevada jury would convict. Then,
he turned around and shielded dad with his death and
his written confession. From start to finish, it works out,
plain as day. Gosh! Say—it is terrible. Gosh—horrible!
Think of it—But, thank God, it is cleared up, anyway."

"'Cleared up, *anyway*' is right," Sam said, and looked
around at all of us, pityingly, like he'd look at a litter of
sickly puppies.

34
Defense

"All satisfied, then?" Sam questioned. "All satisfied that Martha killed her, and that Chad carried the body upstairs and hid it for her, and left the false clues—including the tatting shuttle, for reasons unknown—and came down, merry and happy enough, until he took a sudden notion to write a false confession and walk out and shoot himself through the head?"

I was satisfied; but I felt like a fool for so being, when Sam put it like that. I said nothing.

Hubert Hand said, "It looks like a pretty clear case, Sam."

"Does? What's become of your clear case against John, unchanged tires, and everything?"

"I had not heard Ollie's story, then."

"Dad," there was pleading in John's voice, "you don't mean to say that you can't see the thing? That you aren't satisfied with this absolutely logical explanation?"

"Yes," Sam answered, with his most dangerous drawl, "that's what I mean to say. It takes more, or seems to, to satisfy me than it takes to satisfy some folks. Satisfied? Not by a damn sight!"

John lost his temper. "For the love of Pete, why aren't you? What would satisfy you? Say? What are you trying to do? Do you like the case against me so well that you can't give it up? You made us all come clean the other day, or tried to. Come clean yourself, now? What have you got up your sleeve?"

"I've got a couple of good fighting arms up my sleeve," Sam answered. "And I've got a daughter, dead, in a grave up there. Since she was knee high to a duck, she's counted on me, for food, and shelter, and protection generally. I don't know—but I reckon she may still be counting on me, somewhere not too far away, for protection. She is going to have it."

Mrs. Ricker began to cry, quietly; but Sam saw her.

"No, no, Mrs. Ricker," he said, "don't get me wrong in this. You believe that she was guilty. I believe that she is innocent. Believing that way, it is my bounden duty to clear her name. It is my fault that she isn't here to stand up for herself. It is my fault, too, I guess, that I've raised John so that he won't stand up for his own womenfolks—"

"That's rotten of you, dad. It is unfair. I'd stand up for Martha till the cows came home. But what's the use of bucking straight facts?"

"Damn your straight facts. We haven't got any. I've a few straight fact questions, though, that will blow this story galley-west. Here's one of them:

"Does it stand to reason that, for two months, Gaby lived right here unharmed by Martha? But that, on the very day, when she feared death from some outside enemy, Martha should kill her?"

"It is coincidental," John admitted. "But, just the same, there are lots of coincidences. We all meet them, all the time."

"It wasn't a coincidence that Gaby was afraid of meeting, when she walked out of this house on the fourth of July. Here's another question.

"Mrs. Ricker, she says, was plumb convinced that Martha committed the murder, and that I helped her by carrying

the body upstairs afterwards. She thought this the night of
the murder, and the next day, and ever since. Why, then,
didn't she come to me and, anyway, put out a feeler or two
in my direction? She knew that I'd go as far to save Martha
as she would go. I wouldn't protect John, nor any other
person on this place; but Martha was a child—younger,
even, than a child in some ways. Mrs. Ricker knew that I'd
save Martha with my last dollar, and, as somebody said the
other day, with my last lie. Mrs. Ricker and I were alone
together for more than half an hour the morning of the
fifth. Why didn't she give me a hint, then, of any of this?"

"I—I was afraid," Mrs. Ricker answered. "I was waiting. I thought that you would give me the hint—the sign.
I was not sure—"

"Not sure then, but sure now?"

"I tell you," Mrs. Ricker flared up, "I was afraid. So
long as she was living, I was afraid of everything—of
everyone. I was afraid of myself. I dared not think; I dared
not look. I scarcely lifted my eyes from my tatting. I—I
was afraid."

"Now, now," Sam said. "I see your point in that, especially since talking had got you in bad once. But—see
here. I said a while ago that I'd always known you were a
good woman. Well, I am going to keep on knowing it, for
the present. There are enough folks around here to jump
at conclusions without me doing it. But you, thinking as
you say you think, directly accused Danny the other day.
That was not the act of a good woman—"

"God, Ollie!" Hubert Hand burst out. "He is going
to try to pin it on you, to save Martha and the Stanley
name—even yet."

"You," Sam said, "are a liar."

"Safe enough. I wouldn't fight you, and you know it,
old man."

Sam jumped to his feet. I had to stumble over John, but I managed to reach Sam first, and to stand in front of him. "Boys, boys," I begged. "Not here. Not in this house to-night. Remember—"

Hubert stuck his hands in his pockets and walked away. Sam dropped into his chair. The telephone bell, in the other room, began to ring.

35

A Visitor

Hubert answered the telephone, and called to Sam.

I followed him into the living-room to hear what was to be heard. I think that John and Mrs. Ricker followed for the same reason.

When Sam said, "Read it, please," I knew that it was another telegram. They telephone all of our telegrams to us from Rattail, and mail them later, when they get around to it, if they don't forget.

We had been pestered nearly crazy with telegrams, on account of all the ruckus Sam had stirred up about Canneziano, on the night of the murder. I supposed this would be another one of them, about some poor Indian or other who had been found at a desert water-hole. But, almost right away, I could tell from Sam's answers that this was about something different. He kept writing things on the telephone pad, and asking central to repeat, and to repeat again, and to spell that, please. Lands, but I got nervous, before he finally hung up the receiver, and turned to us, and asked:

"Any of you ever hear of a fellow named Lynn MacDonald?"

"None of us, of course, ever had.

"Seems he is a kind of detective," Sam explained. "He calls himself a crime analyst, and he specializes in murder cases. Works on his own hook, kind of like Sherlock Holmes did, I guess. He had a list of references, and past cases, long as your arm. They sounded fine. I forget them now. Anyway, he made a straight proposition. He wants to come here and take the case. He wants his expenses, and nothing else, if he fails. If he succeeds, he wants ten thousand, cash. Poor fish, I'd have paid twenty thousand just as quick. Anyway, that's a fair proposition. It is the way I am used to trading; money down if I deliver, nothing if I don't. I'm going to wire him to come."

"Dad," John objected, "you don't know a thing about this guy, except what he tells you. If you have to drag a detective into this, now, after what Mrs. Ricker has told us, why don't you wire to a reputable agency, and have it send someone?"

"I like the tune this fellow sings. I like the straight way he made his proposition. When I wanted the best doctors for Martha, I always got specialists, didn't I? Well, this fellow's a specialist. His references were damn good. I like his name. An honest Scotchman comes pretty close to being the noblest work of God.

"Let's see—Danny is coming up on Friday afternoon, isn't she? I'll wire MacDonald to take the same train. That will save us two trips to Rattail in the heat."

"Listen, dad—sleep over it," John urged.

I hated the quick, sharp way both Sam and Hubert Hand looked at him. I hated him noticing it, and jumping right into an explanation.

"If Mrs. Ricker is right about all this," he said, "and I swear that I think she is, isn't it enough for us to know about it, dad? If you get a detective here, and he comes to the same conclusion, we can't keep it a secret, then."

Sam said, "He won't. And we aren't wanting, nor needing any secrets on the Desert Moon, just now."

He sat down and began to write the telegram. Five minutes, and he was reading it to the operator at Rattail.

He had just hung up the telephone receiver when the doorbell rang, a long, impudent ring.

Nobody, I thought as I went to the door, with any sense of decency would ring our bell, like that, on this evening.

I was right. For a minute I did not recognize the man standing there on the porch. In the next minute I did recognize him. My heart stood stock still. He was Daniel Canneziano.

36
Canneziano

He pushed right past me, into the room, without waiting
for an invitation. He always was a polished-up, perfumed
little fellow, but that evening, what with his gray spats
and a cane, he was right-down dandified.

"Got a chap to drive me up from Rattail," he said.
"Beastly things, these Ford cars. What?"

He gave that explanation of how he had got up from
Rattail, as if it were the only thing any of us could possibly be wondering about him, or wanting to know.

"I left my trunk down there," he went on, taking off
his light gray overcoat, and brushing it, and folding it
across his valise that he had set on a chair. "The Ford chap
couldn't bring it. I thought you could send a truck down
for it, to-morrow, Sam."

"Counting on paying us quite a visit, eh, Canneziano?"
Sam found his voice at last. "Trunk and everything."

"As a matter of fact," Canneziano answered, sitting
down and making himself comfortable on the small davenport, "all that mess you stirred up about me, on the night
of the murder, makes traveling not altogether agreeable
for the present. Yes, I think, all things considered, that
having me for a guest, after having set all the police in the
country on my trail, keeping me safely here, as it were, is
about the least you can do, isn't it?"

"I reckon I could do a little less, in a pinch," Sam drawled. "But, all things considered, as you say—though it might be you and I aren't considering the same things—I'm glad to see you here. Make yourself right at home, for you may be going to stay even longer than you planned."

"Righto! However, if you have some neat little scheme of trying to pin the murder on me, I'd advise you to abandon it. If I hadn't had water-tight alibis, all along the line—"

"Keep your water-tight alibis in a dry place till you need them," Sam advised. "Maybe you will need them. We've got a crime analyst, specialist in murder cases, coming up here Friday. You can give your alibis to him."

"That crime analyst sounds like Lynn MacDonald. That's what she calls herself."

"She!" Sam said.

"If you've got Lynn MacDonald, you've got a woman."

"Hell!" Sam exploded.

"Just the same," Canneziano said, "she's the best dic on the coast. Some say that she is the best in this country. Not that I give a hang. But, this is inside dope, if anybody can find who killed the Gaby, this MacDonald woman can. You should hear some of the San Quentin boys compliment her—in their way."

"We don't want a woman. Better wire her not to come, dad," John urged.

This time it was Canneziano who looked quickly and sharply at John. "You're dead right you had," he said, "if you don't want the murderer discovered."

"Sam," Hubert Hand suggested, "you'd better wire and verify her references, anyway."

Canneziano laughed. "I see what you are getting at. I take it you've all gotten pretty jumpy around here, these last few days. Can't see the woodpile for the n-gg-rs. Now this gentleman—by the by, Sam, you are forgetting your manners; I have not, as yet, met any of your guests—thinks that this coming dic may be a pal of mine; something of the sort. If that were the case, what good would it do to verify her references, by wire? The people you wired to would all answer that Lynn MacDonald was honest, capable, and so forth. She's got a reputation around the bay that is hard to beat. But, if this were a plant, Jane Jones or Amaryllis De Vere could come along, just the same, posing as Lynn MacDonald. If you are really concerned about it, why not have a Burns man bring her up? You shouldn't mind the extra expense, Sam."

"There's generally more than one way to skin a cat," Sam said, "besides the way you are told to do it."

Leaving us to think that over, he went to the telephone and called the office of *The Morning Record,* at Telko, and asked for Mr. Clarence Pette.

When he finally got him, he asked him whether he knew Lynn MacDonald. Evidently he said that he knew who she was, for Sam told him to take number Twenty-one at Telko, Friday afternoon, and to meet him here, and he would pay him fifty dollars for his trouble.

"Pretty work, Sam," Canneziano approved. "Too bad I got you all so rattled. As a matter of fact, I rather fancy myself in the role of a sleuth. If Lynn MacDonald weren't coming, I'd like to take a try at this job myself. For instance, I noticed that, though Dan is in 'Frisco now—according to the papers—none of you suggested that she meet Lynn MacDonald, have her identified, and bring her back here with her. I am trying to decide whether that means that you don't trust the gentle Dan, or whether, though the newspapers say she is to return at once to her home in Nevada, you do not expect her to return."

"It means neither," John snapped.

"Mr. Canneziano," I said, "this is John Stanley, Sam's adopted son. He and Danny are engaged to be married.

This other gentleman is Mr. Hubert Hand, and the lady is Mrs. Ricker."

Things felt real polite, for a minute, as they always do just after folks have been introduced.

"Bad times you have been having around here, lately," Canneziano said, pleasantly, as if he were talking about the weather.

Mrs. Ricker excused herself and went upstairs.

37

Strangler Bauermont

Sam spoke directly to Canneziano. "Did you ever know a man named Bauermont—Lewis Bauermont?"

"Strangler Bauermont? Very well indeed. Has he any thing to do with it?"

"What's that you called him?" Sam asked, sharply.

"Strangler Bauermont, you mean?"

I remembered that Danny had told me his nickname was "Mexico."

Sam said, "That's what I mean. How did he come by a name like that?"

"He is by way of being a wrestler, I believe; and won the name for some particularly clever hold that brought his man down every time. I have never gone in for that sort of thing—can't give you scientific details. He was a jiu-jitsu expert, also. Oh, no, no," as he noticed our quickening interests. "He is a continent and an ocean away, at present. Moreover, murder is quite outside his line—quite. And he was, I believe, rather smitten than otherwise with the Gaby."

"You are sure he is in Europe now?" Sam questioned.

"I had a letter from him, only a few days ago, written and sent from Deauville. A cable to Scotland Yard would locate him precisely for you, I have no doubt. Assuming, of course, that you don't mind spending a few dollars."

"I suppose," Sam mused, "that he could easy teach his strangling trick to another man."

"Undoubtedly. But isn't the entire connection rather foolish, when one stops to think that Strangler has been, for years, badly smitten with the lady?"

"I guess he got over that," Sam said. "Seems, now, as if he was anxious to be shed of her."

"Oh-ho! And he famous for his constancy to the Gaby. Nine, ten, I don't know how many years. However, though I'll grant his name belies it, he was a smooth, diplomatic cuss. I think you can be practically certain that he would draw the line at murder—under any circumstances."

"That letter you had from him," Sam said. "I suppose you destroyed it?"

"I don't tie my letters into packets bound with blue ribbons."

"Was it written in code?"

"No. You see, the hotel where I was putting up just then was, one might say, over regulated. Letters written in code were not favorably regarded there."

"Could you read a letter written in his code?"

"I fancy so. If you have a Spanish dictionary."

"There was nothing Spanish about this one. It was just a jumble of letters."

"I don't know it then. I'm rather clever with codes, however. I fancy I could decipher it, with a bit of study."

"Do they speak Spanish in Mexico?" I questioned; and was rewarded by having all present look at me as if they thought that I had just developed a yearning for cultural, geographical knowledge.

"I am getting at something," I explained. "Was this Bauermont man ever in Mexico?"

"Unfriendly persons," Canneziano answered, "insinuate that Mexico is his native land."

"Did anyone ever call him 'Mexico'?"

"To his fury, yes. Is it relevant?"

Sam asked, "Where were you, do you know, at the time of the Tonopah train robbery, three years ago? You were here, right shortly after that, I seem to remember."

"I stopped for a friendly visit, and you kicked me out, and into my downfall at 'Frisco. My three years in the big house are at your door. But I hold no grudge."

"What I want to know is, where were you at the time of the train robbery?"

"I was in Denver, since you insist."

"Was this Strangler fellow there with you?"

"He was. Pardon my curiosity, but is this leading to something?"

"I don't know. Do you? This Strangler friend of yours told the girls that you and he robbed that train.

Canneziano's face went dark and ugly. "So the girls say, ugh?"

"He told them that," John said. There was threat enough in his voice to make Canneziano come off his perch.

"Is that possible?" he questioned, but pleasantly enough. "I can't see his motive. As a matter of fact, when we read the accounts of how easily the thing had been pulled off, we did rather regret that we had not taken a try at it ourselves. If he had not included himself in his confession to the girls, I would think that he had some friendly reason for preferring me in captivity. . . . No, I don't get it."

"We think he has denied it, since," Sam said. "We think that the code letter, which none of us can read, is his denial. No matter. Your story tots up straight enough with the one we have."

"Gratifying, I am sure. I wonder whether I might see this code letter? As I've remarked—I've a beastly habit of bragging, I hope you don't mind—I am rather clever with the things."

I went upstairs to get it. I am not denying that it gave me the creeps to go into Gaby's room, alone at night. When I opened the door, and saw that the light on the table was lit, and that someone was standing beside it, I all but jumped out of my shoes.

It was Mrs. Ricker. She turned to me, and apologized, quietly, for having startled me. "I was looking at these things," she went on. "They know. They were there. If only one of them could talk—"

"I thought," I am sure I spoke too tartly, "that you knew. You said that you did."

"Sam doesn't believe it," she answered. "Doesn't that give me, her mother, a right to doubt, if I can?"

I was all out of sorts. "It would have been better to have doubted it, in the first place," I said.

"I know. But I didn't—I couldn't. Sam does. And then, that man coming into the house to-night—I can't explain it; but, someway, he made all of us, even Hubert, seem so good. The house itself felt, to me—do you understand?— good. As if any wicked thing would have to come into it from the outside, from far away, just as he came into it to-night?"

I did understand. I had had that feeling of drawing close to the others and away from him, the minute he had come into the room. But I was so put out with her, for startling me, and for being in Gaby's room, anyway, poking around—though land knows she had a right to be there, and I might have done the same thing myself, with my lists of clues, and so on—that I just said I supposed so, and picked up the letter, at the same time looking over the other things on the table to be sure nothing was missing.

"Perhaps," she said, "I should not have come in here? I suppose, when the detective comes, he—she would like to see the room as nearly as possible undisturbed. Do you think it would be a good plan to lock it, and to give the key to Sam, until she does come?"

She went around with me, while I locked the doors on the inside. We had to lock the doors in Danny's room, too, since the two rooms had only the curtained doorway between them. We went into the hall through Danny's room. I locked that door after us. She told me good-night and went to her own room. I went downstairs, and gave the key and the letter to Sam.

"Wise idea, Mary," he said, when I told him that I had locked the rooms, "I suppose Canneziano would tell you, though, that locked doors do not a prison make." He handed the letter to him.

"Looks rather confusing, doesn't it?" Canneziano said, when he had unfolded and straightened the pages. "Still, these things are generally quite simple. What price deciphering it, Sam?"

"No price, to you," Sam answered.

He returned the letter to its envelope and tossed it on the table. "Fair enough," he said.

"I fancy," he questioned, next, "that Lynn MacDonald is going to get rather a good thing out of this, eh?"

"That depends on her success," Sam answered.

"Yes? I understand that she takes jobs on that basis quite often. It is not thoroughly approved in the best criminal circles. Too much incentive to frame a case. However, that theory of framing has been over exploited. My proposition, cards on the table, is this: If I beat the lady to it, discover the murderer before she does, will you pay me what you have agreed to pay her?"

"Canneziano," Sam said, "get this. Get it now. I'll pay you not one red cent for anything. Not one red cent."

"Fair enough," Canneziano repeated. "And my mistake. Undoubtedly, I should have worded it differently. For instance— What will you pay me not to discover the murderer on the Desert Moon Ranch?

A week ago, Sam would have got up and kicked him out through the door for that question. This evening Sam sat still and looked him over, sort of sliding his eyes up and down over his smooth dapperness. Finally he drawled, "Go as far as you like, Canneziano. Only—you won't get anywhere you'd like to be, not on that line."

"Presently, perhaps," Canneziano answered. "No hurry."

I'll be switched if Sam didn't sit there and murmur, mildly, "Said the carpenter," to himself.

38

Lynn MacDonald

On Friday afternoon, late, I went with John and Sam down to Rattail to meet the train. When it came thundering, snorting up, I thought of the last time that Sam and I had met a train together, and of how our entire world had changed in the two months. Was it going to keep on changing, I wondered. I could not bear to look into the past; I found that I did not dare to try to think into the future.

Just before the train stopped, with its usual roar of protest against Rattail, Clarence Pette swung off it. He came over to us with a timid air, like an animal just learning to eat out of a person's hand. He took no risks, until Sam had greeted him, real pleasantly, and politely.

"Miss MacDonald is on this train," he said to Sam and me. "Is there anything else I can do for you?"

"Not a thing, if you are positive that she is Miss MacDonald, except to take your fifty—here it is—and vamoose."

"I'm positive. Thanks. Here she comes now."

I looked up to see her coming. I could hardly believe my eyes. I don't know what I had expected; but I surely had not expected anything to get off that smoke-dirty train, in the middle of a Nevada desert, on a sweltering hot July evening, that looked as she did.

In the first place, in her pongee silk dress with coat to match, and perky little green hat, she looked as if she had been fresh picked, in the last nice California garden, and had been kept under glass, on ice ever since. But that was only a part of it. She looked, too, like linen sheets feel, at the end of a long hard day; sheets that have been hand-washed, and sun-dried, and dew-dampened, and ironed smooth as satin. She looked like very early on a September morning, in our mountains—that was the zip and the zest of her, combined with her comforting freshness and cleanness.

She was tall; taller than most women, and with weight enough to look durable and useful, but not a mite fat. She had eyes that were as gray as pussywillows, and that did no monkey-tricks of changing to green or blue; she had wavy carrot-colored hair, that was so full of life it looked as if it were trying to break the bonds of its neat, boyish bob and go floating off, on its own, to make maybe a tiny sunset cloud. Her nose was small; her mouth was a mite too large, showing freely in a smile her teeth, little and polished white, like a puppy's.

Coming straight from San Francisco, she used no visible cosmetics; which is much the same as if I had said, rising out of the Pacific Ocean, she was as dry as a chip. But you could no more imagine Lynn MacDonald stopping anything, much less herself, to peer at her freckled nose in a vanity-case's mirror, than you could imagine a baseball player stopping between first and second base to take his temperature with a clinical thermometer.

All of this general satisfactoriness, coming through the alkali dust and offering to shake hands with a person, was, I might say, disarming. My impulses were all mixed. I felt like putting my old, muddled head down on that nice high chest of hers and having a right good cry. And yet, I felt for the first time in days, like a broad grin. I managed it, and forewent the other.

Her voice was low and pleasant, but there was something brisk and crisp about it, and about all of her, that seemed to say plenty and plenty of time for everything, but not one precious minute to waste.

In the background, during this meeting, John and Danny had been hugging and kissing, as if the rolling train right behind them, filled with staring people, were a peaceful, flowing river, and the people fishes that were swimming past. At last, to my relief, they came over to join us; Danny, looking paler and more snuffed out than usual, by contrast, maybe, with Miss MacDonald; John beaming with triumph at having her home again.

"But," Danny said, after Sam had introduced her to Miss MacDonald, and had explained why Miss MacDonald had come, "you didn't tell me that you were coming here."

"You girls get acquainted on the train?" Sam asked.

"We had breakfast together in the diner this morning," Miss MacDonald answered.

"Did you know who I was?" Danny questioned.

"It was my business to know that, wasn't it?" Miss MacDonald smiled.

"Only—why didn't you tell me?" Danny persisted.

"I don't wonder that you ask," Miss MacDonald said. "And I hope that you will forgive me for seeming unfriendly, secretive. It is, simply, that I never want my first history of the case to come from the nearest relatives. Of course they feel too deeply to see clearly. Mistaken impressions are so hard to eradicate, that I go to any lengths to avoid them. If I had made myself known this morning, Miss Canneziano, I should have had to seem more rude and ungracious than I seemed by acting as I did. Because, please," she included all of us in her glance, "I have to ask each of you not to talk to me about the case. I should have to refuse to listen. When I need to know anything about it—I shall need to know many things—I'll ask it, as a direct question. Until I ask for more, from you, if you will all do that, simply answer my questions, you will help me immeasurably."

"That's easy," Sam said.

"I am afraid," she answered, "that it won't be easy. And I have to make another request that won't be easy to ful-fill, either. It is, that no one will question me. I am sorry to have to ask that. I am afraid that it seems as if I were trying to surround myself with a glamour of mystery—pretending to false wisdoms and acumens—"

"Not a bit of it," Sam interrupted. "'He travels the fastest who travels alone.'"

"I have always questioned that," she said. "At any rate, I don't intend to travel all alone."

"You mean you are going to take a few days to size us up, and then get some of us to help you?" Sam asked.

"Question number one," she said, and laughed, too.

39
A Trap

We had got into the sedan, by that time, and were riding along the Victory Highway. I declare to goodness, a sound that was pretty much like a ripple of giggles went tittering around. It did us good, every last one of us. It was antiseptic, as laughs so often are. Just as I was thinking how much more wholesome everything felt, since I had shaken hands with Miss MacDonald, Danny, who was riding in the front seat beside John, spoiled it all by emitting a shriek; it was not a very loud one, but it was thick with horror and repulsion.

John talked to her for a minute or two in a low voice, and then explained, over his shoulder to us, that he had told her about "that man" being on the ranch.

"Uncle Sam," Danny pleaded, "do I have to see him?"

"Well, Danny," Sam apologized, "I'm right down sorry about it; but, you see, he is staying on the place. We'll keep him out of your way as much as we can."

"Why can't he stay, if he has to stay at all, down at the outfit's quarters?" Danny asked.

"We'll see what Miss MacDonald says. I kind of thought, maybe, she'd like to have him where she could keep an eye on him. I kind of wanted, myself, to keep an eye on him."

Danny put her head on John's shoulder and began to cry; weak, choking little sobs that hurt like having to watch a sick baby.

"Poor little thing," Miss MacDonald said to me, her voice lowered and rich with sympathy.

I thought she would ask me what the trouble was, and who the man was that was causing it. Instead, still speaking low, to me, she said, "So often I get completely at odds with my profession. And then I hear some woman crying like that, or something else as heartbreaking comes to me, and I know that I am justified. Not because I shall discover this criminal. That won't help this little girl, greatly; but because I am one of an army that is fighting crime."

I didn't say it, but I felt like telling her that she seemed like a whole army herself—an army with banners.

I leaned forward and tried to sooth Danny; told her that we would all do what we could to keep him away from her, and to make it easy for her.

"It can't be made easy," she answered. "You can't keep him away from me. I won't see him, I tell you. I've been so homesick—and now to come home to this. I can't see him. I won't—"

Miss MacDonald, who the minute before, had seemed all pity for Danny, began, suddenly, to talk right through and over her sobs, to Sam; to talk in rather a loud voice about stock raising, paying no more attention to Danny s troubles than she paid to the humming of the motor.

I sat and sulked and nursed my disappointment. If I had been a man—which praise the Lord I am not—it would have been a case of love at first sight with me toward Lynn MacDonald. But now I told myself bitterly that I had been a fool to expect real womanly sympathy and kindness from a person in her profession. Ferreting out criminals would make anyone as hard as nails. I was right, in a way. That was not the last time I was to see her turn, suddenly, from a sympathetic woman into a crime analyst. It was sort of a pity, though, that I had to see that side of her so soon; so long before I could begin to understand it.

Not until Danny had quieted down, and had turned to us with stammered apologies and attempted explanations, did Miss MacDonald ask, "Who is this man?"

"Dreadful as it must seem to you," Danny answered, "he is my father. But he has brought sorrow, and fear and trouble to my mother, and to my sister, and to me, whenever he came near us. He is a wicked man."

"Wouldn't it be possible," Miss MacDonald turned to Sam, "to have someone go ahead of us to the house, and ask him to keep to his own room, this evening?"

"Well—" Sam hesitated. "But Danny will have to meet him, sooner or later."

"Better later, in this case, I should say. She will be rested to-morrow. Possibly, too, it would be easier for her if their first meeting could be in private. Shouldn't you rather see him alone, just at first, Miss Canneziano?"

"Oh, no!" Danny exclaimed. "I hope I need never see him alone. Please—don't any of you ever leave me alone with him, not for a minute, if you can help it."

For all the fuss she had made about it, I will say that Danny did very well when we all went into the house and she saw Canneziano, standing over by the east windows, smoking a cigarette.

"What-ho, Dan," he said, smiling his smooth, smirking smile at her. "You are looking seedy. Bad times around here, lately."

She didn't go near him. She edged closer to John; but she answered, looking at him straight and lifting her chin in a pretty, dignified way she had, "Very, very bad times indeed." She and John walked through the room to the stairway, and up the steps, and out of sight.

Canneziano stood watching them, a dark, ugly look on his face. "There's filial affection for you," he said. And then, with a half laugh, as he lit another cigarette, and shook the flame from the match, "The girl is a fool."

40
The Missing Box

Miss Macdonald came down to breakfast in the morning, trim and white as a new candle. She ate heartily, complimenting the food. She asked after Danny, who had not come down for breakfast. She talked about how splendidly the high altitude and the marvelous Nevada air made her feel. She told us, who had lived here all our Eves and didn't know it, that the air in Nevada was supposed to be the best in the entire United States for growing things. And, all the time, she was either not noticing, or pretending not to notice, how we were all hanging on her every word, and watching her every movement.

I guessed the others were doing as I was doing; watching for penetrating glances, and listening for catches in her innocent questions. But, at that, I blushed for them; particularly for John, who sat and stared at her as if she were something he had to learn by heart, before the meal was over. She caught him at it, several times; but, though he would then have the grace to blush, and go glancing about, he'd begin again, at the beginning, the minute she looked away.

When we had finally finished breakfast, she asked Sam if she might detain him. I stayed on, when the others had left the dining-room. She said pointedly, though politely and to Sam, not to me, that she wanted to speak to him alone.

I took myself off. But the open window in the pass pantry was too big a temptation; so I went in there, softly, and stood far back and to the side.

Her very first words took me right off my feet. "Mr. Stanley," she questioned, "do you trust your housekeeper?"

"Mary?" Sam drawled. "Well, now, I don't know as to trusting—"

I don't know how to express what my feelings were when I heard Sam say that. Pulverized is a word that would edge it, I guess—as if I had been caught in a sausage machine, and ground up into small pieces, each one hurting on its own hook.

"But," Sam continued, "if Mary was going on a long journey, to indefinite foreign parts, and felt the need of my right eye to take along with her, I'd loan it to her for as long as she wanted it—no questions asked. I can't say that I'd go much further than that, though."

I was whole again, and warm and glowing. Sam, the old ninny, getting his dander up, and to a beautiful woman like that, just because she had asked him a simple question.

She laughed; a cheery, escaping sort of laugh, like something with bright wings suddenly flying loose.

"Come back into the dining-room, then, Mrs. Magin," she called to me. "You can hear better in here."

I came in, a mite shamefacedly. "It was my overweening curiosity," I explained.

Sam murmured, "'Satiable.'"

"I like people with curiosity," she said. "I understand them, too; because, I suppose, I am one of the most curious persons in the world. Another thing, I have never found a truly curious person who was a wicked person. As much as any generalization can be made, all criminals are egotists. Curiosity means interest in the affairs of others. Of course, one has to be able to discriminate between innate curiosity and the slyness of self protection—But, forgive me, Mr. Stanley, I am chattering away your time. Now then."

(Later we became accustomed to that brisk professional opening of hers, that "Now then," as a signal for getting right down to business, but it was as surprising, heard for the first time, as biting your tongue.)

"Gabrielle Canneziano was last seen, alive, where and at about what hour?"

We told her.

"Did she seem at ease, happy, untroubled?"

Sam said, "I was playing chess. I didn't notice."

"I did," I said. "She was unhappy, troubled, and frightened."

"Frightened? Are you positive that you had that impression at the time?"

"Yes. I spoke to Mrs. Ricker about it, right then."

"Did she agree with you, then?"

"She didn't say."

"Did Gabrielle Canneziano speak to any one of you, as she walked through the room?"

I told her about Gaby's gesture to Chad, and about him following her to the porch and talking to her there.

"Chadwick Caufield? The man who killed himself when the body was found?"

"Yes."

"Did he leave the porch with her?"

"No. He came straight back into the house."

"What other members of the household were in the room at that time?"

Sam told her.

"That leaves her sister, and your son and daughter as the only members of the household who were absent at the time. How long before Martha Stanley returned to the house?"

Sam said, "I was playing chess. But I know it wasn't long."

"It wasn't more than five or six minutes," I said.

"How long before Danielle Canneziano came downstairs?"

I told her about Danny's calling after Gaby. "It wasn't much more than ten minutes after she called, not fifteen minutes, I am sure, before Danny came downstairs."

"Since you are a cook," she said, "you probably have more than the average ability in estimating time."

"Good cooks," I told her, "don't estimate. They know. When I'm boiling three-minute eggs, I use my watch, and always have."

"At least, then," she said, "you know how difficult it is to deal accurately with minutes. With every desire and reason to be honest, five minutes, in the testimony of a witness, may be anything from two minutes to seventeen; ten minutes, anything from five minutes to twenty-three; twenty minutes, anything from nine minutes to forty-five; forty-five minutes, anything from twenty-odd to an hour and a half. Now then."

She went on with her questioning. We had finished breakfast at eight thirty o'clock. At eleven thirty, I felt that she knew everything that Sam and I knew about the case, and, probably, a deal more.

She knew about the two girls searching for something.

She knew about Gaby's getting the code letter; about her peculiar actions afterwards. She knew about the quarrel with Sam.

She knew about John having gone to Rattail for medicine that Danny said she had not sent for.

She knew about him taking four hours, instead of two to make the trip; about the reasons he had given for that; about him going straight upstairs, the back way, and staying there for half an hour. In answer to her questions, it was Sam and not I who told her about John's acting so bothered and troubled when he came down for supper.

She knew about all of our actions between five and six o'clock. She knew that Sam was unwilling to swear that Hubert had been in the barn during that entire time. Sam insisted upon telling her about Danny's suspicions concerning himself: that he had left Chad, the ventriloquist, in the barn to hood-wink Hubert, and had gone off somewhere.

She knew about me asking Chad to close the attic; about the locked door; the key in my pocket. She knew that I had found the body, and had stopped to clean away Sam's pipe ashes.

She had seen the note that Chad had left. She had compared it, through her magnifying glass, with other specimens of his handwriting. She had stated, positively, that the note had been written by the same hand that had written the names and jokes under the pictures in his kodak album. She had spent ten minutes, or more, looking at these pictures. Then she had asked Sam to explain, in detail, why he had entirely discounted Chad's note of confession.

Sam said, "The body was cold and stiff when we found it. That is proof, isn't it, that she had been dead more than an hour?"

"If you are certain of that, it is positive proof that she had been dead much longer than one hour."

"I am certain. Well, until seven o'clock that boy had not been out of my sight for one minute, after Gaby walked through the room, alive, for us all to see her, at four o'clock."

"Twice," Miss MacDonald objected, "you have told me that you could not answer a question because, at the time, you were absorbed in your chess game. How, then, can you be certain that Chadwick Caufield was not out of the living-room for a short time, say fifteen minutes, between four and five o'clock?"

"Because he was playing the piano all that time."

"You are certain that you would have noticed it, had he stopped playing?"

"Certain. He was spoiling my game, and driving me half crazy with his noise. I kept hoping that he would stop. Kept forcing myself not to ask him to stop."

"Why shouldn't you ask him, if it was annoying you to that extent, in your own home?"

"Well, it was Chad's home, too. He had as much right, I reckon, to play his music as I had to play my chess game."

I liked the look Miss MacDonald sidled at me when Sam said that.

"You, too, are sure," she questioned me, "that Chadwick Caufield was at the piano during that entire hour?"

"I know it."

"What sort of music was he playing?"

"He was improvising. It was happy, cheerful sort of crooning music—if you know what I mean."

"Yes. He did not seem worried, depressed?"

"Not a bit. He seemed happier than usual, I thought."

She went on with her questions. They brought us to Martha's death. She took what seemed like a long time asking us questions about Martha's health. Had she ever complained of dizziness? Shortness of breath? Indigestion? And all sorts of other seemingly unimportant things.

"Where," she finally came back to the powders again, "was this sleeping medicine purchased?"

Sam told her in San Francisco, with a doctor's prescription.

"Have you still some of them left, in the original box?"

"A few, I think."

"Good. Will you get it for me, Mr. Stanley?"

"I'll get it," I said, and my opinion of her as a detective was lowered, then and there. If she had not found out, by this time, that it was useless to send a man to look for anything anywhere, but, most particularly, in a bathroom medicine closet, she still had too much to learn.

I had seen the powder box, left out of place on the table, the morning of the fifth of July, when I had gone into the hall bathroom. I had picked it up, out of habit, and replaced it in the medicine closet. I thought that I could put my hand right on it.

I could not. When I opened the mirror door, the box was not to be seen. I searched and searched. I might have spared myself the trouble. From that day to this, the box, with the remaining powders in it, has never been found.

41

Questions

"I was afraid of that," Miss MacDonald said, when I returned with my information and nothing else to the dining-room. "Now then: Would it be possible for you to remember who last took one of these powders, and when, with no ill effects?"

"Danny and Mary each took one the night of the fourth, when Martha did," Sam answered. "I've asked them about it, and both of them say that they did not feel queer at all, afterwards. They were both wide awake in the morning."

"My word!" said Miss MacDonald.

"I think," I offered, "that something was all wrong with Martha's heart before she took the powder. She acted sleepy, stupid, all afternoon."

"From noon on, you mean?"

"No—at least, I didn't notice until later in the afternoon. Mrs. Ricker said that she had a hard time keeping her awake between seven and eight o'clock."

"I see. Mrs. Ricker did not take one of the sleeping powders that night?"

"She didn't need one," Sam explained. "She is naturally calm. She didn't go all to pieces like the other girls did."

"And yet, I have gathered that she was far from calm when her daughter died?"

"She went clear, raving crazy," I said.

225

"Yes. Now then—"

"Hold on a minute," Sam said. "I think that you think, from the questions you have been asking, that the sleeping powder, like I gave the other girls, would not have caused Martha's death. Now I want to know—"

"I am sorry, Mr. Stanley," she interrupted, "but I have explained that I can not answer questions."

"Suppose I insist on a few common sense questions being answered, right now?"

"You can't do that. You can hamper me in my progress. You can dismiss me from the case, right now. But you aren't going to do either, are you?"

"I won't hamper you, if I can help it. I won't dismiss you, as you say, now, either. It wouldn't be right, without giving you a chance, after you came all the way up here, and you know it. That's why you should try to be reasonable."

"I am trying to be reasonable, Mr. Stanley." Her smile at Sam, just then, looked as if she might be trying to be something a mite more charming than reasonable, besides. "Now then—"

She was off again, leading us with her questions, through Mrs. Ricker's confession and her suspicions of Martha.

"After Martha came into the house with the bracelet," she asked, "was she out of the room again within the hour; or even within the second hour, between five and six?"

"She was not out between four and five," I said. "She might have been any place, for all I know, between five and six. I was in the kitchen."

"Did you have any particular reason for watching her between four and five o'clock?"

"No."

"Then, I am afraid that you can not be positive that she did not leave the room."

"I am positive," I insisted. "There weren't any goings nor comings. We all stayed right in the room. It was too hot to move around. I know that Martha did not leave the room. She sat beside Chad on the piano bench, for a while. She sat on the arm of Sam's chair, watching the chess game—"

"Gosh!" Sam said. "I remember that, now. She was fooling with my hair. I kept smelling the blacking on her shoes."

"You couldn't have," I said. "Because, Sam, she was wearing white shoes."

"She used some preparation to clean her white shoes, I suppose?" Miss MacDonald asked.

"Some stuff called 'White-o-clean.' We all use it."

She asked for the bottle. When I brought it, she smelled of it, and asked Sam to. "Is that the odor you noticed?" she questioned.

"Nothing like it."

"Now then."

"Hold on," Sam said. "I've got two things to tell you that you are overlooking, and I know that they are both mighty important."

"What are they?"

"The first one is this. Gaby had lived here close to two months. Martha had never harmed her. Does it stand to reason that, on the very day Gaby was afraid she was going to be killed, Martha would do it? There's too much coincidence in that, isn't there?"

"I think so," she answered, breaking her rule for once, at least. "Though we can not ever discount coincidence. In the first place, what appears to be coincidence usually proves not to be coincidence at all, in the end. In the second place, genuine coincidences are much more frequent than is generally supposed, or admitted. But, Mr. Stanley, unless the other thing you have to tell me is a fact, and not an opinion, I am going to ask you not to tell it to me, at least not until later."

"It is straight fact."

"Very well, then?"

"I'd rather show you," Sam said. "Then you wouldn't have to take my word for it. Will you come out to the rabbit hutch with me?"

"But," she questioned, "can that be necessary?"

"You can judge for yourself. Martha was always trying experiments with feeding her rabbits. I guess she thought that they might like grain. Maybe they do. I don't know. Anyway, she, or someone, had tugged a half sack of grain up there. A lot of it had spilled out under the berry bushes. It is all fresh sprouted, and growing fine. Is that important, or not?"

Her brows puckered. "I'm sorry—I don't follow you."

"There wasn't a spot out there, except under those bushes, where Martha could have hidden the body. A body, even as small as Gaby's, would have smashed down and broken those fresh sprouts of grain."

"But—the body was never there."

"Mrs. Ricker said that she thought it was. We just told you."

Her mouth popped open with surprise. "But, Mr. Stanley, you couldn't have considered Mrs. Ricker's opinion seriously? Is it possible that you don't know that Gabrielle Canneziano was murdered right there on the stairs, where she fell, and where she was found?"

42

A Revelation

"How in blazes could I know it?" Sam said. "What's more, I don't believe it. I think that she was murdered outside, and carried in, afterwards."

"My word! Weren't you present when the body was moved?"

"No. I—well, I didn't care about being."

"The fingers of her right hand were clutching the stair tread with the grasp of death. Nothing can disprove that. Dead fingers can not be made to clutch."

"How do you know that?" Sam demanded. "About her fingers, I mean."

"To prove to you," she said, after an instant's hesitation, "that my refusal to answer questions is not merely an attempt to appear wise and mysterious, I am going to answer this question.

"When I saw the body in the crematory in San Francisco—"

"What!"

"I always do that, when I can. Before I sent you my telegram, I had gone to see the body."

"Did—does Danny know that?"

"No. It might be better not to tell her. It is a necessary part of my profession. The crematory people realize that; but, since people are often very sensitive about it, they prefer that the relatives should not know that they allow it. As I was saying, I saw, then, that the fingers on the right hand had been broken. The undertaker had done that, you understand, in order that they might look natural to fold.

"When I had received your telegram engaging me to take the case, I telephoned to the coroner and the undertaker in Telko. I asked them to come to the train and talk with me for the twenty minutes that the train stops in Telko. I took a drawing-room for the purpose; so that we could talk undisturbed and unnoticed. That will be the reason for the day's drawing-room charge on my expense account, Mr. Stanley. I don't want you to think that I was unduly extravagant."

"Extravagant! Hell!" Sam exploded, forgetting himself. "What do I care about a drawing-room? What I want to know is, what those fellows told you, and why they didn't tell me."

"They corroborated the opinion I had formed, from the fingers, about the death clutch, among other things. I don't know why they didn't tell you that. Probably, because they assumed that you already knew it. What information I got from them, they gave with extreme reluctance, due, I think, to their long-standing friendship with you, and their desire not to incriminate any member of your household. I got nothing from them—or, to put it more fairly, perhaps, they were able to tell me nothing except the facts concerning the position of the body. Those facts proved that she had been killed on the stairs, by someone who had been coming downstairs behind her. How did it happen that you did not know this?"

"As soon as I realized what had occurred," Sam explained, "I cleared everybody right out and locked the door. I knew that it was necessary for the coroner to examine the body before it had been disturbed."

"How very, very sensible," Miss MacDonald said. But I did not quite like the way she said it.

"If you mean," I spoke up, "how unfeeling, I want to say that, though she had been living here for two months, she had not exactly endeared herself to any of us."

"No? I had understood that Chadwick Canfield was deeply in love with her; that Mr. Hand was more or less enamored. There can be no doubt that her sister loved her devotedly. That leaves Mr. Stanley, his son and daughter, Mrs. Ricker and yourself, as the people to whom she had not endeared herself."

Sam and I received that in silence. It was one of those odd things that was true, but that did not sound so.

I looked at my watch and said that it was time for me to be starting to get dinner. She asked if she might help me. I thought that she was trying only to be polite, and I was making my refusal just as polite, when she interrupted me.

"Please, Mrs. Magin," she urged. "You mentioned at breakfast that you had only one inefficient girl to help you, just now. I love housework, of all sorts. And I want to get intimately acquainted with this house. The best way to do that is to work in it, isn't it? You know—you can't know a stove until you have cooked on it, nor a room until you have cleaned it. Won't you let me help you, as a special favor to me?"

Sam winked at me. "She isn't going to let you out of her sight, Mary."

Miss MacDonald tried to smile, but she made a failure of it.

"But you don't need to worry, Mary," Sam went on, "because one thing, now, is dead certain. If Gaby was murdered there on the steps, it is impossible that any member of this household could have done it. It was, anyway. But now it is sure. That clears us all."

Miss MacDonald flashed out, in one of her rarely shown tempers. "What utter nonsense," she said.

43
A Shadow

When it came to helping in the kitchen, that girl was more help in five minutes than Belle, Sadie and Goldie, all three of them together, had been in half a day. She didn't ask questions. She didn't say where is this, and how do you do that? She pitched in as if she had been working in that kitchen with me for the past twenty years. How she knew where I kept the potatoes, where the best paring knife lived, and the particular kettle that was best for cooking the potatoes in, I don't know, and I never shall know. Most mystery stories, especially of late, have an element of the supernatural in them. I tell you, that girl's knowledge of my ways, and the manner in which she took hold in the kitchen, are as supernatural as anything ever brought to my notice. The first thing I knew, she was peeling the potatoes, and peeling them thin and clean. She didn't ask how many would be enough. When she got them peeled and washed, she put them on, in boiling water, with no inquiry as to where I kept the salt. She did not talk as she worked. I was glad of that; for, after three solid hours of conversation, I needed, badly, a silent space. I wanted to think. Those last words of hers, "utter nonsense," in answer to Sam's statement, kept ringing in my ears.

I tried to think whether there was any way a person could get upstairs without coming through the house. We had no fire escapes. There were no trees close enough to the house so that even Douglas Fairbanks could swing to an upstairs window from one of them. There were no vines growing on the house. Without about a twenty-foot ladder, which we didn't have on the place, and which would be hard to go conveying about, to say nothing of disposing of it afterwards, there was not any possible way for anyone to get to the second floor of our house, except by means of the back or the front stairway.

Since Gaby had been killed on the attic stairway, and since all who knew about that sort of thing agreed that she had been dead at least two hours when we found her, she must have returned to the house sometime between four and five o'clock, and have stolen upstairs with none of us seeing or hearing her. Since she could do that, there was no reason to suppose that someone else could not have done the same thing; either coming in with her at the time, or coming before or after she did. I had to conclude that another person certainly had done just that; had entered the house and had gone upstairs during that hour. Who? The person whom she had been fearing? Not one of us, that seemed a certainty. And yet, Miss MacDonald had said, "nonsense."

I remembered, again, her strange, mad actions immediately after she had received the code letter. I remembered how she had looked in the hall that day, when I had told John that I thought I had seen the ghost of Sin. In Gaby's note to Danny she had written that she had purposely kept her fears and her danger a secret from Danny. Undoubtedly, the secret was written in the code letter. Had she told Danny partly the truth about the contents of that letter, or had she told her falsehoods from beginning to end? Or had Danny told us only a part of the truth? Why did we all keep forgetting how Danny had tried to call Gaby back, when Gaby had started on that fatal walk?

I have said before, and I say again, I knew that Danielle Canneziano had not murdered her sister. But I knew,
too, that if she had some reason, some better reason than
I could conceive, for keeping quiet, for not telling everything she knew, Danny was capable of so doing. I remembered our talk in her room on the morning of the fifth of
July. I remembered how she had acted when her engagement ring had slipped from her finger—and I tried to turn
my thoughts into different channels.

There was Chad's suicide and his confession. It could
be possible that he had killed himself because he had loved
Gaby. But that would not account for his confession to
the crime. It could mean but one thing—a desire to shield
someone. Would he have cared about shielding some unknown scoundrel who had crept into the house and killed
the girl whom Chad loved? Had Chad, then, mistakenly
suspected Martha, or Sam, or John, and killed himself and
left the note to aid one of them? Not likely. Men do not
kill themselves, leaving a written confession to a crime of
which they are innocent, because of some mere suspicion.

I remembered my conversation with Hubert Hand in
the hall that morning. What was it that he had thought I
had overheard in the cabin and had bribed me not to tell?
It was reasonable enough to suppose that, at that time, he
had hoped to keep his entire story, his prison records, his
reason for coming to the Desert Moon, his relations with
Mrs. Ricker and Martha, a secret; just as I had hoped to
keep the fact of finding Sam's pipe ashes a secret.

Sam's pipe ashes, again. If someone had put them there,
in an effort to implicate Sam, it would have had to be
someone who knew Sam's ways. My thoughts were off
again. You can't, I told myself, get shed of a following
shadow by running away from it. You have to turn and face
it, before you can go the other way. I faced it.

John. He had left the ranch at two o'clock. He could easily have gotten back by four, or shortly after. Suppose that he had left the machine down the road, quite far down the road in the spot where the tire tracks showed that the machine had been stopped and started again, the spot where we thought he had changed a tire? He could have climbed the fence, taken a short cut to the house, and gotten here in half or three quarters of an hour. He could have met Gaby; could have stolen into the house with her. He could have killed her, and stolen out of the house again. A short cut across the fields, and a drive to the house would get him here by six o'clock—the time he did get here. If he could be wicked enough to murder, he could be wicked enough to arrange clues to throw suspicions on his father and his sister. If he were low enough to do that, he would be low enough to rob her of a little money. In other words, grant that John is a blonde, and you can go along and grant that he has blue eyes and tow hair. It was all of it false, I told myself, from its wicked beginning to its wicked end; false and unfair. But I had faced it. Now I could turn and go in another direction.

I had not realized how deeply I had been thinking, dawdling over my work in consequence, until I saw that Miss MacDonald had taken up the pork chops, and had them in the warming-oven, and was making gravy, as smooth and tasty looking pan-gravy as I ever saw.

"Good lands!" I said. "I've certainly come to one conclusion."

"It is a little early for conclusions, isn't it?" she asked.

"It is a lot too late for this one."

"Pleas—" she began; but, for once, I got the best of her.

"My conclusion is," I said, "that, by hook or crook, Sam Stanley has got to get me some efficient help in this house. When I think of what I've put up with, all these years in the way of help, and then see the way you pitch in, it makes me mad all over."

"I wish," she said, "that I might drop this case, right now, and stay here for all time, and be your assistant and a thoroughly domestic person, and forget that there were crimes and criminals in the world."

"Maybe," I said, eagerly, but knowing of course that it was too good to come true, "when you've finished with this case, you could do that. You'd be one of our family, and Sam would pay—well, I guess anything you'd care to ask."

"No," she smiled, "it is tempting—now. But that desire of mine to give up my profession is a phase that I always pass through at the beginning of each difficult case. In a few days, when I begin to get hold of something, and when things begin to take shape, all my love of the work will return. It is only at first, when I seem to be in a maze of mystery, like this, that I get so discouraged. I always do it, right at first; and I always think that here is the case of which I am going to make an absolute failure."

"Have you ever failed on a case?" I asked.

"Indeed I have, on several. It is queer, though; in each case that has been a failure, it has seemed that the solution was written plainly from the start. It was written all wrong. Judging from that, I should be unusually successful in this case."

Poor girl, no wonder that she was discouraged. She has given me leave, now that it is all over, to use any of her notes that I care to use in the writing of this story.

"Far be it from Lynn MacDonald," she said, when I asked her about using the notes, "to refuse advertisement of one of her banner cases. My rivals will say that I succeeded in this because, as often happens, my luck stood by me. But you and I, we understand about luck, don't we, Mary?"

"If you aren't afraid," I said, "that your notes may give away some of the secrets of that luck of yours, so that your rivals will be able to lay their hands on some of the same brand?"

She laughed. "I never write down a secret. That is a safe enough rule for an honest person, who plans to remain honest. For a dishonest person, or for one who contemplates any sort of evil, or admits the possibility of such a course, the safe rule would be: 'Never, under any circumstances, put pen or pencil to paper.'"

As Sam would say, "It is a poor rule that won't work both ways."

The notes that Miss MacDonald had made, before this conversation of ours, that day in the kitchen, and on the evening of that same day, July eleventh, are as follows.

44
The Notes

JULY 7. Saw body in crematory late to-night. Cause of death, strangulation. Probably work of expert. Look for Japanese on ranch. Broken fingers on right hand. Beautiful, costly gown, lingerie, etc., indicating wealth and good taste.

JULY 8. Rose, who has shadowed twin sister reports nothing verging on suspicion. She attended services at crematory. Evidence of genuine grief. Returned to hotel. One telegram sent to Desert Moon Ranch. Received no company. Mailed no letters. Did no shopping.

I received telegram from Desert Moon Ranch engaging me on case. Explicit directions concerning train probably due to inconvenience of meeting trains in rural community, and not due to a desire to have me on the same train with Miss C. However, note.

Telephoned to coroner and undertaker, requesting them to give me conference in Telko. Also, had coroner verify list of names, as published in "Examiner" of all persons present on ranch at time of murder. Note—absence of all ranch employees at the time. Note—extreme reluctance of both coroner and undertaker to give information, or to meet me in Telko.

July 9. Spent day in shadowing Miss C. myself. R's observations, as usual, excellent.

Rose's research through back files of Nevada papers provided following information.

Samuel Stanley, ranch owner. Very wealthy. Exemplary character. High standing throughout state of Nevada. Philanthropic.

John Stanley, adopted son of S. Stanley. Distinguished himself on University of Nevada football team, 1916, 1917. Enlisted in air service for war, 1917. Mather's Field when armistice was declared.

Hubert Hand. Winner of chess tournament held in Reno, 1914, 1915.

Mrs. Ollie Ricker. No report.

Chadwick Caufield. No report, except mention as guest at Desert Moon Ranch.

Mary Magin. No report.

Danielle Canneziano. No report, except mention of her arrival with sister, Gabrielle, at ranch last May.

Inspection of Miss C.'s room in hotel after she had turned in her key revealed no clue. Unusually neat and orderly person. Wastebaskets empty. Newspapers folded on table. Magazine, "Ladies Home Journal" on table. No heavy perfume. Hotel soap unwrapped. Fastidious. Silver dollar left on table for chambermaid.

Rose reports: Miss C. went from hotel to Ferry Building in taxicab. Crossed alone on ferry. Spoke to no one. Boarded train at eight thirty o'clock and went at once to her berth.

July 10. Afternoon. Breakfasted with Miss C. this morning. No conversation. All the evidences of good breeding.

Had conference with coroner and undertaker. Think that they strongly suspect John Stanley because of their repeated efforts to keep me from sharing the suspicion.

Information gained from them: Girl murdered on attic stairway. Position of body and marks on throat prove an attack from the rear. Members of household declare that rigor was complete when body was discovered at eight o'clock the night of the fourth of July. Amateur testimony, however. If fact, death must have occurred at least three hours before discovery of body.

JULY 10. Night.

Allowed sudden "hunch" to betray reason and common sense. Usual silly mistake at beginning of case. Set a trap to catch hawk. Got caught myself. Luckily, no harm done.

Met members of household. First impressions, before hearing history of case other than gained from newspapers, coroner and undertaker.

Danielle Canneziano. Impressions previously noted sustained. Charming, lovable character. Innocent.

Samuel Stanley. Honest. Likable. Kindly. There is a slight chance that he might be involved, unwittingly. He is not stupid; but, decidedly, he is not clever.

Mary Magin. Intelligent. Imaginative. Honest. Innocent.

John Stanley. Too handsome, but unconceited. Bashful. Likable. Judgment suspended.

Hubert Hand. Egotistic. Clever. Judgment suspended.

Ollie Ricker. Life has treated her badly. She has put on armor against it. Stupid. Perhaps sly. Judgment suspended.

Daniel Canneziano. Criminal type. Alibi proves him not guilty of the murder, but he is probably involved. Why did he come here?

JULY 11. Evening.

Heard case history to-day from Mr. S. and Mrs. M.

Tempted to destroy all first impressions as recorded. Remember, however, the value of mistaken impressions is usually important.

Multiplicity of clues most amazing in my entire experience. Would seem to indicate that many of them are false
clues.

Most Important Clues. (Definite.)

1.—John's unnecessary errand.
   A.—Length of time gone.
2.—Victim's evident fear as she walked through room.
   A.—Unusual costume for short walk on the place.
3.—Miss C.'s calling after her sister.
4.—Caufield's suicide and confessional note. (Probably
   most important of all clues.)
5.—Victim's note to Danielle Canneziano.
   A. Proof of her fear.
6.—Death of Martha Stanley.
   A. Missing box containing sleeping powders.
7.—Canneziano's presence on the ranch.

Clues of Less Importance. (Definite.)

1.—Contents of beaded bag.
   A.—Empty purse.
   B.—Missing bill-fold.
   C.—Crumpled handkerchief.
   D.—Broken cigarette holder.
   E.—Note from Hubert Hand.
   F.—Cigarette case with two cigarettes missing.
   H. Empty matchbox.
2.—Code letter.
   A. Destroyed caps for typewriter.
3.—Pipe ashes on bag and carpet.
   A.—Not necessarily Mr. Stanley's.
   B.—Probably fixed false clue.
4.—Tatting shuttle. (Doubtful.)

Clues of Most Importance. (Indefinite.)

1. Entire story concerning the money from robbery being hidden on Desert Moon Ranch.
2. Victim's peculiar actions after receiving code letter.
   A. Quarrel with Mr. Stanley.
3. Mrs. Ricker's story.
   A. Her reason for telling it.
   B. Did she believe it?
4. Mrs. Magin's desire to remove pipe ashes.
5. Miss C.'s reluctance to tell of them. Her final complete confession of her suspicions concerning Mr. Stanley.
6. Hubert Hand's unnecessary confession concerning his past life.

Clues of Least Importance. (Indefinite.)

1. C. Caufield's powers of ventriloquism.
   A. Probably greatly over-rated by members of household.
2. Playing of radio between two and four o'clock that afternoon.
3. Martha's reference to a surprise in which she and Chadwick Caufield were involved.
   A. Possibly untrue.
4. Mrs. Magin's evident antagonism toward the victim.
5. Mr. Stanley's prompt action in locking the attic door and his refusal to have the body touched until the arrival of coroner.
6. Reason for victim's having given bracelet to Martha Stanley at that time?

Negatives.

1. No clues of any sort discoverable in victim's room.
2. No clues of any sort discoverable in attic.

3. Lack of motives for crime by persons at present in-
stinctively suspicioned.
4. No dogs on a ranch of this size.

Now, as I read over these notes, my good opinion of
myself rises until it runs over the pan. I declare to goodness, the list of clues made out by Lynn MacDonald, Crime
Analyst, is not much better than the list made out by Mary
Magin, Cook and Housekeeper. She has done hers in better form, and she has included a few things that I left out.
But, most of the included things were unknown to me at
the time I made my list. Many of the other included things
did not amount to shucks. For instance, we have no dogs
on the ranch because the dogs in northeastern Nevada have
a habit of running out and associating with rabid coyotes,
contracting rabies, coming home and biting whoever is
conveniently to hand. For instance—but never mind. As
I said before, poor girl, no wonder she was discouraged.

45
Another Key

As indicated by her notes for July eleventh, on that afternoon Miss MacDonald had cleaned the attic, thoroughly, and had found nothing to pay her for her trouble. Keeping me in the dark, as she had, I supposed, when she said early the next morning that she wanted to clean the living-room, that she had got at least a hat full of clues from the attic.

Land knows, the way I had been neglecting things, the living-room was badly in need of a good cleaning. I wanted her to allow me to help her, but she would not. It was luck that I happened to come in with the floor wax just as she was looking at something that she had dug out of the ashes in the fireplace.

"What's that?" I questioned.

"I believe," she answered, "that it is the missing key to the attic door."

She got up, shook out her skirts, and went straight upstairs. I trailed along. I stood by and watched her while she fitted the blackened key into the lock. It turned both ways, as smoothly as you please.

Without bothering to say anything to me, she went up and down the hall, trying the key in the locks of the other doors. It fitted none of them. She went downstairs again, with me trailing after her, and tried the key in all the locks downstairs. It fitted none of them, either.

"Do you know," she asked, showing at last that she was conscious of my presence, which I was beginning to doubt, "when you last had a fire in that fireplace?"

I thought a minute, and then told her on the night of the fourth of July, during the storm.

"Do you remember who kindled the fire?"

"It had been fixed there, ready for the match, for weeks. Things have gone to rack and ruin here lately; but I always used to see to it that the fire was set in the fireplace, ready to light when needed."

"Do you happen to know who applied the match to the fire that night?"

"Sam did."

"But surely, even though the rain had come up, a fire on the fourth of July could not have been necessary?"

"We don't have fires here when they are necessary," I told her. "We have them when they are possible without absolute suffocation. Half a pint of rain is plenty of excuse for Sam to light a fire at any time, even if he has to open all the doors and the windows to cool off."

What I was saying was the honest truth; but I had a mean feeling that she didn't believe me.

Right here, with apologies to Miss MacDonald and others of her profession, I want to say that if they would just remember that nine times out of ten a person who pretends to be telling the truth is telling it, it would save them a lot of mistakes, and a lot of worry. The man who spends his time biting his money to see whether or not it is genuine doesn't, usually, have much of it to bite; to say nothing of the wear and tear on his own teeth, which would be considerable.

I was standing by the living-room windows, trying to keep my temper down with some such consoling thoughts as these, when I saw a car drive up and the coroner and the undertaker getting out of it.

I told Miss MacDonald the news, and asked her what in the world she supposed they were coming here for, at this time in the morning.

"I needed to see them again," she answered. "Mr. Stanley telephoned to them last evening."

"Well," I said, "that means that I've got about half an hour to disguise a family meal as a company dinner—"

"Don't bother," she interrupted. "They won't be here for luncheon—dinner. I need to see them only about ten minutes."

I didn't bother—answering. If she didn't know any more about the ways of people in this country than that, I didn't see why I should take it on myself to teach her.

But she was right. She talked to them a few minutes; and, though I insisted that they stay for dinner, off they went. It was an insult to the Desert Moon Ranch. Everyone on the place, but Miss MacDonald, knew it. Two weeks before, if a couple of friends had left the ranch at eleven-thirty in the morning, with no reasonable excuse for so doing, Sam would have blown up and burst with rage. That noon he was not even decently indignantly interested.

He had plenty of interest, though, concerning the finding of the attic key. He had had it all settled, and was satisfied that, since it had been proven that Gaby had been killed on the stairway, it had also been proven that no member of the household could have been implicated. Now this second key coming to light, the key that must have been put over back of the wood before the fire was lighted that night, and that must have been blackened in that one fire, because there had been no fire in that fireplace since, dragged, to quote Sam, not wishing to use such words on my own hook, "Every damn one of us back into the damn mess again."

"Sam," I said, and I guess my only excuse is that I was still angry at having my honest word doubted, "do you know what I think? I think that Miss MacDonald—though land knows she is a nice girl, and a living wonder as help in the kitchen and around the house—is going to be a flat fizzle from start to finish when it comes to discovering the murderer."

"That's kind of the way I got it sized up, too," Sam said. "But if she's good help to you, she's worth a lot more than her expenses."

"It isn't the cost of her," I said. "I'm afraid she is going to do a lot of harm around here."

"Good-night, Mary!" he said. "If anyone can do any more harm around here than has been done already—why, leave 'em do it."

"Not much with your 'leave 'em do its,'" I said. "My idea is that we've had about enough trouble. What I'm getting at is this, Sam: I think that fool girl, at present, is suspecting you more than any other one of us."

"That's the way I had that sized up, too," he said. "But let her go ahead. If she can prove I'm guilty, I'm willing to hang for it."

"Don't be a fool, Sam," I snapped. "Did you ever happen to hear of circumstantial evidence?"

"You bet. But they can't hang more than one innocent person on circumstantial evidence, and there's enough of that stuff around here now to hang about five or six of us. I'll take my chances with the rest of you, Mary."

"Lands, Sam," I was taken aback, "do you think she suspects me?"

Something pretty close to the old twinkle came into Sam's eyes. "Well, Mary, Gaby was one extra to do for and she came late to meals and pestered you quite a lot.

Furthermore, though it hasn't been made a point of, you were all alone in the kitchen for the hour between five and six o'clock. You might have slipped up and have done the deed between the time you put the meat on and took the biscuits out."

I knew that he thought he was being funny; but I didn't like it. "See here, Sam," I began, "Danny was going back and forth all the time—"

"'Now then,'" Sam interrupted, mocking Miss Mac-Donald. "Did Miss Canneziano have any particular reason for watching you? No. I see. Then, I am afraid, she can not be positive that you were not out of the kitchen. Twenty minutes often seem like two hours and sixteen minutes—

"I'll tell you what, Mary," Sam got suddenly serious. "I'm going to wait a few more days, and then if this lady isn't progressing a deal faster than she is at present, I'm going to pay her off, full amount, of course, and wire to 'Frisco for a plain, ordinary, he-man detective to come up here and take hold of things. By the way," he went on, "does it seem to you that Danny and Canneziano are getting along all right?"

"I judge it isn't a case of their getting along, much," I said. "So far as I know, she hasn't spoken a word to him since she greeted him the evening she came home."

"Well," he hesitated, "well—I know a mite further than that. I'll tell you, sometime that isn't dinner time—maybe."

He went into the dining-room, and I followed him.

All during that dinner, and the same had been true of every meal since the first breakfast I've mentioned, John hardly took his eyes off of Miss MacDonald. I made a way to speak to him about it, alone, right after dinner.

"John," I said, "for Mercy's sakes, what do you want to sit and stare at Miss MacDonald for, during meals, like she was the place where you had lost something?"

He blushed. "Gosh, Mary! I haven't been doing that, have I?"

"You certainly have. It doesn't look nice, John. Why do you do it?"

"I didn't know that I did. But, on the square, did you ever see anything as pretty—I mean, as clean and—well, kind of comforting looking? She changes so, too; like a diamond, or a desert, or a sunrise, or—something. Did you ever see anyone as interesting to look at, Mary?"

"Never mind asking me," I said. "Just you go and ask Danny some of those questions."

"Danny," he answered, "is—well, Danny is Danny, of course. She's different."

"Better take to watching how different she is," I advised, and left him to think it over, and went into the living-room.

Canneziano was loafing around in there. "Mary," he said, "I'll make a dicker with you."

46
A Dicker

"Not with me," I said, and started up the stairs.

Curiosity like mine is a curse. I'd gone about four steps up when it caught me. "What's your old dicker?" I said.

"If you'll persuade Sam to give me the ten thousand for producing the murderer, I'll split it with you."

I am tired of apologizing for myself. I will state, merely, that I managed to say the one thing, under those circumstances, that I should not have said. "Do you know who the murderer is?" Thereby proving that I was possessed of about as much diplomacy as an alarm clock.

"Certainly not," he answered. He had not hesitated; he had looked straight into my eyes. But I knew that he believed that he had lied.

"See here," I said. "I take it that one five thousand dollars is as good to you as another. If you know who committed the murder, and will produce him, I'll give you the five thousand dollars myself."

"Don't say that, Mary," Danny stepped out from behind the long curtains at the end of the south windows.

Canneziano jumped like a spurred bronco. "Spying, eh, my lady?"

She spoke directly to me. "Listen, Mary; don't ever, for any reason, enter into any sort of an agreement with this man. If he knows, or thinks that he knows, who the murderer is, he can be forced to tell without a bribe. If he had known for one day, one hour, and had withheld the information, he is, in effect, an accomplice—there is a legal term for it, but I have forgotten it. I am going out, now, to find Uncle Sam, and to bring him here and tell him that this man says that he knows who committed the murder. Mary, you telephone to the sheriff in Telko—"

"Just a moment, please," Canneziano spoke smoothly and smilingly. "I have said, definitely, that I do not know who killed the Gaby. And—I do not know. I am bored, unspeakably bored. I should like to try my hand at detecting this—er, villain. But," he shrugged his narrow shoulders, "with no impetus—"

"The fact that she was your own daughter—" I began, hotly.

"Don't, Mary," Danny interrupted, with a sigh. "There is no use. You and he do not speak the same language."

"How is this?" Canneziano said, and went on speaking, very rapidly, in some foreign language.

Danny stood and stared at him without a mite of expression on her face. He paused for breath. She said, "I have forgotten my Italian. I do not understand you, and I am glad that I do not. Come, Mary, shall we go upstairs?"

In the upper hall she said that she wanted me to go with her to Miss MacDonald, because she wanted to tell Miss MacDonald what had just happened.

We knocked on her door. She greeted us pleasantly enough, but there was a pucker between her eyebrows.

"You have asked us," Danny began at once, "to tell you nothing about the case. Does that mean that you do not wish to have us tell you of day-by-day developments, which seem to have a direct bearing on the case?"

"As, for instance?" Miss MacDonald questioned.

Danny told her about what had happened, from the time she had stepped behind the curtains, until she and I had come upstairs together.

Miss MacDonald's first question was, "Why were you watching him?"

"Because," Danny answered, straight, "I think he came here with some evil purpose. I should like to find out what that purpose is."

"Why were you so eager to prevent Mrs. Magin's making a pact with him?"

"Miss MacDonald, a woman who has dealt with criminals, as you must have, should not need to ask that question."

"But," Miss MacDonald persisted, "you have not dealt with criminals."

"I have dealt with this man. I know that he is bad and crafty. For five thousand dollars he would perjure himself over and over again. He would produce witnesses who would perjure themselves. You know the ways of criminals better than I do, Miss MacDonald. I know, as Uncle Sam knows, that it is unsafe to deal with them."

"Has this man approached you with offers similar to this one, Miss Canneziano?"

"He has had no opportunity."

"You are sure of that?"

Danny's chin went up a trifle. "I don't understand."

"I think that you do."

Danny turned to me. "Mary," she said, "yesterday afternoon that man came to my room when I was alone. He slipped in, closed my door, and locked it. I ran into Gaby's room, but I could not get out of it because the doors were all locked. I went into Gaby's bathroom and locked myself in. I stayed there for half an hour, or longer, until he left. Miss MacDonald evidently thinks that he and I were in conversation during that time. I have no proof that we weren't. Do you believe me, Mary?"

"I do, with all my heart," I said.

Miss MacDonald persisted. "You told no one about this?"

"I did not dare to tell. If John thought that that man—" She stopped short.

"Yes?" questioned Miss MacDonald.

"I mean that John would fight with him; would whip him within an inch of his life."

"Why should you care?"

Danny looked at me.

"She'd care," I said, answering the appeal in her big, hurt eyes, "because she is a woman, Miss MacDonald. It may be hard for you to understand; but women, who aren't crime analysts, don't want their men fighting."

"Thank you, Mary," Danny said, and walked hurriedly out of the room.

47
An Aid

"Mrs. Magin," Miss MacDonald began, right off, the minute the door had closed behind Danny, "I want to ask you to help me with this case."

"I couldn't be any help to you," I said. I guess I was rather tart about it.

"Why not?"

"One reason is," I said, "that anybody who doesn't know any better than to suspicion Danny, in this affair, would need a lot more help, to get anywhere, than I could give them."

"My only suspicion concerning Miss Canneziano," she answered, "is that she knows more than she is willing to tell. I may be wrong about that. Have you any other reason for refusing to help me?"

"Only that you don't believe a word I say. If you would consider that I am, anyway, trying to be honest, and if you'd do the same with the others, until you are sure that you have reason to do otherwise, I'd consider it an honor to help you, and I'd thank you kindly."

"I am afraid that I don't entirely understand."

"Crime and wickedness," I told her, "aren't the general rules of the world. If they were, all the good people would have to be locked up, for safety's sake, while the criminals ran loose for lack of space to confine them. Why, instead

of doubting my simple word, this morning, when I told
you how Sam always lighted a fire, for any excuse, couldn't
you have believed that I was telling the truth, and that
whoever put the key in there knew that Sam would light
the fire, and so throw suspicion on himself?"

"That is possible," she admitted. "But the key, there,
leads me to suppose that whoever put it there, to hide it,
would be too stupid for much subtle reasoning. Keys, you
know, don't burn."

"They don't," I agreed. "But we never take the ashes
out of the fireplace as you did this morning. We open the
ash-dump and shoot them down into a barrel in the base-
ment. Every few months the ashes are emptied in starva-
tion field, eight miles or more away from here. Not a bad
way to get the key carried off the place, if that was what
he wanted. Not a bad way, either, to throw more suspicion
on Sam, if the key was found."

"Most criminals are stupid, though," she clung to her
point. "Try as they may, they always make some stupid
blunder."

"It seems to me," I said, "that the ones who get caught
are stupid; they are the ones who have made the blunder,
left the clue. But look at the number of criminals who get
clean away. Not long ago, I was reading some statistics—"

"You know what Mark Twain said about statistics?
'There are three kinds of liars: liars, damned liars, and
statistics.'"

I had to laugh. I think she said that to put me in a good
humor, for she went right on to say, "But you haven't told
me, yet, that you will be my assistant in this case."

She couldn't hoodwink me. "I told you that I'd be no
use to you, as long as you doubted every word I said."

"But," she argued, "by your own admission you tried
to shield Mr. Stanley, immediately after the murder; stopping to clean away his—the pipe ashes. If you tried, once,

to shield him, wouldn't you try again to shield him, if you needed to?"

"No," I said, "I wouldn't. I'll tell you why. That night, and for several days after, my mind was like a dirty cluttered kitchen. I couldn't get enough space cleared in it to start thinking, let alone working at it. I have tidied up a place, since then, and I've done a batch of thinking. I know, now, that Sam doesn't need me, nor anyone, to shield him. Any evidence found against him, will be good evidence, in the end, against whoever fixed it to throw blame on him."

"I am inclined to agree with you," she said. "Now then: Is there anyone here who would benefit by his conviction?"

"Am I," I questioned, "your assistant, or am I not?"

"Does it make a difference in your answer?" she questioned in return.

"A deal of difference. Being your assistant honor would bind me, wouldn't it? If I know that you are believing that I'll help, and tell the truth, I'll try to. If I think I am to be doubted, anyway, maybe I'll say what I'd like to say."

She sat and looked straight at me for at least half a minute. "I do believe you," she said, "and trust you. I have, since I first met you at the station. I can't help myself. You're all right, Mrs. Magin, and I know it. I'll agree to your terms. Now then: As my assistant, is there anyone on the place who would benefit in any way by Mr. Stanley's conviction?"

"In a way," I said, though it all but choked me, "John would. He is to inherit everything Sam has. But John loves Sam. And John didn't do it."

"Miss Canneziano would also benefit, then, wouldn't she, since she is to marry young Mr. Stanley?"

"It doesn't make sense," I said. "John has plenty of his own, right now; and Sam would give them anything and everything they wanted besides, as long as he lived."

"I had understood," she said, "that Mr. Stanley objected to the marriage."

"Not a bit of it. He has asked them to wait a year.
That's all."

"Is there," she asked, next, "any person at present on
the ranch whom you would concede might, possibly, com-
mit a murder?"

"Canneziano."

"Yes, I know. And leaving him out of it?"

"Well," I had to hesitate, "I am not sure. Every instinct
I have tells me that neither Hubert Hand nor Mrs. Ricker— No. It is an awful thing to say; but, do you know,
Gabrielle Canneziano herself was the only other person
who has ever been on this ranch whom I could even imagine doing such a terrible thing."

"I wonder why you disliked her so much?" she said.

"Because she didn't have any of the decent, ordinary
virtues," I answered. "She didn't know anything about
them. Not charity, nor gratitude, nor kindness, nor honesty, nor modesty, nor—nor anything."

"Isn't it strange that twin sisters, who looked as much
alike as these girls did, should be so entirely different as
to character?"

I had not seen her notes at that time. I did not know
that she had written "Innocent" after Danny's name. I
spoke up, pretty hotly.

"Strange or not, it is true. In character those two girls
were as different as night and day. I never even thought
that they looked alike. Who told you that they did?"

"I have seen their photographs," she reminded me.
"Chadwick Caufield's album is filled with them."

"Their photographs may look alike. They didn't."

"But they *did,*" she insisted.

"I tell you," I said, "that they acted so differently, and
talked so differently, and dressed so differently, that there
was not one bit of likeness."

"A most unusual state of affairs for duplicate twins. These sunshine and tempest relationships are seldom found, outside a Mary J. Holmes' novel. Miss Danielle Canneziano came here on a most doubtful errand; an errand that amounted to robbery, nothing else—"

"If you are accusing Danny—" I interrupted.

"Oh, I am not!" There was a flash of temper in that. "Making all allowances for mistakes in time, Miss Canneziano could not have committed the murder herself. But, suppose that her past was not as innocent and blameless as she would like to have you all think. Suppose that a revelation of all she knows, or suspects, concerning her sister's death, would also bring to light things that she can not afford to have brought to light concerning herself. It is at least reasonable to think that she knows more than she is willing to tell."

"Maybe," I had to admit. "But I doubt it."

"Why do you so dislike that admission?"

"Because John loves her. John is a good boy. I'd hate to see his heart broken."

"Will you forgive me for saying that young Mr. Stanley does not impress me as a man who is very deeply in love?"

"I know," I agreed. "Just now he is a mite put out with Danny. He has been, ever since she accused Sam."

"Considering the circumstances under which Miss Canneziano made that accusation, young Mr. Stanley is acting most unjustly—if that is the case."

"All men are unjust to the women they love," I told her. "It seems to be a part of it, like a rash with measles."

She smiled at that, and changed the subject.

"I wonder whether you noticed," she said, "that coming up from the station I set a trap for Miss Canneziano. Just for an instant, I fancied that there was more fear than grief in her attitude toward meeting her father. I suggested, you remember, that she see him alone? I wanted to see whether she desired a private interview with him. Her prompt refusal made it evident that she had no secret to give to him, and expected to get none from him. That is in her favor. Still—

"Before you go now, since you have agreed to help me, do you mind if I direct a bit? I want you to keep one eye on Miss Canneziano. I want you to keep the other eye on Mr. Canneziano, Mr. Hand, and Mrs. Ricker. Will you do that?"

"One whole eye for Danny," I questioned, "and only a third of an eye for each of the others?"

"For the present," she smiled. "Will you do that?"

I said that I would. It was not until after dinner the next day, when I was resting in my own room, feeling as virtuous as the three monkeys, who see no evil, hear no evil, speak no evil, pleased as Punch over my failures of the past twenty-four hours, that I realized that I just naturally could not carry through a job that went as much against the grain as that job went.

We are, I thought, allowed to know some things—just simple, honest knowing. And I knew that keeping a suspicious eye on the girl who had said "bless your heart" to me, on the evening of the second of July, was as sensible as sitting up for Santa Claus.

Someone knocked on my door. I answered the knock. Miss MacDonald, all smiles, was standing there.

"Let me come in," she said; and, as soon as my door was closed behind her, "A most fortunate thing has happened."

48
New Clues

"Someone," she went on, "has been to my desk and has stolen the code letter."

I could manage nothing but an echo. "Fortunate!" I said.

"I had a careful copy of it, locked up, of course. I have been leaving the letter in plain sight on my desk for bait. Don't you see, Mary," she forgot her formality in her excitement, "this is the mistake I have been hoping for. I have found a beginning—at last. It is bound to be easy from now on. Oh, Joy!"

She was almost doing dance steps. I wasn't. I was thinking, hard, in the tidy space in my mind; trying not to get it cluttered with her excitement, trying to cook up some common sense.

"The letter," she went on, "could not have concerned anyone in this house except Miss Canneziano, her father, and, possibly, not probably, young Mr. Stanley."

"I guess," I said, "that was likely what you were wanted to think."

Her gray eyes questioned me.

"Supposing," I answered, "that Mrs. Ricker, or Hubert Hand, or anyone of us, wanted to get you clear off the track, suspecting especially Danny, could one of us do better than to steal the code letter?"

"My word!" she said. "And you, with a mind that works like that, spending your life doing cooking."

"Doing cooking," I told her, "is how my mind comes to work like that. If anyone ever told you that it didn't take brains to cook, he was making a big mistake."

"But such quick, sure thinking, "she said, "is marvelous."

She laughed. "Listen to me doing a Dr. Watson for your Holmes," she said. "Golly, but I'm lucky to have you at hand, though."

I love to be flattered. I sat and preened myself.

"All the same," she went on, "it does prove one thing. That the murderer, or his close accomplice, is right here on the place, now."

"Chad's confession proved that. The key in the fire-place proved it, too."

"Dear me, no. Not conclusively. Now, let me see." She took a folded paper from the front of her dress. "Here is my copy of the letter. It does look a mess, doesn't it?"

I looked at the paper and read, as before:

"Paexzazlytp! f-y nyx ogrgrago, rn fgao atf jan j-asn, ahzgo zkg c-. ahhalo, vkgt nyx clplzgf rg zkg kypulzae, zkaz nyx. . . ."

It surely looked a mess.

"The fact that it was written on the typewriter," she said, "makes me suspect that the typewriter may unwrite it for us."

I told her then what I had not thought to tell her be-fore; about my having heard the typewriter going, slowly, in Gaby's room right after she had received the letter.

"Fine!" she said. "She had burned the caps for the keys, too—all but the curly 'Q' that rolled away. May I use the same typewriter that she used?"

We went together into Gaby's room.

"I should have thought you'd want to clean this room, first of all," I said.

"Mr. Stanley unlocked it for me that first night. I spent five or six very busy hours in here, and I slept here that night, too."

"Upon my soul! Doesn't that go to show? I'd have taken oath in any court that you spent the night in your own room."

"That is exactly it," she said. "Honest people are so sure that they know things, which they don't know at all, and that they have seen things, which they haven't seen."

I have wished, since, that I had said something else instead of saying, "Well, I might think I knew something which I didn't know; but I'd never make a mistake about what I had seen or had not seen."

"Perhaps not—" she said.

"Did you find anything in here that night?" I questioned.

"Nothing. The burned papers were completely burned, as they usually are. Of course, the complete absence of clues should be made into a valuable clue—but I haven't quite worked it out. For instance, though, you insist that she was a vain, conceited person?"

"If ever there was one."

"Vain women usually have photographs of themselves about. I found not one in here."

"She used to have one, in a silver frame," I said. I looked around and saw the frame lying face down on the mantel. I picked it up. An old faded picture of Sam and Margarita in their wedding togs confronted me. I had seen it plenty of times before, but in the old album downstairs.

When I had shown it to Miss MacDonald, and had told her about it, she took it and carried it to the window.

"The glass has been washed, carefully," she said, "since the picture was put in here."

She pressed on the purple velvet back and took the picture from the frame. Across the bottom of the picture, where the wide silver frame had hidden it, written in Gaby's bold handwriting, were these words.

"My one deadly enemy."

"My word!" said Miss MacDonald.

"Are you certain," she questioned, next, "that the girl's mother is not living?"

"Don't ask me to be certain of anything," I said, and looked for a chair to sit down in.

She came and put one of her capable hands on my shoulders. "You shouldn't let this trouble you," she said. "It is more than likely that Gabrielle Canneziano had nothing to do with it. I must verify the handwriting."

In the next instant she certainly gave me a fine turn. Her eyes went big and round, her cheeks blazed with blushes, and she clapped her hands to them and stood staring at me as if I were the original human horror. "I—" she gasped out, "I—have made a mistake."

I felt like rising and giving her a good shaking. "Lands!" I snapped. "Who hasn't?"

"I would discharge one of my assistants like that," she snapped her fingers, "for such a mistake. Crime analyst! Confounded ass! Conceited amateur! Oh!" She went running out of the room, leaving me sitting there to do what I liked with that talk of hers.

She was back in two minutes. She had Gaby's last note to Danny in her hands. "I have been assuming," she said, and her cheeks flamed up again, "that Gabrielle Canneziano wrote this note. I have had a pleasant little assumption. Now I will get some facts. I must find a sample of her handwriting—"

She began to search through Gaby's desk. I helped her. Gaby had made a thorough job of her burning. There was not a scratch of her writing to be found.

"Danny will have something," I said. "I'll see whether she is in her room."

Danny was in her room, sitting at her own desk, writing out checks and addressing envelopes. I told her I had come to ask her for a sample of Gaby's handwriting.

"I am sorry, Mary," she said, as she finished addressing an envelope, sealed it, and looked for a stamp in the stamp-box, "but I haven't anything, except, of course, the last note she wrote to me, and Miss MacDonald is keeping that."

"Please dear," I urged, "won't you search through your desk and your papers? It is really very important."

"But I have looked, Mary. Mrs. Ricker had the same idea, yesterday. She thought that Gaby might not have written that last note. I am certain that she did; but I searched and searched to satisfy Mrs. Ricker. I destroyed Gaby's letters to me, when we came to the United States. She has had no reason for writing anything to me since then. Hubert Hand had several notes from her; but he says he has not kept them."

She addressed another envelope, and added it to the pile beside her. "It isn't," she said, noticing my reluctance to leave, "that I am not interested, Mary. It is only that I know that I haven't a scrap of her writing."

I turned to go. I had reached the door when she called to me and asked me to take her letters downstairs for the mailbag, when I went downstairs.

I returned to Miss MacDonald with my information.

"Dear me!" she said. "Mrs. Ricker indeed? If only they would work with me, Mary, instead of by themselves, or— against me. At any rate," she put aside the photograph, a ruler-like thing, and her magnifying glass, "the note to Danielle Canneziano, and the writing on the photograph were done by the same person. What are the letters you have there, in your hand, Mrs. Magin?"

I told her they were some that Danny had asked me to take downstairs. She held out her hand for them. I had to allow her to have them. But first I read the addresses. They were the names of mail-order stores in Portland, Oregon, and in San Francisco, California.

Miss MacDonald looked at them closely. Then she took up a flat paper knife, from Gaby's desk, and deliberately opened the envelope by lifting the flap.

"She surely does not seal her letters carefully," she said, and took out a check, nothing else, from the envelope.

"It is dated to-day, the thirteenth of July," she said.

"Of course it is," I answered, tartly, not liking any of this. "She was writing them just now, while I was in there."

"Did you see her writing them?" she asked.

"I certainly did."

She sighed and moved her head with an impatient gesture, rather like John's worried gestures. "Then that is that," she said, and returned the check to the envelope, sealed the envelope, and gave it, with the others, back to me.

"Now for the code letter," she said, and sat down in front of the typewriter. I left her there, and went to look for Sam.

49
New Suspicions

I found him in the living-room, playing solitaire. Mrs. Ricker was in the chair by the window, tatting. "Lands, Sam," I said, sitting down across the table from him, "when did you take to sitting around and wasting good time like this?"

"I am helping Miss MacDonald," he said. "Making it easy for her to watch me and convincing her that I'm more or less of a nut, at the same time. Two birds with one stone—"

"She isn't watching you," Mrs. Ricker spoke up. "She is watching Hubert and me."

Queer that with all the years I had known Mrs. Ricker as a dumb person, now that she had begun to talk, her talking seemed only natural.

"I reckon," Sam said, "that she is watching all of us pretty closely."

"No," Mrs. Ricker insisted, "she is watching Hubert and me. Chiefly me. I can't stand it much longer. I am losing my mind. If I don't leave here, before long, I shall be quite insane."

I can't say that Sam's ears actually pricked up when she said that, but they gave that impression.

"I didn't know that you were thinking about leaving here, Mrs. Ricker," he said.

"I am thinking about it; because, if I don't leave here, soon, I shall have to be taken—to an insane asylum."

"Now, now, Mrs. Ricker," Sam urged, "don't be feeling like that. It is just a case of watch and let watch around here, now—"

"It certainly is not a case of live and let live," she said. "I tell you, I can't stand it!" She jumped up from her chair, and went rushing out of the room through the front door. On the porch she dropped into a chair, and hid her face in her hands.

As I looked at her, sitting there, I remembered that it was she who had found the body. Her story had sounded straight enough; but, before she had told it, she had had plenty of time to make it a straight one. Perhaps she had had help in making it a straight one. . . .

Hubert Hand. He had, by his own admission, served a term in prison for forgery. He had had notes from Gaby, and had destroyed them. Was it possible that he might have written the farewell note to Gaby, and the inscription on the photograph? Sam could not swear that Hubert Hand had been in the barn the entire hour between five and six o'clock. That meant, then, that no one knew, positively, where he had been between five and six o'clock. I remembered how eager he had been, at first, to prove that John was the guilty person; how readily he had accepted the theory of Martha's guilt. That theory had been Mrs. Ricker's. Mrs. Ricker loved Hubert Hand. She had loved Martha, too; but Martha was dead.

Would it have been possible for Hubert Hand to have slipped into the house, through the front door, during that hour between five and six, without Danny's having seen him? Possible—that was all. Danny had cut the bread, in the kitchen. She had emptied jelly from its glass to a dish; had cut the butter. Each task a matter of minutes; but coming through the front door and getting upstairs would be a matter of minutes, also. Mrs. Ricker, of course, would have seen Hubert Hand pass through the room; but Mrs. Ricker could keep a secret.

Again, what had he thought that I had overheard that day in the cabin?

What motive could he have had for killing Gaby? Suppose that Gaby had lied to Danny about the entire contents of the code letter, and that, after all, the money had been hidden on the place. That would be an explanation for Canneziano's coming to the ranch. But suppose that Hubert Hand had found it, or had known that Gaby had found it——

"Come home, Mary," Sam's voice, speaking extra low, cut in on my reverie. "I want to know what you think about this.

"I set Canneziano to mending the south clover fence this morning. I told him I was going to north clover. On my way there, I passed the house. I happened to remember how slick Miss MacDonald had cleaned the attic. It seemed a shame not to use it; so I went up, taking my field glasses with me, for luck. I'd watched about five minutes, out of the window, when I saw Canneziano leave the fence and make up toward the cabin. I came down, jumped on Bobbie Burns, and circled around the hill, back of the cabin. Just as I got my glasses trained, I saw Danny, walking to beat time, coming away from the cabin. I don't know whether she had been in it or not. I didn't see her come out of it. I rode straight down. Before I had quite reached the cabin, Canneziano came out of it. He was carrying a fishing rod, and he went right down to the stream with it. What I'm wondering is, had he and Danny met at the cabin, and had a talk?"

"I know exactly what Mrs. Ricker means," I said, "about losing her mind on this place. It has come to the pass that no one can do any simple thing without being spied on and suspected. Danny always takes her walks in the direction of the cabin. We all do. It is the prettiest, coolest walk on the place."

"Does she always walk so fast, trying to keep cool?"

"Probably not," I said, "unless she has seen Canneziano, and is walking fast, trying to get away from him."

Sam rubbed the back of his head. "By Joe! I hadn't thought of that."

"Think about it now, for a minute," I advised. "When you get through, try to think whether you know of any place where we could get hold of a scrap or two of Gaby's handwriting. We have the last note she wrote to Danny, but we want something more."

"You've come to the right place, for once," he said, and took a long envelope out of his pocket.

"I guess I never happened to mention to you, did I, that I fixed up a small checking account for the girls in the Telko Bank? It was just a matter of my own convenience— saved me the pesky trouble of buying money orders at the post-office. Their bank statements and canceled checks came in a few days ago. I was going to look them over, soon as I could get around to it. Here they are. Do you want me to take them up to Miss MacDonald?"

"I'll take them," I offered, "and save you the trip." I longed to see how much of Sam's money the girls had spent in one month, and what they had spent it for.

I don't know yet whether it was cunning, contrariness, or courtesy that propelled Sam up those stairs, with the envelope tight in his hand, and without having allowed me as much as a peek at its contents.

50
Shovels

I went into the kitchen and put through a fairly good batch of baking, considering that I'd got a late start at it. I had intended only to stir up a sunshine cake for supper; but when a thunder shower came, washing everything cool and sweet, I opened the kitchen wide to it, and made an angel cake out of the whites of the eggs, and baked a big pan of ginger bread. Zinnia did the washing up; so I was all through and frosting the cakes, when Miss MacDonald telephoned down to the kitchen and asked me to go for a walk with her.

Between times, I'd roasted three chickens and got a salad in the icebox. I wouldn't need to turn a hand to supper for an hour; so I told her that I'd like nothing better than a breath of the clean, sage-seasoned air, and that I'd be ready in ten minutes. I gave Zinnia a few directions, and went upstairs to change my shoes.

As I came down the front stairs, into the living-room, I saw Mrs. Ricker coming up the steps to the porch. She was toting a big old shovel; carrying it out in front of her, and carefully, right side up, like it was a pancake turner and she had a pancake on it. I stopped in my tracks. There are some connections that the mind refuses: President Coolidge with a six-gun, for instance, or Chief Justice Taft with a saxophone, or Mrs. Ricker with a heavy, dirty old shovel.

She stopped to turn sidewise and open the screen door with her foot, and then she came straight along into the living-room, poking the thing toward Miss MacDonald.

"I want you to look at this," she said.

Miss MacDonald, all crisp in white linen, backed away a mite; but she looked, as directed.

I came hurrying to look too. I don't know what I expected to see—nothing less than a dead scorpion; but, certainly, something more than I did see: an old iron shovel with dirt on it.

"Well?" Miss MacDonald questioned.

"I was going to Martha's grave when the shower came up. I stopped in the cabin. This shovel, and another one, were inside the door there. Look at that earth—it is fresh earth. Now I tell you, two people have been digging around this place; and they were at it not longer ago than yesterday, more likely this morning."

"My word!" said Miss MacDonald. It seemed to me there was more annoyance in her voice than there was interest or astonishment.

"Somebody," I pronounced, "still believes that there is money hidden around here."

Mrs. Ricker nodded her satisfaction.

"But surely," Miss MacDonald said, "around a farm, a ranch, that is, around a place of this sort there must be a great deal of digging going on. Gardens—vegetables, you know. That is—one thing and another." She fumbled it, like that.

"We don't make garden here in July," I told her. "The vegetable gardens and greenhouses are about three miles away from where Mrs. Ricker found the shovels."

"To be sure." She puckered her brows. "But—Mr. Stanley spoke of fishing. Don't the men dig worms for bait?"

"Anyone," I told her, "who did bait fishing on the Desert Moon, would be about as popular as an S.P.C.A.

convention at a round-up. Likely you'll learn our ways, in time. Bait fishing isn't one of them."

While I had been getting this off my mind, Danny had come downstairs. I guess we must have looked funny, the three of us, standing there and staring at the shovel, which Mrs. Ricker was still holding as if it were a pancake turner.

"But—what is it?" Danny inquired.

"It is a shovel," said Mrs. Ricker.

"Yes, I know. But what about it?"

"It has fresh earth on it," Mrs. Ricker explained. "It means that someone is still hunting for something on this ranch."

"I—don't understand," Danny faltered.

"You do, if anyone does," Mrs. Ricker said, trying to make it sound off-handish; but it did not.

To my surprise, Miss MacDonald answered, "I think that you are mistaken, Mrs. Ricker. Miss Canneziano knows, I fancy, no more about the shovel than you do."

Mrs. Ricker's face flushed. She carried the thing out and threw it into the yard with a gesture of furious anger. When Miss MacDonald and I passed her on the porch, she turned her head away and did not look at us.

"If we hurry," I said, "we'll have time to walk to the cabin and see the other shovel."

"Bother the other shovel! We don't want to hurry. Can't we get down to the stream, somewhere close here, and find a place where we can be alone to talk?"

"Right down this path," I answered, and started down it. She followed me. For fifty yards or more neither of us said a word. I was too put about to feel like talking.

Why should she have told me to "bother the shovel"? Why had she acted so peculiarly about the shovels, anyway; choosing to assume that they were unimportant? If, as I supposed she was thinking, Mrs. Ricker, had gone to the trouble to fix up those two shovels, and to carry one of them in, to hoodwink us, that was important. I was sure in my own mind that Ollie Ricker had not done that. If she had not, and if two people were digging around the place, they were digging for something, weren't they? For what? For exactly what I had said—for money. Worms!

I must have made a sound that was suggestive of my disgusted annoyance, for Miss MacDonald stepped up to walk beside me on the narrow path.

"I am sorry," she said, "that I have seemed so exasperatingly stupid: but I know that those shovels are of no importance."

"I don't see how you could know that," I said.

"I am sorry again: but I have promised not to tell you how I know it."

"Not to tell me!"

"I meant, of course, that I had promised not to tell anyone. My promise was made to Mr. Stanley. Since this has come up, I am sure that he will allow me to break it and tell you later what it is that I can't tell you now."

"Sam!" I said. I was mad all over. I had thought that, anyway, Sam was open and above board with me.

"You'll understand all about it, later," she said. "Please don't be vexed. I have some really good news. First, the handwriting on the checks, the photograph, and the note all tally accurately. That must mean, that Gabrielle Canneziano wrote all of them. Next, I have worked out the key to the code letter—"

"Lands alive!" I said, my astonishment and admiration getting the best of my bad humor. "In this short time? Talk about wonders—"

"Not a bit of it. The code is so simple that I am surprised that people, who have wits enough to use a code at all, would use it.

"The keys on typewriters, with a standard keyboard, are arranged, you know, for the touch system of writing:

a, s, d, f, g, so on. All that this code amounts to, is taking the letters straight as they come along: a, b, c, d; and so on. From the center line of letters, they skip to the upper line, making the 'q' be a 'j' and from the upper line down to the lower line, making the 'z' a 't.' They use only the letters on the keyboard, and the punctuation marks as they would rightly be used. Generally they put a hyphen after the letter to be capitalized, though occasionally they use the capital letter. It is so childish that I fancy it is only a friendship code, and that it is not used for matters of any real importance."

"Then this letter is of no importance?" I asked.

"Not to the writer. Of vast importance to us, I believe. It explains why the original letter was stolen, among other things. Here is one of the copies that I made of it."

51
Danielle's Secret

We had come to the stream, and to the shade of the aspen trees. I sat down on one of the rocks, above the first fishing hole, and unfolded the papers she had given to me, and read:

"Salutations! Do you remember, my dear and gay Gaby, after the V. affair, when you visited me in the hospital, that you said, with your imitated Mona Lisa smile, 'Sorry, old dear, I made a trifling mistake, did I not?' The incident has probably passed from your memory. It has not passed from mine, because I did not believe then, and I do not believe now, that you intended to fire that shot at V. instead of at me. You proved your innocence, however, like the expert you are; so, 'let the dead past—' et cetera. Particularly since I did not die, but have lived to make, also, a trifling mistake.

"I find that I was in error concerning the train robbery. After due reflection, I have remembered that, reading of the details in the Denver papers, your respected father and I merely regretted that we had not had the forethought, and the cleverness, to have pulled the affair ourselves. Since this is the case, we could not have hidden the money, as I seem to recall telling you that we did, on the Desert Moon Ranch. It was a pretty dream of ours—that was all.

"Shall I explain? Do you remember the sweet cocotte with the colored sash at Cannes? Very young, very exquisite, and almost very innocent? She watched us, from her table, out of the violet corners of her long, long eyes. When we left the place, you and I, my gloves were missing and I returned for them. You were duped, my dear, were you not?

"She is not as lovely, not as gay as you were at eighteen. But you are no longer eighteen. And you have grown exacting, and a bit vicious (recalling, again, the V. affair), and a bit selfish, too. (I knew that you collected the final five hundred pounds from Baron T.)

"These, and all things considered, I seem to myself to have acted rather nobly, rather compassionately. I spared you the heartache of witnessing your supplantation. Ours was a tender leave taking, was it not? I paid the expenses of a long and costly journey for you and the gentle Danielle. (Gad, Gay, I'd have paid twice as much to be rid of you for half the time!) I sent you to fond relatives. I provided you with an interesting and romantic occupation—treasure hunting. I gave the righteous Danielle the opportunity for which she was pining; the opportunity to try her hand at turning you into 'an honest woman.'

"Tell her, by the way, that her lover, or as she virtuously insisted, her husband is still with me, and that he is behaving himself admirably. I suspect that my Lili is a bit over fond of him; but I have warned her that one who has had the chaste affections of the little nun would be unlikely to succumb to her ardencies.

"Lili now inquires to whom am I writing. She is eighteen; she has seen you; so I dare tell her, to you, in a far country with an amusing name—Nevada.

"She mispronounces it, deliciously. She blows it, and you, charmingly away from the tips of her tiny pink fingers. She kisses my ears. She tells me that she owns me. So,

I suppose, I should not sign myself, as of old, Yours, with an ever increasing devotion, Bimbi."

"Good lands alive!" I said. My stomach hurt me, and my head ached.

"I am sorry for young Mr. Stanley," Miss MacDonald said. "But, you see, I was right in thinking that Miss Canneziano's life might hold a secret."

"No! No!" Danny stood there in front of us, holding to an aspen tree for support.

"I wondered whether you were coming out from behind the tree," Miss MacDonald said.

"I saw you looking at me. You are cruel. You are very cruel."

For a minute all I could be was sorry for Danny. I got up and went to her and put an arm around her.

She tucked her head down on my breast. She was so small that I could look right over it, at Miss MacDonald, sitting there, undisturbed and triumphant. She was in the right, and was a good girl; so it was queer that the sight of her made my heart go straight out to the wrong, bad, little Danny, with her brown head underneath my chin.

"Danny, honey," I said, "are you planning a divorce, after you've had your six months in Nevada? Was he cruel to you? Unfaithful?"

"No, no," she said. "Nothing like that, nothing at all. I can explain every word of it. But will anyone believe me?"

"You just try it," I urged. "I'm all set for believing you, right here and now. Come over here, and rest, and tell us all about it."

I led her across to the rock where I had been sitting, and made a place for her beside me.

52

An Explanation

She began, right straight forward and sensible: "I knew that was in the letter, and I longed to destroy it, on that account, but I was afraid. I knew that its disappearance would throw all sorts of suspicions on me. But this morning, when I saw the thing, right there on her desk, the temptation was too great. I never thought of her having made a copy of it. This afternoon, when I heard her at the typewriter—I knew. I've been in torment ever since. I have prayed and prayed that she might fail to work out the code. When I came downstairs, just now, I knew that she had not failed. I thought she would tell you about it; so I followed. I thought, perhaps, if I'd tell you both the truth, and plead with you to believe me— But now I am ashamed to offer it.

"You won't believe me. John won't believe me— But, it was only a doll: one of those funny, long-legged, floppy things, with an adorable face. I saw him in Paris, and loved him, and bought him for mine. I called him Christopher Clover, and said that he was my husband—because I had always said that I would never marry. Lewis he was so horrid about everything—used to tease me about my lover, until I got so tired of it, and so ashamed, that I put him away on a closet shelf.

"After we were all packed, and the trunks were locked, that last day, I found him there on the shelf. Gaby wanted me to carry him on my arm—that was done quite a bit over there. She thought it was *chic;* but I thought it looked silly. I was going to leave him in the apartment; but Lewis asked me to let him have him. I did. That is all. But—will you let me see the copy of the letter? Gaby read it to me only once."

I gave it to her.

"See," she said, eagerly, "he calls me righteous. See how he speaks of the doll and his—Lili. He wouldn't have spoken like that about a man, nor said that he was behaving himself. See, too, he calls me a nun. If you'll be fair—it seems to me you can easily believe me."

"Honey child," I said, and spoke the truth. "I do believe you. It is sensible and reasonable. I believe every word you've told us."

"And you?" she appealed to Miss MacDonald.

"Your explanation is reasonable. You have told the truth about everything else in the letter. Certainly, I shall give you the benefit of the doubt."

"You won't tell John?" Danny pleaded.

"Of course not. Nor anyone else, just now. Shall we go back to the house?"

Danny and I sat still.

"I'll run along, then," she said, and went away without us.

"Danny," I began at once, "you take my advice. You get to John as quickly as you can and tell him the truth about this. He loves you. He'll want to believe you. Men always believe whatever they want to believe. Don't you worry another mite about it."

"Have you noticed," she questioned, slowly, "that John has been different—very different, ever since—"

"We've all been different, dear," I told her.

"Yes, I know. But—John has been more different. Mary, tell me, am I silly? Have you noticed that John seems to be very much interested in this Miss MacDonald? He looks at her all the time. And he jumps about, waiting on her, rather as Chad used to do with Gaby. Of course, he feels that I have changed, too. And I have. I can't keep from showing how unhappy I am, and how worried. I suppose I constantly disappoint him. And yet . . ."

"Danny," I said, "it is just this. Men don't wear well in times of trouble. They can't help it. It is the way they are mixed. So we women put up with it. We have to, if we put up with men at all. Everything is going to come out all right. But I want you to tell John, yourself, about your doll and not wait for someone else to do it."

"I'll try to," she agreed. "But we are so rarely alone together any more."

On our way back to the house, Sam and John overtook us. I got Sam to walk along fast with me, and left them lagging behind us.

"I'm a mite worried," Sam said, "about those two young folks. I don't quite make them out, here lately. I suggested to John, a while ago, that considering Danny's trouble, and all, it might be just as well for them to have an early wedding. Told him to talk it over with Danny, and that any date they set would be all right with me.

"I was all braced against being carried off and drowned in a torrent of gratitude. No, siree. That young whelp evaded it. Said that he'd see; and that she'd say that right after so much trouble might not be a suitable time for a wedding. I'd give a pretty to know what he has on his mind. I can't think that the boy is just rotten fickle. And yet—he has been shining up to Miss MacDonald, here of late. Have you noticed it, Mary?"

"Noticed, nothing!" was the best that I could do.

53
Another Murder

Canneziano did not come down for breakfast the following morning. I thought that a little strange, for meals were the one thing he had been real polite to ever since he had been on the Desert Moon.

As soon as breakfast was over, Miss MacDonald spoke to Sam and asked him, as she had asked him that first morning, if she might detain him. "You, also, Mrs. Magin," she smiled at me.

"I wonder," she said, as soon as we three were alone together, "if Mr. Canneziano could have given us the slip, last night?"

"Not likely, with ten of the boys all drawing wages for watching the place, and him in particular, is it?" Sam questioned.

"Not at all likely. Still. . . . Will you go and see whether or not he is in his room, now, Mr. Stanley?"

Sam went. When he came back he had to drawl a lot more than usual to keep his voice steady. "His door is locked. He doesn't answer when I pound on it."

Miss MacDonald said, "I have an excellent pass key. Let's go up and try it."

Curiosity dragged me along with her and Sam, though every bone in my body protested.

Miss MacDonald's key unlocked the door. The three of us went into the room.

The blinds were tightly drawn. The electric fan was whirring and buzzing away in the gray gloom.

Miss MacDonald crossed the room, quickly, and snapped up the blinds. There was one long, hard, dusty shaft of yellow sunlight. Sam walked through it to the bed where Canneziano was lying, huddled up under the covers. I looked the other way.

I heard the rattle of Sam's pipe as it fell on the floor. I heard the rustle of Miss MacDonald's quick movement. I heard a queer, throaty note that she uttered. Something dragged my hot, aching eyes open. I looked toward the bed. I saw Canneziano's swollen, discolored face. I saw the deep yellow throat, with great brutal bruises at its base. The shaft of sunlight moved up and down, up and down, carving through the swaying blackness like a long sharp knife.

I felt Sam's strong hands on my shoulders, pressing me down into a chair. I heard myself saying, shrilly, over and over, "What are we going to do? What are we going to do?"

It was Miss MacDonald's voice, cold and clear as spring water that brought me to my senses. "We are going to find the murderer on the Desert Moon Ranch."

Sam said, "You're damn right we are. And we are going to have half a dozen he-men detectives on this place by to-morrow night."

"Very well," Miss MacDonald answered. "Will you telephone, at once, for the coroner, Mr. Stanley?"

"Hell!" Sam said.

I had my face covered; but there was a hollowness in that oath of Sam's that told me, plainer than any looking at him could have told me, that he was frightened; scared to the marrow of his bones.

It took Miss MacDonald, though, to understand the reason for his fear.

"Yes, Mr. Stanley," she said, "these men, when they come this time, in spite of their friendship for you, are not going to be as easily satisfied as they were last time. They were able to blink at one murder. They can't keep on blinking. They dare not—even in Nevada."

"Who wants them to blink?" Sam bluffed.

"You do. We all do, for the present."

Sam did not answer that. He stood, and looked stupid.

"Won't you listen to reason," she urged, "before you go downstairs to telegraph for other detectives? In talking to you this way, I am putting all of my pride behind me, and I am violating my own code of professional ethics; so I want to say, first, that if you will allow me to remain on this case, I'll take not one cent in payment. Wait— Let me have my say out, and then you may have yours. My motives are not entirely unselfish—motives seldom are. For one thing, I have never been dismissed from a case. It is a humiliation I would pay any price to avoid. I have other reasons—but no matter. That is my side of it.

"Your side of it is this. If, when the coroner and the others arrive to-day, you confess that no progress has been made, they will undoubtedly step in and take matters into their own bungling hands. I think that they would make an arrest. That would be fatal, now. For I am positive that they would arrest an innocent person, and that the guilty person would then have an excellent opportunity for escape.

"I have a certain reputation, Mr. Stanley, and these men—particularly the sheriff—respect it. If you will keep me on this case, I will tell them that I am making definite progress. That I believe I shall be able to turn the criminal over to the state within a comparatively short time—"

"Would that be the truth?" Sam demanded.

She hesitated. "If you mean, is that what I believe now—my answer is yes. I may be wrong. I have, at least, a very definite suspicion. I have no proofs."

"You wouldn't," Sam questioned, "give these men that assurance if you knew that I was going to get some men detectives up here to work with you?"

"I couldn't," she said. "I can speak only for myself. I do not, can not work with detectives not of my own choosing. I would give any one you brought here my notes—the definite results of my investigations so far. I would have no right, now, to give him anything else."

"In other words," Sam said, "you don't care a whoop about having the murderer discovered unless you can do the discovering yourself, and get the credit for it?"

"Sam Stanley!" I said.

Her cheeks flamed. "Please get your other detectives here as soon as possible, if you wish them to consult with me before I leave for San Francisco."

John's voice came calling down the hall. "Dad? Are you up here?"

"Wait!" Miss MacDonald commanded. "Tell him to wait a moment."

Sam opened the door a crack. "I'll be with you in a minute, son." He closed the door, and stood looking questions at Miss MacDonald.

She walked quickly across the room, and stopped close to Sam, facing him. "I'm sorry I lost my temper, just now. I'm not going, unless you force me to go. Please don't. Please give me my chance. Do you realize what it means to be tried for a murder, even if one is acquitted? I am not asking this for myself. I wouldn't stoop to beg for anything for myself as I am begging for this, now. I am sure you mean to be a fair man. Be fair to me, and to all of the innocent people here on your ranch. I don't say that other detectives might not be able to discover the murderer. I do say that I am certain they would do irreparable harm before they succeeded. . . ."

"If you stayed," Sam had the cheek to question, "and worked along with them—that was my idea—couldn't you prevent their doing any harm?"

"I could try to. I will try to, if you insist. But I am doubtful of my success. Consciously, or unconsciously they work against me, because I am a woman. You don't know them as I do. You don't know their methods, as I do. If you feel that you must have others here, working on the case, allow me to send, at my own expense, for my own assistants; the girls whom I have trained—"

"We don't need any more girls around here," Sam said. "It is pretty certain that we do need someone to protect the lives of all of us on this place—"

"When you telephone for the coroner," she said, "won't you telephone for a locksmith to come out with him, and bring strong bolts for all the doors—"

"You admit, then, that we are all in danger?"

"Nothing of the sort. You are all perfectly safe—at present. I do believe that before long, my own life may be in danger. I want no one to think that I suspect that. I need the protection of the bolts. It must seem that I think that everyone needs the protection."

"You believe," Sam questioned, "that your own life is in danger. And yet—"

"Please re-consider, Mr. Stanley. Please allow me to have the case alone, at any rate for a little while longer."

"Game!" Sam had muttered it to himself, but I had heard it. I knew that she had won, for the present, at any rate.

"You honestly think," he questioned, "that you can manage this single handed, and keep us all safe, and produce this murderer—pretty shortly?"

"I do, Mr. Stanley."

"And you honestly think that other detectives coming here now might make a peck of trouble, arrest the wrong person, and mess things up generally?"

"I have never been more certain of anything. I think the fact that you dismissed me, now, and sent for others, would be damning evidence against innocence, to the men from Telko.

"Let me meet them, in my professional capacity, to-day, Mr. Stanley. Let me meet them, not as a failure, but as a person confident of success. I know that I can manage them, and send them away satisfied. Mary, can't you say something? Won't you help me to persuade Mr. Stanley?"

"You don't need any help," I told her. "He's persuaded."

"Is that true, Mr. Stanley? May I have the case alone, for a little while longer?" She was all breathless with eagerness.

"Drat it all, yes," Sam said. "I'm damned if I know what I ought to do. But you are dead game. I—Well, shake on it, Miss MacDonald. You'll do the best you can for us, I know that."

The hand she held out to him was trembling, and her voice as she thanked him trembled. But still I was amazed when, right after Sam had gone out of the room, she said to me, "Mary, I believe on my soul that I have just had an experience that is too strong for me," and hid her face in the crook of her arm and began to cry.

54
Delay

I myself heard the sheriff say to Sam, late in the afternoon of the day we had found Canneziano, strangled in his bed, "I tell you what, Sam, this is a pretty dirty business—all of it. If you had anyone but Lynn MacDonald on the case, I reckon it would be up to us boys to step in and take a hand. But she has sure given us some pretty good dope—and we're waiting. She's got the rep. There's that Doling-fetter movie murder. She put that through when all the police force and all the dicks in the country had failed for a year. And the Van Muiter case—and a dozen others. I know you're square, Sam. All us guys around here know it. But I'm damn glad you've got Lynn MacDonald on the job to prove it to the country."

As I say, I heard that conversation with my own ears. And yet, in the week that followed, I had times of thinking that, anyway, Sam had likely made a mistake in keeping Miss MacDonald on, alone.

I couldn't begin to describe the horror of that week. It is, I suppose, what books call a paradox to say that the worst thing about the week was that nothing, just nothing, happened. To all outward appearances the Desert Moon Ranch was as peaceful as an empty grave: hollow peace, false peace, and all of us conniving at the falsity made it worse.

One day, for instance, when we were all at dinner, Zinnia dropped the teakettle in the kitchen. We women all screamed. Sam whipped his six-gun from his back pocket. John rushed to the kitchen. He came back, wiping the sweat from his forehead.

"Zinnia dropped the teakettle. It didn't hurt her."

We all looked foolish, and began to be very busy, passing things, and pretending that our actions had all been the ordinary, conservative actions of people who had heard anything heavy dropped.

Sam locked up the house early every evening. Then, trying to make it casual, one and another of us would go sauntering around to make sure that he hadn't overlooked a door, or a window. People were constantly jumping, and starting, and looking behind them at nothing. None of us women ever went far from the house, except Mrs. Ricker to visit Martha's grave. For one thing, Sam had increased the guard around the place, and I never felt sure, when I ran down to the dairy, that one of the cowpunchers wouldn't think I was trying to escape and take a shot at me. For another thing, though both murders had been done in the house, there was a feeling of safety about four walls that I couldn't get in the open air.

As I have said, Mrs. Ricker went every day to visit Martha's grave. She went alone. I would not have gone with her, not for any price. I was afraid of her. I was afraid of Hubert Hand. By Wednesday of that week I was afraid of everyone in the house except Miss MacDonald and Sam. Friday found me doubtful of Sam.

Losing my mind? Of course I was, or it was losing itself in the black shadow of crime, by which the Desert Moon had been eclipsed. A mind can't go straight, in darkness, any more than a body can. None of our minds went straight, those days. I am sure that the mind of each one of us on the place—always excepting Miss MacDonald's—

did as mine did. It went groping in the dark; it bumped
into obstacles of doubt; it tripped over fear and fell into
senseless stupidities; it lost its way, and wandered into
wild suspicions. I tell you, there were times, during those
frightful days, when I found myself seriously considering
whether or not I had committed the two murders.

On Thursday evening, of that week, Mrs. Ricker said to
me, with no concern at all in her manner, "I wish I knew
just how that lethal chamber that they use for executions
in this state, felt. Whether it hurts to be executed that
way, and how long it takes to die in it, and all about it.

"Because," she went on, still unconcernedly, "if it
didn't hurt too much, I'd much rather confess to the murders, and get it over, than to keep on living like this. I am
going insane. I think that I can't stand another week like
this one. Every hour, now, is worse than a quick, painless
death. Too, I'm afraid of what I might do, if I go clear
mad, with all these horrors in my mind. Though, perhaps,
I have already gone mad. Do I seem to you to be insane,
right now, Mary?"

I told her no. But it was a flat lie. At that moment I was
certain that everyone on the place was more or less insane,
especially Miss MacDonald. I think yet that I was right
about the others. I know, now, that I was wrong about
Miss MacDonald; but she had certainly given me plenty
of reasons for thinking either that she had lost her senses
entirely, or else that she had never had any to lose.

Apparently, after Sam had agreed to keep her on the
case, she had at once given up all interest in it. She had a
short talk with me, and told me that she would no longer
need my help, and expressly instructed me to stop watching Danny and the others.

"As far as it is humanly possible," she said, "I want you
to go about the business of living as if nothing at all un-
pleasant, even, had happened. I don't want this to be an
appearance. I want it to be a fact."

Then, as if she knew I couldn't follow those fool instructions, and as if she were bound to have them followed at any cost, she began to follow them herself. She got sort of childish about it.

On Tuesday evening she produced a bunch of paper and some pencils. When we had all thought that something important was going to happen, she suggested that we play that old, silly game of "Consequences." And when we one and all had other things to do, she was none too pleasant about it. Said that she was tired of reading, every evening, and that the radio made her nervous. She fussed about, until Danny, feeling as she did, got John and Hubert Hand to make up the four to play Bridge.

All week I could see Sam watching her and growing more and more impatient. On Thursday he said to me that she was too busy flirting with John to have time for anything else. That was not fair. She didn't flirt with John— she wasn't the sort who would flirt with anyone. But she surely did begin to notice him, and his attentions to her. It was not that she treated him too well, in any way. It was, only, that she did not treat him quite according to our standards for the way unengaged girls should treat engaged or married men. Not once did she encourage him to neglect Danny; but, after John had neglected her, Miss MacDonald seemed to be, usually, right on the spot, ready, waiting and willing, to be pleasant and friendly to him.

I tried to make excuses for John. Poor little Danny wasn't, I had to admit, much like the girl he had fallen in love with. She had lost practically all of her prettiness, and she looked, all the time, too white and wan and generally dragged out to seem quite wholesome. Like the rest of us, the strain of fear and suspicion was too much for her; but she was frailer than any of us, so the strain told harder on her.

She had explained to John about the reference to her and to her doll in the code letter. He had taken it all right, and had been, as she said to me, "sweet" about it, and about never doubting her word at all. Still, I sort of thought that a grain of suspicion might still be bothering him. And I knew that he had not been quite able to forgive her, not for telling of her suspicions concerning Sam, but for suspecting Sam in the first place.

Yes, I could make some excuses for John. But the process of trying not to blame him, personally, resulted in my opinions of men in general being forced down several degrees. As I may have suggested, that took them just about to where the thermometer stops registering.

On Friday morning, when Sam came zigzagging into my kitchen, ordered Zinnia out of it, his voice all thick and husky, and fell down into a chair, I did not doubt for a minute that he was dead drunk. I knew that he had not touched a drop of liquor for forty years; but what men could do, men might do, and worse.

"Mary," he said, "we've got the report from the 'Frisco chemists."

55

The Third Murder

Miss MacDonald had thought it necessary to have Martha's body exhumed and sent to San Francisco. That is what the coroner and the undertaker had been about on their second trip to the ranch. Sam had not wanted any of us to know about it, particularly he had not wanted Mrs. Ricker to know. That had suited Miss MacDonald better, too; so they had had the men do the work while we were all at dinner that day. They had been careful to fix the grave so that it would not show that it had been disturbed; and then, being men, they had left their shovels right there in the cabin for the first person to find. As you know, the first person had been Mrs. Ricker.

We had been waiting ever since for the chemist's report. Sam's looks and actions, now, kept the question from my lips. I thought that the report must have contained some new horror. In a way, it had; but Sam's first words were reassuring.

"It is too good to be true," he said, and repeated, dazedly, "too good to be true. Miss MacDonald had her assistants trace the prescription from Doctor Roe. The powders were harmless. I didn't cause my girl's death. The report proves—Miss MacDonald says— The report proves—"

"Take it easy, Sam. What does the report prove?"

"Somebody gave her a deadly poison. The chemists found two traces. One they can't analyze. That's why they've kept us waiting so long for the report. They are still working on it, hoping for results. The other was nitrobenzene. Miss MacDonald says that, in small doses, induces coma and takes as long as twenty-four hours to act. But it is apt not to be deadly by itself. It was combined with this other drug—the one that must have made death certain."

Miss MacDonald came hurrying into the kitchen. She was holding the monkey charm bracelet in her hand.

"See here," she said, "this bangle thing opens. I think we can be certain that the poison she took, or was given, came out of it. There is a trace of the odor. Smell it."

She handed it to me. It smelled a little like shoe polish, with sort of a faint almond flavoring, underneath. I gave it to Sam, who had been reaching out his hand for it. He smelled it, and then knotted it up in his fist.

Remembering, I can't think of anything that he said which would do to quote. The gist of it was, that if Gaby had given Martha the poison, he was not sorry that Gaby had been killed, because justice had been done. He went on to say that, if she had not given it to Martha purposely, but only carelessly, forgetting its deadliness, he reckoned that things had turned out for the best, as far as Gaby was concerned, anyway. Not satisfied with that, he expressed, violently, his regrets that vengeance had been taken out of his hands.

"It isn't vengeance you want, Mr. Stanley," Miss Mac-Donald reminded him, pretty sternly, "but justice. That is within our reach. I am practically certain that the person who poisoned Martha, who strangled Miss Canneziano and her father, is right here on this place—"

"Hold on," Sam interrupted. "Considering that this person is a poisoner and a strangler, and that he is around loose and careless, and that we may all be murdered in our beds, or out of 'em, or poisoned at our meals, it seems to me the next move is to telephone to the sheriff, and have him out here in a hurry, with some men—"

"Nothing of the sort," Miss MacDonald snapped at him. "I have told you before, and I tell you again, that as matters stand now I am the only person on the ranch who is in the least danger. I did not say that I was certain. I said that I was practically certain. I can't be certain until I have some proof, some evidence. At present, I have not one scrap of either—"

"Then you can't know who the guilty person is."

"Exactly what I have just said. My work from now on is to get that proof. If you would help me, instead of—"

Sam interrupted, his whole body straining forward with his eagerness. "Tell us who he is, and where he is, and we'll help you, right enough."

"I can't tell you. Not unless you want to have still another murder on the Desert Moon Ranch. But you can help me. First, by keeping the discovery of the poison a secret. Second, by allowing everyone else on the place to suppose that I am still in a state of entire bafflement concerning the crime. Third, and most important, perhaps, by having patience with me."

"Ye'a," Sam said, "and while we are sitting around, having patience, this bird will walk off to some green hill far away. I think the boys are doing their best to guard the place, but this bird's a slicker. What's to keep him from, say, dressing in my clothes some night, and riding merrily away on Bobbie Burns or Wishbone? All he'd have to do is to give the boys a high-sign and they'd let him ride to hell, if they thought he was me. Another thing—I can't trust all my punchers. Some of them are greasers, some half-breeds. Money, and not much of it, talks pretty loud to some of those boys."

"At present, the person I suspect has no intention of leaving the place."

"When you don't know anything else, how can you know that?"

"I didn't say that I didn't know anything else."

"Do you know, and will you tell me, why you can't put this fellow where the dogs won't bite him, while you are collecting the proof, evidence, and so on that you think you need?"

"For one reason, because I am not a police detective. Sometimes it is necessary to use their methods of arresting each suspect and getting the evidence afterward—third degrees, so on. That method, by the way, accounts for the number of criminals who are able to make complete escapes. It is a stupid, bungling method—and a brutal one. I detest it. I have used it only twice in the seven years that I have been in this work. I used it then because it was necessary. I will not use it now, because it is not necessary. This case will come to the grand jury complete, with indisputable proofs. If I had known—suspected I mean, before Mr. Canneziano was killed, what I now suspect—" She stopped short, evidently afraid of saying too much.

"Ye'a," Sam argued, "but nothing has happened since then. What I can't get, is how you think you are ever going to find the proof—the evidence."

"Well—" she began. "Because," she finished, quite tartly, and walked out of the room.

"'Because,'" Sam mimicked, almost before she was out of hearing distance. "It was a black day for me, and for the Desert Moon, when I put this thing up to a 'because' woman."

I more than half agreed with him, but I was not going to let him know it. "Did you notice," I questioned, chiefly to turn his mind from the subject of "because" women, "that she kept saying that she thought the person she suspected was on the place? I mean—she didn't say that he was living in the house."

"House! Hell! Of course she didn't say house. Why should she say house? Haven't we been over and over it? Aren't we fair frazzled out, every last one of us, from climbing up those front and back stairs, with our minds, all day long and half the night? Counting minutes, counting seconds; going to the barn and back, over and over. Nobody who lives in this house could have done it. That is settled. That is fact. Not unless some one of us was able to be in two places at the same time between four and five o'clock that day."

Something clicked in my mind. I declare to goodness, I felt the click, plain as a twinge of toothache. It scared me. I put both my hands over the place in the front of my head. I felt as dazed, and as shaken, as if I had been sleep-walking, and had bumped into a door, in the dark, and wakened to find myself in a strange, brightly lighted room.

"No sir-ee," Sam went on, too busy with his own ideas, "I suppose, to notice my actions, which must have been peculiar, "if the murderer is still on the place, he is skulking around here in hiding. It is that strangler fellow, all right. I'll bet my last dollar on it. For some reason, he is trying to clean out the Canneziano family—all of them. I'll bet he told Martha to give the poison to Danny, not knowing what a child Martha was—or, maybe, knowing it. Martha, supposing the poison was candy, or something nice, ate it up herself. I tell you what, I'm going to do some proof hunting, now, on my own hook. If I find some stranger hiding out on this place, that will be good enough proof for Sam Stanley, and for any jury in Nevada.

"Of course, Mary, it hasn't been so hard on you—not having to feel the responsibility the way I have. But I've come to the end of my rope. I'm going to use my own head, now. I've got to get an expert here, for one thing, to watch and guard over Danny. . . . Say, what's the matter with you, Mary? You look so funny. Do you feel sick, or something?"

"'Something,'" I said, "but, at that, I suppose it isn't near as bad as feeling responsibility."

If I'd stayed there listening to him for one more minute I'd have burst. I left him, and went running, like the crazy thing I was, up the back stairs to my own room.

56

A Whisper

I stayed in my room for half an hour, thinking with all my might that I was thinking. At the end of that time, discovering that I had not turned out one single rational thought, I gave it up and went to find John.

I forgot all about the men who were guarding the ranch. I went straight down to the outfit's quarters. I hadn't been on the back of a horse for more than ten years. I got a lazy puncher to stop doing nothing long enough to saddle an old nag for me, and boost me up on her, and off I went.

Jogging along through the clean, clear air, I at last began really to do some thinking. I came to my senses in consequence. It was high time. I turned the nag around and rode back to the outfit's quarters. I slid off of her, and left her there, and went walking to the house.

It was fortunate that I had given up my wild goose chase. There on the porch sat John, talking to Miss Mac-Donald. When I got close enough to them to see how he looked, I felt as if my heart would break for him. He looked, in spite of his tan, like death.

When I had reached the foot of the steps, both of them, without saying an aye, yes, nor no to me, got up and went into the house.

My legs were shaking under me. I had to go slowly up the steps. Neither John nor Miss MacDonald was in the living-room when I got there. I went on into the kitchen.

Miss MacDonald was putting on her big apron. Zinnia was clattering the silver in the dining-room.

"John knows, doesn't he?" I questioned.

"Knows?"

"I think that I know what you—"

"Don't!" she shot out at me, and I wouldn't have jumped any higher if she had shot a gun instead of a word.

"Don't," she calmed down and came over to me and spoke in a whisper, "say anything in here. Not anything."

"I've got to," I said. "I'm human. You listen to me." I whispered it, right into her ear.

I hadn't half finished what I had to say before she moved away from me; but she nodded her head, with those quick, short little nods that always mean confidential agreement.

For almost an hour I had been thinking that I knew it. That nodding of hers made me realize that I had only feared it; that I had believed that she could deny and disprove it.

I had planned biscuits for dinner. I went and got out the bread-board, and opened the floor bin, but I couldn't do it.

"I'm sorry," I said, and to my disgust I began to cry. "I guess you'll have to make out to do alone, for a while. I—I'm not feeling well. I'll have to go and lie down—"

Still blubbering and blind with tears I went upstairs, and bumped into Sam, standing outside John's door. I dried my eyes and saw that he was holding his six-gun, ready for shooting, in his hand.

57
Grief

"What is the matter with you?" I demanded. "What are you doing with that gun?"

"John is in there packing his valise. He says he is going to leave the place. I say he is not."

"Going to say it with the six-gun, if necessary, ugh?" I asked.

"If necessary, Mary, by God, he put it up to me, straight. He came to me, and said that he had to get off the place for a while. Had to. I baited him along. Asked him where he wanted to go. He didn't even try to hide his feelings. Didn't bother to make up an excuse. Said it was all the same to him where he went: 'Frisco, Reno, Salt Lake, anywhere, just so that he could get away. When I reckoned he'd stay right here, he up with the idea of going down to live with the outfit. He's a fool; so he thinks that I am. Thinks I don't know he could get a good horse, the first night—"

"If John thinks you're a fool," I said, "he's paying you too much respect. I can't think of anything much worse, or more dangerous than a fool, but whatever it is, you are it. It turns me all over to look at you. Give me that gun."

I reached out and took it. His fingers didn't stick to it very long. I judged that he was not quite as eager to shoot John on sight as he had been pretending to be.

"Now get yourself away from here," I said. "Get on downstairs, if you know the way, and eat your dinner. I'll look after John."

"If you help that boy to escape—"

"Escape your foot!" I slipped into John's room, shut the door in Sam's face, and pushed the new bolt into its slot.

John's things were all strewn about; his valise was standing open on a chair, but he had stopped trying to pack it. He was lying face down on the bed.

I went and sat on the bed beside him and put an arm around his shoulders.

"Mary?" he questioned.

"Yes. There, there now, John dear. Try to brace—"

"You don't know!"

"Yes, I do know, dear. I know just what you know."

"My God," he groaned. "It is certain, then? I still had a little hope. I—I can't keep on with life, not after this. When I think of these last weeks I—I'm filthy, I tell you."

"John, dear," I tried to comfort. "You didn't know— you couldn't. You aren't to blame. You are young—"

I knew that I had no comfort for agony such as his, but I could not bear to leave him; so I stayed, hoping, as I suppose foolish women have always hoped, that just plain, quiet loving him might help a little.

After a minute or two, he said, "Mary—if you don't mind, I—I've got to fight this out alone."

I went to my own room. I put a cold-water compress on my eyes, and pulled down the window-shades and lay on my bed. I was mortal tired from sorrow, and the hurt in my heart for John was sharp as a neuralgia pain, but my mind went working right along, independent of my feelings; straight on, like a phonograph, if somebody had started it, might keep right on grinding out a tune while the ship that it was on was sinking.

When Miss MacDonald came up, bringing me some dinner, which I couldn't touch, I said to her: "It seems true, but I know that it can't be. It is too impossible. I mean—too far-fetched."

"Not a bit of it," she said. "The only impossible thing about it is the length of time it has taken us to discover it. Of course—forgive me, Mrs. Magin, I was almost on the trail once, I had at least started in the right direction, and then you threw me completely off."

"I! How?"

She smiled at me. "By seeing something which you did not see. But you are not in the least to blame for that. The fault is all mine."

She went and shut my transom. She looked through my clothes-closet. She looked under my bed, saying, as she did so, "The proverbial practice of old maids, you know." She came and sat close beside me, "Now then . . ." she said.

58
The Puzzle

"Listen. Bit by bit it works into the whole, like a picture puzzle—each segment slipping right into place. There is just one hole in it all, and I think your Danny's kindness and unselfishness will supply that necessary bit."

She began then—to use her own way of saying it—to put together the pieces of the puzzle. She was right. Bit by bit it fitted together. Almost at once she came to the place that she had called a hole.

"There is no hole there," I told her. "Under those circumstances, Danny would have been just sweet, and unselfish, and foolish enough to have done that very thing. She did it. That was why she was worried and unhappy, all that day."

"I'm sure of it. Now then . . ." She went on: Danny's calling after Gaby that day—easy to understand now, of course, and leading straight to Chad's suicide and confessional note. Gaby's fear; Martha's murder; Sam's ashes on the bag; Gaby's note to Danny; each one fitting right into place, until spread in front of me was one of the most hideous pictures that any human being has ever been forced to look at.

"Only," I gasped, "there can't be such wickedness in the world! I mean—not such long wickedness."

"In all my experience," she said, "I have never investigated another murder case where the thing was so cruelly, vilely premeditated; so wickedly, cunningly carried out. If this is true, it will be, also, the first time that I have found a really brilliant mind belonging to a fiend."

"If it is true!" I echoed. "But it is proven. You have just proven it all to me."

She shook her head. "We have a seemingly perfect fabric made up, wholly, of circumstantial evidence. As yet, we have nothing else. Now I have a question to ask you. It will seem to you that I should have asked you this at least a week ago. I did not, because I was certain that, unless I shared all of my suspicions with you, your answer would be exactly the answer that you gave me before. Now, thinking as you think, I want a very careful answer to this question."

When she had asked it, I refused my first impulse to answer it, at once, and sat thinking carefully for several minutes. The answer that I was forced to give, then, made me sick with shame.

"No," I said, "I didn't. I thought, honestly, that I did. But now I know that I didn't. That—that," I knew I was chattering it, "puts Canneziano's murder right at my door—"

"Nonsense," she folded one of my trembling hands in her steady, capable hands. "We can't go poking about like that, into the machinery of fate, and stay sane. The blame in this case is entirely for me. But, if I had not allowed myself to be misled then, but had worked straight on, something equally tragic might have happened. We don't know. What we do know is, that no more time must be wasted.

"I have spent this past week in trying to obtain the necessary proof. I have failed. Now, I am going to ask you to help me. Will you?"

"I will, and gladly. Bull you'll have to tell me what you want me to do. I haven't the faintest idea."

She told me.

"Lands alive!" I said. "That ought to be easy."

I could see that she was annoyed. "I haven't found it so," she said. "I have made three attempts, as many as I dared make, this week, and have failed. Do you realize that it must come simply, and naturally? You must realize that—"

"See here," I interrupted, "why not do as Sam wants you to do? Why not arrest the criminal now, and force the proof, afterwards? This sort of evidence could be gotten then, as well as now, and a lot safer, too, it seems to me."

"Mrs. Magin," she said, "until we have evidence of guilt we have no criminal to arrest. Incredible as it seems, we might still be wrong concerning every bit of this. I once made a horrible mistake. It was on my third case—that is, after I began to work for myself. I don't talk about it. I can't think about it. But I made myself a promise then, a promise that I have never broken, and which I never will break. Except in extreme necessity, proof, positive, and perfect, must come before any accusation or arrest in a case of mine. Twice, as I have said, I have had men arrested because of circumstantial evidence. Each time the evidence was far stronger than anything we have in this case. The first time, the man would have undoubtedly escaped if he had not been put in confinement. The second time was on my third case, which I have mentioned. If you force me to make this the third time—"

"I can't force you to do anything," I reminded her, hoping to cool her down a bit.

"Yes, you can. If you go at this so clumsily that you give the thing away, and so endanger your own life, I shall have to force matters. I must, of course, risk a reputation—I'm not speaking of my own, you understand—in preference to risking a life—again I am not speaking of my own. But, if we are wrong in this, and remember *we may be*—circumstantial evidence is the trickiest thing in the world—it would be bitterly cruel and wrong. It would be even worse than the other mistake of mine. Will you remember that, when you make your first attempt?"

"Yes, I'll remember. When do you want me to make the first attempt?"

"As soon as possible. This afternoon, if you can do it."

"But—how shall I do it?"

"I am going to leave that to you, and to your natural wit. You can do it much more spontaneously if you are not attempting to follow set directions. But do, do be careful. Don't make a mistake."

With that she left me. I am ashamed to say that excitement had made me forget my sorrow. I sat there saying my prayers, planning, and shaking in my shoes, for a good half hour before I could get up enough courage to go downstairs. In all probability, the next hour would bring me face to face with the murderous fiend; and not by the blink of an eye, not by the ghost of a shiver, must I betray my horrible knowledge.

59
The Fatal Mistake

When I finally did get myself downstairs, I found Sam, seemingly alone in the living-room, playing solitaire. I judged, from the look he gave me, and from the way he had his shoulders hunched, that he was still in a right ugly humor.

"Where's everybody?" I asked.

"Out committing murders, somewhere, likely."

"That's a nice way to talk, isn't it?"

He mumbled something.

"What?" I said. "I can't hear you when you mutter like that."

"I didn't talk much louder when I told Miss MacDonald about John's trying to make a getaway. She heard me all right. That's all the good it did. Do you know how much I trust that woman?"

"No, I don't know. I don't care, either."

Sam got out that silly, shrill voice he has for talking when he is trying to mock a woman, any woman, and in using it he spoke up, real loudly. "'Well, Mr. Stanley, why not allow your son to go down and live with the ranch hands, in their houses, for a time, since he is so eager to do so?'"

"Well, what about that?"

"Ahk!" Sam barked. "She is head over heels in love with him, that's a part of what is the matter with her.

I said, "I wish I thought so."

"Why do you wish that, Mary?" It was Danny's voice. Her white face, with the big, sorrowful eyes, peeked around the high back of a chair near the fireplace.

I was too taken aback to answer her.

"How long have you been sitting there, eavesdropping, young lady?" Sam asked.

"I didn't mean to eavesdrop," she answered, quietly. "I am sorry. I was reading, and didn't hear anything until you began to mimic Miss MacDonald. I heard all of that. Why does John wish to go down and live with the outfit?"

"John and Sam had a little trouble to-day," I told her.

Sam, with his usual helpfulness in embarrassing situations, pushed back his chair and went walking fast out of the room.

"Mary," she questioned, "why aren't you my friend any more?"

"Lands, child," I said, "if you mean that because I was wishing Miss MacDonald was in love with John, it was only because I've always reckoned that the more women in love with a man the better for him. John loves you. What do you care how many women love him?"

"John doesn't love me any more. I suppose that was what he and uncle were quarreling about? John wants to get away from me, is that it? And Uncle Sam is so good, and so loyal, that he won't allow it?"

"Nothing like that," I scoffed. "It was—" I left that sentence unfinished, and went into the kitchen.

She followed me. I went straight to the stove and picked up the lid-lifter, which, as usual, when I'm not there to watch, someone had left sticking up in a stovelid to get red hot, instead of hanging it on the hook where it belonged. I dropped it with a howl; and, wrapping my hand in my apron, told her to run and get the linseed oil and limewater, up in the hall bathroom, for me.

I am not saying that I was not to blame. I do say that, if that fool child Zinnia had not jumped around shouting, "Sody! Sody! Wet sody's the best for burns—" and that, if Mrs. Ricker hadn't heard her screeching, and come in, too, and begun asking questions, I certainly would not have overlooked the fact that, before she went to minister to my needs, Danny had picked up that lid-lifter, from where I had dropped it on the floor, and had hung it on its hook.

She made a quick trip upstairs and down again, with the bandages, and the lotion. She offered, sweet and sympathetic, to do up my hand for me. I had noticed, by that time, that my hand was not smarting much, but I was too excited to account for it reasonably. I asked Mrs. Ricker to attend to the bandages. I had another job for Danny.

"I just came out here," I said, "to make my weekly list to send to Telko for supplies. I can't write with this wadded up hand. Will you make the list for me, Danny? Zinnia, please hand her the pad and pencil from the shelf."

Zinnia brought it. Danny sat down by the table and picked up the pencil. My heart thumped in my throat.

"One crate of Fallon melons," I said.

Danny pushed the pad and pencil across the table to Mrs. Ricker. "Perhaps you'd as soon make the list for Mary? I have something to attend to upstairs."

"Go on, now you've started it, Danny," I said. "You write such a neat, pretty hand."

"I presume my writing can be read," Mrs. Ricker replied, as she picked up the pencil. "A crate of Fallon melons, did you say?" She wrote it down. I heard Danny running up the back stairway.

I felt flat as rolled dough from my disappointment. In the next minute I had something more than disappointment to bother me.

"I don't see," Zinnia said, "how you made out to burn yourself on that stove, Mrs. Magin. Miss Canneziano was out here, just a while ago, wanting to make some tea. The fire was dead out. She boiled the water on the electric plate."

I ran to the stove. It was as cold as winter time.

60
The End

I suppose it takes more than a minute for one's wits, particularly if they happen to be thick wits, to drain entirely away.

Before mine had completely left me, I had attempted to telephone to Sam, down in the outfit's quarters, and had failed to get a reply to my call. I had told Mrs. Ricker and Zinnia, trying with all my might to hide my fear, to run out and find Sam, or Miss MacDonald, or Hubert Hand, or John—I had forgotten that John was upstairs in his room—and to bring one or all of them to the house as quickly as possible. To this day I don't know why they went, without a question; but they went, running. It was the slam of the screen door behind them, I think, bringing with it as it did the realization of my aloneness and the memory of Miss MacDonald's warning, that turned me clear over to terror.

I shall not describe what I did, nor what I thought, during the time that I was alone there, downstairs, before help arrived. The humorously inclined might think such a description amusing. To me there is nothing amusing in the spectacle of an old woman being gripped and wrung by fright. I longed to run from the house; but I felt that I must stay there to explain the situation to the others when they came, if they ever did come, and to do my poor best, since I had made the fatal mistake, to prevent catastrophe. By clock time, it was only thirty-six silent minutes that I had to wait before Miss MacDonald came, alone and unhurried, up the front steps and into the living-room.

Still holding Sam's thirty-thirty rifle in my hands—I had known that I could never use it to shoot at any living thing, but I had hoped that it might make me look dangerous—I turned to meet her.

"Don't point that thing at me," she commanded. "Put it down. What are you doing with it? What is the trouble here?"

Before I could answer her, Sam, Mrs. Ricker and Zinnia came clattering through the kitchen.

Mrs. Ricker was wringing her hands and saying over and over, in a voice all broken and mutilated with horror, "I have gone insane, I have gone insane. I have gone insane."

Sam said, "Gabrielle Canneziano just now waved at us from her window."

Miss MacDonald turned and ran like a wild thing up the stairs. Just as she disappeared from our sight the sound of a pistol's shot cracked through the place.

I followed the others. I ran up the steps. I stumbled down the hall, behind them, and into Gabrielle Canneziano's room.

I saw Gabrielle Canneziano, her cheeks painted; her lips reddened, long earrings dangling from her ears, lying on the couch. Over her breast was a widening spot of color, staining the fringes of the soft white silk dressing-gown that she was wearing. On the floor was a smoking revolver.

John came. He said, "She told me what she was going to do. I allowed her to do it. I did not want Nevada to have to execute a woman."

61
Epilogue

Sam says, bitterly, that the only thing I need to explain is the one thing that can ever be explained: how one girl, by changing her clothes and by washing her face, could turn a houseful of supposedly sensible people into a packet of blithering, bat-blind fools for a generous period of time. I can explain that, I think; but I am going to leave it until later, and go clear back to the second of July, the day that Gabrielle received the code letter.

In her talk with John (John says it was in no sense a confession, that it was nothing but a taunt for us all, a final, regretless, high fling of defiance) there in his room, during the twenty minutes or so that she talked to him, before she shot herself, some things, which might still not be clear to us, were made plain. Also, many of Miss Mac-Donald's previously formed opinions were directly or indirectly verified. Miss MacDonald had said, you remember, that the murder had been wickedly premeditated.

"When I read that letter," Gabrielle said to John, "and found myself penniless and planless on a Nevada ranch, I at once made up my mind to kill Danielle, the little fool, and take her place."

How she persuaded Danny to accept the idea of the masquerade, and to change clothes with her, on the fourth of July, we do not positively know. That is the "hole" that

319

Miss MacDonald mentioned in her puzzle. To my mind, there is little doubt that she gained her way very easily, by using her own unhappiness and disappointment as tools with which to remove Danny's scruples and prod her pity. I am sure, remembering Danny's troubled manner at the time, that she consented unwillingly, that she thoroughly disliked the idea, and that she was afraid of its consequences.

When the two girls went upstairs together, on the afternoon of the fourth of July, they must have gone to effect the transformation. Perhaps, then, for a brief minute or two, the thing did seem amusing to Danny; for I know that I heard the girls laughing together, as I have mentioned, when I was on my errand upstairs.

We do not know, when the disguise had been completed, by what pretext Gabrielle lured Danny into the attic. Their trunks were in the attic. There could be a dozen simple reasons why Danny might consent to go up there with her. Coming downstairs again, Gabrielle caught her by the throat, and strangled her, instantly, by means of the deadly jiu-jitsu hold, which she had learned from her "Strangler" lover. It is a hold that requires little strength—though Gabrielle's trained fingers were strong enough—but much scientific skill.

She took the earrings from Danny's ears—or, perhaps, Danny had not yet put them on—went to her own room, arranged her make-up, got into the wrap, which completely covered Danny's clothes that she was wearing, pulled the hat down over her eyes to conceal the change in hairdressing, and walked through the living-room, for us all to see her, at four o'clock.

When Chad went to the porch with her (this John found out by insistent questioning) she told him that Danny had left the house, earlier, by the back way. That she and Danny had arranged a joke on the rest of us, to enliven the dull afternoon, and asked him to help with it by calling, in

Danny's voice to her, when he came back into the house. Chad did it. That was why, since he was standing down by the front doors, the voice supposed to come from the upper hall had a strained and an unnatural sound. Gabrielle had reckoned that Chad, in spite of her request, would be too stupid to discover the facts. Probably she thought that, at any rate, she would be able to impose silence upon him. It was one of her many mistakes. We think that he must have known for the remainder of the afternoon that Gabrielle was masquerading as Danny. His happy mood was caused by the fact that Gabrielle had given him a confidence and had allowed him to perform a small service for her. When he saw what had happened, and when he realized that the girl whom he had worshipped was a murderer, he killed himself. Strange, that in spite of everything, he still loved her enough to leave the confessional note to shield her. The men think that he left the note to shield the rest of us, rather than to shield her. I do not believe it.

She had planned to go straight around the house and re-enter it through the back door. Martha's being by the rabbit hutch was something she had not counted on. It was necessary to distract Martha's attention, and to get her to come at once into the house. She gave her the monkey bracelet. As she did so, probably because of the act of kindness, Martha made one of her frequent mistakes and called Gabrielle "Danny." Gabrielle told John (concerning Martha, John also questioned her insistently) that she then showed Martha the poison in the charm, and told her that it was a love potion that would make Chad love her, "like a lady," if she would swallow it, and never tell anyone anything about it. That, of course, was Martha's secret concerning the happy surprise that had to do with herself and Chad.

Martha out of the way, Gaby must have run quickly around to the back of the house and up the back stairway.

To toss the hat and wrap back on the body, replace the earrings, scatter the pipe ashes over the beaded bag (I declare to goodness, I can more easily think of her lying there in her white silk dressing-gown, than I can think of her, brushing those pipe ashes up, from somewhere, in order to save them for that purpose), and drop the tatting shuttle there, required not more than one or two minutes of time. Another two or three minutes to wash her face thoroughly and to douse on some of Danny's perfume, and she was coming downstairs again, with the headache that necessitated the drawing of the curtains—to make her safety a bit safer, just at first.

She told John that those few minutes when she had to walk through the room, make the trip around the house, and get upstairs again, were the only moments of fright that she had had, from the first to the last. Once safely established in the role of Danny, she said, she knew that she had nothing to fear.

I think, however, that there were other times when she was afraid. I am certain that real fear was there in her room, that day, when the engagement ring dropped from her finger. Though I believe that her fear, then, was caused wholly from superstition, and not from any dread that the slight difference between her hands and Danny's hands might be noticed.

I am sure that her fear for John, on the fourth of July, was real enough. She knew that each minute he was away, longer than the time necessary for the trip, was a minute lost from the perfect alibi she had so mistakenly tried to arrange for him by sending him away from the ranch. She had not known that Danny's fingers had closed on the stair's tread. When John came in the back way she was afraid that it would be remembered later—as it was—and that someone would suspect—as Hubert Hand did suspect—that John had carried the body in at that time.

She had counted on her note to Danny, and on the fact that, as Danny, she was downstairs within ten or twelve minutes after the time we had seen Gaby walking down the path and had heard Danny's voice calling after her, to prove her own innocence. They, and the gentleness of Danny's disposition, did this to perfection.

Her original plan had been to prove that Sam was the murderer. With Sam out of the way, and with John in possession of his fortune, she had thought, I suppose, that she would have no trouble in persuading John to leave the Desert Moon. But she was afraid of the idea. Knowing John's devotion to Sam, she could not reckon, with any sureness, how disgrace and sorrow might affect John. It was too big a risk to take, unreservedly. So, though she picked the quarrel with Sam, strewed the pipe ashes on the bag, put the key in the fireplace, wrote on the photograph, she left loopholes in the shapes of the many other false clues. It is only my own notion that, if she had not thought the definite accusation of Sam, which she made during the session on the fifth of July, was necessary to protect John, she would have backed out, by that time, and not have made it.

It is again only my notion that the request, which she put in her note to Danny, to have Danny take her body to San Francisco for cremation, was made because she thought that it would be desirable for her to be able to leave the ranch at once—perhaps for several weeks. Mrs. Ricker's expressed suspicion probably made her realize the wisdom of returning as rapidly as possible to the Desert Moon.

Gabrielle Canneziano was a born criminal. Almost all of her life had been spent among criminals. She knew their ways, and she knew the ways of honest people toward them. Consequently, she was too clever to drop her disguise, even for a minute, in San Francisco. When, on the afternoon of the fourth of July, she had come downstairs as Danny, she had come resolved from that time forth to be Danny, in thought and in deed, up to the level best of her ability. That she never doubted her ability to turn from black to white within the space of an hour, is a splendid example of Miss MacDonald's contention concerning the egotism of criminals.

Miss MacDonald says that her first real clue was the one I gave to her when I said that no one, except Gaby herself, who would do such a wicked thing, had ever been on the ranch. If she had been on the ranch, she might have committed the murder. She had all three of the primary motives for murder: love, revenge, and greed. The unique feature in this case—Miss MacDonald says that each case has its unique feature—was that the murdered girl had been a duplicate twin.

The hazy, incomplete notion, Miss MacDonald says, had just come into her mind; she had not begun to accept it, she was only allowing it, dimly, to take form, when I returned to the room that day with my hand full of letters written by Danny. Handwriting, as surely as fingerprints, Miss MacDonald says, proves identity.

She asked me, straight, whether I had seen Danny writing the checks and addressing the envelopes. I answered, straight and positively, that I had. (And not twenty minutes before that Miss MacDonald had warned me that people often thought that they saw things they did not see.)

I had not. I had seen the person whom I supposed was Danny writing checks and addressing envelopes. I had turned my back on her, and had walked to the door, when she called after me and gave me the envelopes containing the checks.

Danny herself had written those checks and had addressed those envelopes on the third of July. Owing to all the furor that had been going on in the house that day, she had left her desk before she had torn the checks from her check-book, and had never gone back to it to finish her task. It is possible that Gabrielle had deliberately arranged that, also; but I think not. At any rate, she had had the checks in her possession, and had waited for a date that had a three, or an eight in it, to produce them. Circumstances and I played well into her hands that day; she had only to insert a one in front of the three to make me her fool.

Miss MacDonald, as you have seen, blames herself and not me for the mistake. She says that she should have known better than to believe me; or, to quote her exactly, she should have "doubted your accuracy of observation." But, not until the morning that we found Daniel Canneziano murdered did it occur to her to doubt it.

She says that it was not clairvoyance, not intuition, not even common sense, that it was nothing but a memory that took her, that morning, straight back to the idea that Gabrielle Canneziano could be the guilty person. Oddly, the conviction had come to her before we found Canneziano's body.

Sitting across the table from Gabrielle, posing as Danny, that morning at breakfast, she had thought, idly, of the breakfast that she and Danny had had together in the dining-car. She had taken her chair, that morning, just as Danny had handed the order slip for her breakfast to the waiter. Too vaguely to be certain that it was really a memory, she seemed to see that slip of paper covered with writing. Just then, with the aroma of coffee in her nostrils, and with her iced grapefruit and rolls in front of her, she remembered that it was the same breakfast both she and Danny had had that morning. Would such a small order cover an order slip with handwriting? Not, it was certain, with the neat handwriting that had made out those checks and addressed those envelopes. Right then she resolved to lose no more time; to get, as soon as possible, a sample of the handwriting of the girl who was sitting across the table from her.

Canneziano's murder, discovered in the next half hour, strengthened her vague suspicions into as much of a certainty as she ever allowed herself before she had positive evidence.

As I have written, she spent the following week in efforts to get that evidence; at last, fearing that she was suspected, she detailed the task to me.

You have seen how I failed. How Gabrielle at once saw through my trick of attempting to disable my right hand by burning it; and how, realizing that she was trapped, she had run upstairs, first to satisfy her longing to be herself again, even for a few brief minutes, then to taunt John, and, finally, to take her own life.

For I think, in spite of her denials to John, that she killed herself because she knew that she was trapped, though her vanity and her audacity held to the end.

"I knew I should have no trouble in making you believe that silly doll story," she said. "It was the truth, I knew, too, that the dick would read the code letter. She was so slow about it, that I had to steal it to make her do it. It was time, you see, for the gentle Danielle's story to be verified. I knew that the dick had a copy of it—she'd been baiting me with the thing. I have kept a step or two ahead of her lumbering pace, all the time.

"Don't fancy that I had overlooked the matter of the handwriting. I'm not a fool. I thought of it before I killed the girl. There were a dozen ways I could have gotten around it—could yet get around it. If necessary, I could even have disabled my own right hand. I had rather planned, at first, to do that. But, later, I found that I loved my pretty little white hand better than I had supposed. Just as I have discovered that I loved the gay Gaby better than I had supposed—so well, indeed, that I have decided that death as Gaby is infinitely preferable to life as the shiny nosed Danielle. I have seen this coming. I have not cared.

"I got rid of that cur, Canneziano, not because I was afraid of him, but because he tried to double-cross me. I had promised to do much for him, after you and I were married; and he would have sold me out for a few thousand dollars. He came here, hoping that Danny might pay him a pretty sum for his silence about my past. He knew his muttons. She would have been fool enough to have done it; poor slain sister stuff; more to be pitied than blamed—all that, you know. He should have played with me, instead of against me. I had a few old scores to settle with him. Most of my rage about the money was because I had thought it would be such good fun to get the best of him. And I did—so that is all right. I hid in his room early that evening. It was frightfully amusing to watch him locking his door and his windows to make his sleep a safe one. It was. I did the job so neatly that he never woke at all.

"For that matter, it has all been amusing. You have all been such utter fools. But I am tired of it now. Oh, very tired. Particularly, I am tired of my cruel plan to destroy the gay Gaby by burying her alive. I am going now to do it in a swifter, kinder way."

Sam insists that her success, even for so short a time, is an indictment against all of us; that it shows that none of us was capable of looking deeper than clothes and face paint. I do not agree with him. Gabrielle was a professional actress. She had lived with Danny long enough to learn all her ways, her mannerisms, her habits in conversation. She did not dupe Chad, who loved her, and who was an expert in voices. She did not dupe Canneziano, who had known both of the girls all their lives.

The murder itself, by stupefying us all with horror, with fear, with suspicions, did much to help her. But without

that dulling of our perceptions, I think that the imposture
would have been successful. At the time of the murder,
the two girls had been on the ranch with us less than two
months. Strangers never get much deeper than surfaces in
so short a time. There was nothing remarkable, it seems to
me, about her being able, quite easily, to deceive all of us,
with the single, glaring exception of John.

John is one of a large class of people who could all be
filed under the recipe for simple acceptors. It is a necessary class; a class that acts as an oil to the hinges of the
world, making it move smoothly: the gentle, thoroughly
honest class that by quietly believing what it is told to
believe, keeps us out of revolutions, and rebellions, and
the like. I am not saying that the doubters and the rebels
are not necessary (as Sam would say, "It takes that sort to
make all sorts"), but Heaven help us if they predominated.

When John came home from Rattail, on the fourth of
July, he was faced with the apparent fact that Danny, in
the course of a few hours, had changed essentially. That
was what had bothered him so; what had made him jerk
his head, and blink his eyes, and complain of a touch of
sun. John had never recognized, much less admitted to
himself, that there was the slightest similarity between the
two girls. Consequently, in spite of a change, Danny must
be Danny; she looked like Danny, she talked like Danny,
and we all said that she was Danny. John believed.

Very shortly after that, John was faced with another
apparent fact. Gaby had been murdered. He could see that,
with his own eyes, as we all could see it.

He at once set the fact of Danny's change against the
fact of Gaby's murder—and there he stuck fast; too loyal
to go further; too dismayed to retreat. He did not believe
that Danny had killed Gabrielle. He had known Danny
too well to harbor such a belief. He was forced to believe

that she knew who had done it. Consequently, her accusation of Sam could be nothing but a wicked accusation. Only—Danny could not be wicked.

The mystery was a torture which Danny's presence intensified unbearably; so he avoided her; and, unable to blame her for anything, blamed himself and hated himself for his suspicions and for his failing loyalty. I'll venture, though it can be only a venture, that the realization of his interest in Miss MacDonald, and his inability to be rid of it, was another cause for John's befuddlement.

That interest, of course, has all disappeared for the present. Though he despised himself for it, John might have been untrue to a changed, living Danny; might, in the end, have jilted her meanly. John is male. But to a Danny who is no longer living, John, now, must always be true. John is young. I reckon he has fine honest plans for being faithful to her memory for the remainder of his life. Miss MacDonald is also young, and lovely, and heart whole. She has promised to come and visit us for a month next June.

Just now, with our thermometers at fifty below zero, and our chilblains burning, and the coyotes piercing the nights with their lank, long, frozen screeches, and the cold old owls always grieving forth their mournful "chuck-a-loo, whoo, whoo, whoo's" June looks mighty far away.

But, five fingers and a thumb, and she will be here, smelling of sunshine and tasting like smiles; painting our deserts with rainbow colors for as far as the eyes can see; spreading sunsets that catch you right up into their midsts; offering dawns that share their youth with you and that make you believe all over again in things which you had long ago stopped believing. Now I don't know shucks about romance; but I have a notion that June, in our northeastern Nevada, stirs up whole batches of the stuff. I am counting on her to serve it, fresh and sweet, this year.

It isn't June, though, and it isn't romance that I am trusting for the final chore: it is something more lasting than either, something sturdier, something for which I can not find a name. But I know that it is induced by a mixture of long years of right living, and clean thinking, and sanity, and courage; so I am expecting it to clear away the shadows from the Desert Moon and leave it, riding high as it used to ride, high and proud, a brave, shining thing in our valley.

THE
SARA ELIZABETH
MASON
MYSTERIES

MURDER RENTS A ROOM

THE CRIMSON FEATHER

DEATH
ON THE CAMPUS
**ADDISON
SIMMONS**

FEAR OF FEAR

FLORENCE RYERSON
COLIN CLEMENTS

VIRGINIA RATH

FERRYMAN,
TAKE HIM ACROSS!

Coachwhip Publications

CoachwhipBooks.com

The Jekyll-Hyde Murder Case
MADELON ST. DENIS

THE DESERT LAKE MYSTERY
KAY CLEAVER STRAHAN
Author of THE DESERT MOON MYSTERY

KILL 'EM WITH KINDNESS
By FRED DICKENSON

LADIES IN BOXES
GELETT BURGESS

Coachwhip Publications

CoachwhipBooks.com

I'll Hate Myself in the Morning

Murder on the Left Bank

Elliot Paul

THE BAND PLAYED
MURDER

EDITH HOWIE

CRY MURDER

EDITH HOWIE

NO FACE TO
MURDER
EDITH HOWIE

Coachwhip Publications

CoachwhipBooks.com

FULL CRASH DIVE

ALLAN R. BOSWORTH

GRIMM DEATH

LADY IN LILAC

SUSANNAH SHANE

MURDER IN THE WPA

ALEXANDER WILLIAMS

Coachwhip Publications

CoachwhipBooks.com

Coachwhip Publications

CoachwhipBooks.com

Coachwhip Publications
CoachwhipBooks.com

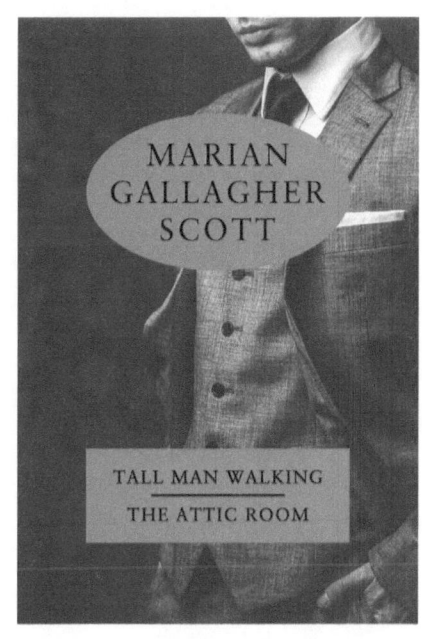

Coachwhip Publications

CoachwhipBooks.com

Coachwhip Publications

CoachwhipBooks.com

The Hollow Tree Mystery

MADELON ST. DENIS

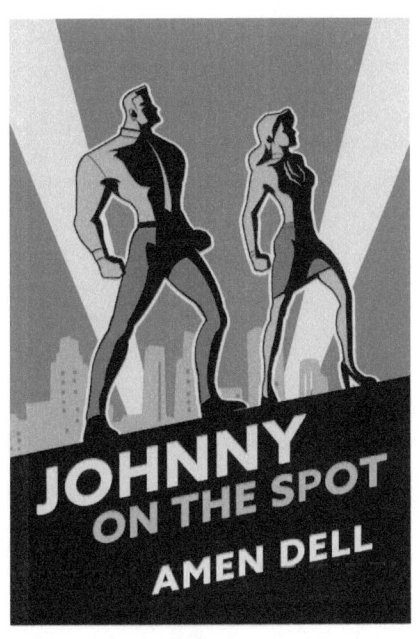

JOHNNY ON THE SPOT

AMEN DELL

VULTURES IN THE SKY

A HUGH RENNERT MYSTERY

TODD DOWNING

SAMUEL ROGERS

YOU'LL BE SORRY!

YOU LEAVE ME COLD!

Coachwhip Publications

CoachwhipBooks.com